Dark Passions is a single author collection of some of my short stories pulled together from other out-of-print anthologies. There are no new stories in this collection, just time-worn, in some cases award-winning, shorts.

They feature one of my favorite characters to write about – vampires. I love their power and allure. I like them dark and dangerous. I insist they are passionate and protective. I find it interesting to write powerful, immortal creatures who can be tempered by the strength of love. Love is totally unpredictable and amazingly powerful. It should never be underestimated.

Maybe there is an unexpected creature with dark passions in your future!

Featuring a roll call of some of the best writers of gay erotica and mysteries today!

Derek Adams	Kyle Adams	Vicktor Alexander
Simone Anderson	Victor J. Banis	Laura Baumbach
Ally Blue	J.P. Bowie	Barry Brennessel
James Buchanan	TA Chase	Charlie Cochrane
Karenna Colcroft	Ethan Day	Diana DeRicci
Taylor V. Donovan	S.J. Frost	Kimberly Gardner
Kaje Harper	Stephani Hecht	Alex Ironrod
Jambrea Jo Jones	DC Juris	AC Katt
Kiernan Kelly	K-lee Klein	Geoffrey Knight
J.L. Langley	Vincent Lardo	Cameron Lawton
Anna Lee	Elizabeth Lister	William Maltese
Timothy McGivney	Kendall McKenna	AKM Miles
Robert Moore	Jet Mykles	Jackie Nacht
N.J. Nielsen	Cherie Noel	Gregory L. Norris
Erica Pike	Neil S. Plakcy	Rob Rosen
George Seaton	Riley Shane	Richard Stevenson
Christopher Stone	Liz Strange	Lex Valentine
Haley Walsh	Lynley Wayne	Missy Welsh
Ryal Woods	Stevie Woods	Sara York
Lance Zarimba	Mark Zubro	

Check out titles, both available and forthcoming, at
www.mlrpress.com

DARK PASSIONS

LAURA BAUMBACH

mlrpress
www.mlrpress.com

Published by
MLR Press, LLC
3052 Gaines Waterport Rd.
Albion, NY 14411

Visit ManLoveRomance Press, LLC on the Internet:
www.mlrpress.com

Cover Art by Winterheart Design

Print format: ISBN# 978-1-944770-18-1

Second Editions 2016

TABLE OF CONTENTS

Sin &
Salvation

The snow fell in huge flakes, each light bit of fluff looking rough as sand but touching his face as if carried on a baby's breath. Ian Flynn couldn't remember seeing snowflakes this big in over three hundred years. During that time, he'd become something of a connoisseur of snowflakes. He favored cold climates that reminded him of his birthplace in northern England, ensuring there would be snow in the winter, especially for Christmas.

If he had to spend the holiday alone—and he had for over two hundred years despite having a steadfast, beloved lover for all those decades—he was determined to have the comfort of a white Christmas. This year was no different; it would be a lonely, if white, Christmas.

Ian knew all he had to do was call to Trevor through the strong bond they shared as master and child, lover to lover, friend to friend, and Trevor would come to him, compelled and unable to resist.

But Ian never pulled Trevor away for trivial reasons, especially from Trevor's single-minded, yearly, seasonal mission of hunting down the murderous riffraff and gang members that still haunted the same London streets where Trevor himself had met the end to his own mortal life so long ago. Christmas Eve had a different meaning to Ian and Trevor than to most people.

Trevor celebrated by taking revenge on the same type of men who had murdered him, and Ian spent the season contemplating his greatest sin. Even vampires had ghosts that haunted them and demons that needed excision. Dirty blood soothed Trevor's pain; snowflakes eased Ian's.

"Are you coming in soon, sir? It's a bit chilly and I have almost completed dressing the shrub in the main living room. The lights need your approval before the baubles are hung."

The smooth, cultured tones cut through the cold night air in a neat, precise, clipped voice, but Ian could hear the slight chatter of his manservant's teeth. Sighing, Ian blinked the remaining flakes off his eyelashes.

He glanced over his shoulder at the waiting man and, not for the first time, marveled at Stuart Graves's capacity for understatement. The temperature had been hovering slightly above two degrees for the last week, the "shrub" was a twelve-foot blue spruce with an eight-foot span at the bottom, and the "baubles" were hand-blown, one-of-a-kind antique glass ornaments. Nodding, Ian gave Stuart an exasperated smile.

"I'm sure you've done an outstanding job, like every year, Stuart. Nobody has the eye for color and details that you do."

Ian turned back to watch the flakes fall from the sky, each frozen droplet riding the sharp gusts of frigid air. He tried to lose himself in the warm memories of long ago holidays and happier times. Things would be better in a few days. They always were.

When his hearing told him Stuart hadn't moved, Ian softly added, "Go on back inside before you freeze. I'll follow you in a second. I just wanted to watch it snow for a bit."

Stepping to the vampire's side, Stuart lowered his voice. Clearly uncomfortable, he suggested, "If you're concerned…for his safety, maybe…you should call him home." Hesitant, Stuart glanced up at Ian and caught his gaze. "Just this once."

After a moment, Ian lowered his gaze, then stared up into the falling snow. He didn't need to intimidate Stuart. The man had been his servant and confidant for over twenty years. Ian knew he had lost any real fear of him long ago.

He sighed and studied the cloud-cloaked, inky night sky. He wished he could see the stars. His mother had always told him as a boy that the stars were actually prayers on their way up to heaven and God's ear. He'd believed that if he prayed hard enough and was a good son, his prayers would become stars, too. But that was all in the past. Ian was pretty sure that heaven didn't answer the prayers of demon spawn, even if a little part of him still believed in his mother's tales.

He wondered if it was snowing for Trevor right now. The dirty back streets of London were far away from his cozy, New York City penthouse.

"He can take care of himself."

Stuart didn't move. His voice stayed low, but grew firmer, concern and conviction in each word. "He can't continue to haunt the same alleyway Christmas Eve after Christmas Eve, year after year without running the very probable risk of capture. Not in these modern times, sir."

"He'll be all right." Ian swallowed past the lump in his throat, almost smiling at the thought he could still feel terror after all these years of existence as an undead creature of the night. He could feel terror, and pain and love and concern, too. But mostly tonight, like every other Christmas Eve, he felt guilt and acceptance. "He's very good at this."

"He's being hunted as a serial killer." Surprised by the ring of desperation, Ian turned to study the man's face as Stuart tersely added, "They call him the 'Yuletide Terror.' A madman. They'll hunt him down like one, too."

Ian didn't outwardly flinch, but he felt his eyes narrow and his vision grow yellow-tinged with the first signs of his vampire nature coming forward.

Stuart paid the warning sign no heed. "They almost captured him last year." He stepped one pace closer. Ian let him, taking comfort from the man's concern, if not his words. "This year the London police are sure to be even more prepared."

"I can't interfere." Last year's brush with the police frightened Ian just as much as it did Stuart, but he refused to let it show. He did appreciate Stuart's concern. Not many humans grew to care about vampires the way Stuart cared about Ian and his mate. He sighed and stared off into the night, resigned and unhappy. "I don't have the right."

Fastidiously dusting the fine layer of snow off Ian's broad, firmly-squared shoulders, Stuart let his hand linger a moment on the vampire's arm and gently said, "He doesn't blame you."

Spine curving under the weight of the centuries-long guilt he carried over what he considered to be his greatest sin, Ian slumped under Stuart's comforting touch, gold-tinged eyes staring unseeingly up into the silent heavens and whispered, "I blame me."

His voice sounded old and raw, reflecting all the years his age had gathered in the time since his turning. It was old and raw, but also strong and primal, leaving no room for argument. He knew Stuart would heed it and as if on cue, the man stepped back, sighing.

"I'll tend to the fire. It will have faded by now." Stuart turned and walked back to the balcony doors, but paused in the open doorway, concern etched into his aging, aristocratic face and dark, caring gaze. "I'll have a goblet of something warm waiting for you when you come in." He shivered, rubbing at his upper arms. "Please, don't stay out here too long." His tone lightened a touch and he briskly added, "The blood will congeal and you'll have to eat it with a spoon. And I'm not staying up to watch that."

With a huffed, halfhearted chuckle, Ian dropped his chin to his chest, nodded, and then turned to face the man.

"I wouldn't want to put you through that, Stuart. I'll be in soon. I'm going to count the stars for a while." He turned back to look up at the sky, snowflakes collecting on his dark lashes and hair, blinding him. He glanced one final time over his shoulder at the waiting man. "Thank you, Stuart." Ian stared at a small snowdrift gathering in one corner of the penthouse patio, suddenly unable to meet Stuart's imploring gaze. "For everything."

Silence was his only answer for a second longer than he thought was reassuring, but then a firm but sad "Yes, sir" banished his fears. Stuart did understand. That was important to Ian. Stuart was the second most important person in his life, a trusted servant, a father figure and a confidante.

The door shut softly behind him and Ian knew Stuart had retreated into the warmth of the apartment. Within moments, the mellow, moody sound of Bing Crosby's "White Christmas" drifted out to him. The phrase "I'll be home for Christmas" reached his ears, and he had to give an ironic chuckle at Stuart's pointed lack of subtlety in songs. Beneath his formal manners and acid-tipped tongue, the man cared very much about him and Trevor. The fact that he would be so brash proved it.

Next to Trevor, Stuart was the only other person Ian had allowed himself to have feeling for. He dreaded the moment when the man would grow infirm with age and die, leaving Ian to face the world and future Christmas Eves on his own again. Loss was the hardest part of being immortal. If he hadn't had Trevor by his side all these years, he would have walked into the sun long ago. Trevor was his salvation.

The desire to have Trevor at his side was nearly overwhelming. Something powerful and compelling told him to search the black, clouded skies, and with a childish sense of hope and anticipation he did, memories of his first meetings with Trevor piling like the snowflakes in the corner of the balcony wall.

§ § §

It was three weeks before Christmas and the streets of London were clogged with people, carts, street vendors, and filthy slush. The year would be turning to 1824 with the approaching New Year celebration, but the Christmas season had yet to be played out, and for that Ian Flynn was immeasurably happy.

Despite having been a vampire for over two hundred years, he still took pleasure in the sounds and smells of the season. Even the cold was welcomed, its icy hands bringing a tingle to his sensitive skin and a touch of color to his perpetually pale cheeks.

Even as a creature of the night, his olive skin and dark good looks still hid the outward signs of his demonic affliction from the human world he existed in. Only the slight yellow tinge to his eyes warned of his unearthly nature, but it was only revealed when his need to feed consumed him or his temper outdistanced his practiced hold on his fiery nature.

A sharp gust of December wind battered at Ian's long, heavy cloak and threatened to tear the top hat off his head. He stepped out of the carriage and landed on both feet on the dirty cobblestone lane, the controlled power in his large, square frame evident in every movement. He had been a miller's son, his days spent lifting and hauling sacks of grain and assisting the huge grinding wheel in his father's mill in its grueling job of grinding grain to flour.

Standing six foot three, Ian's shoulders were broad, his back strong and straight, and his legs were thick and long. Brushed back off his handsome face, his brown hair hung past the nape of his neck, its dark mahogany color matching the gold-speckled depths of his keen, mesmerizing eyes. A square jaw and high broad cheekbones completed Ian's solid look and commanding presence. He turned heads, both male and female, wherever he went.

Even the dark of night and the poor torchlight of the gentlemen's parlors and stage halls he frequented couldn't mask his compelling aura. More than one young lass, and lad, had lost more than their virginity to him, but never their life.

In all his decades as one of hell's unnatural children, Ian had never killed while feeding, never taken more than his unsuspecting and usually willing victim could spare, careful to never spawn a child of his own, or bind a thrall to his will. Raised by hardworking, loving parents and being born with a calm, easygoing nature, Ian didn't want a servant or a lover who was compelled to stay at his side for reasons outside of true loyalty or love.

To Ian, the curse of the vampire was best unshared past a moment of carnal pleasure and the satisfaction of feeding well from a comely bed partner. Being alone was never a problem for him. He had accepted being lonely as his accursed fate.

Fresh from a heavy sleep induced by a prior evening of fun, frolicking, and feeding, Ian was out to enjoy a night of cultural entertainment and bask in the delights of the theater. He had always enjoyed listening to the tales his mother told to him at night or when the harsh winter storms kept them all barricaded behind their stone walls and thatched roofs.

Once he had found the thrill of the theater, where stories came to life on the bright stage and in the colorful costumes of the players, there was no going back. He attended every theater and playhouse in every town he traveled through. He marveled at the skill and courage of the actors on the stage and their ability to become someone else for an evening, occasionally longing for that same ability to transform him from creature of the night to a fanciful hero in one of the fairy tales acted out when the curtains opened and the lights fell.

Tonight's play was a well-hailed effort by the playwright Richard Brinsley Peake, with an adaptation of Mary Shelley's much-gossiped-about novel Frankenstein. It was billed as a romantic drama, but Ian doubted there was anything romantic about it. He was looking forward to seeing if the fictional story of life after death took on a new perspective under the kerosene lamps and costumes. He lived his own version of it every day, giving him sympathy for the monster in the novel. He, too, had been thrust into an unholy afterlife he hadn't asked for nor wanted.

The carriage pulled away and he ascended the steps outside the playhouse, allowing the footman to brush off the sprinkling of snow on his coat as he climbed to the building's entrance. The place was old and only moderately kept up, but the hall was spacious and well lit and the decor bright, neat, and well polished. He handed his hat and cloak off to a young, eager attendant who appeared at his side. He smiled at the young man and flipped a coin into the air, allowing the attendant to catch it and pocket it as he walked away.

"Thank you, sir. It's very good of you, sir." Ian inclined his head toward the boy, and the young man winked and brashly added, "Name's Jules, sir. If you need anything at all, sir. Jules." Jules gave a suggestive smile and then sauntered away to store Ian's things, making sure Ian caught his flirtatious glance.

Ian smiled and kept walking, knowing it had been coin well spent. It assured him good service and no waiting for his cloak at the end of the performance. And if his tastes ran to snacking on lamb later between scenes, he knew he had a willing sheep in hand for the shearing. The young man was crude, but he showed experience and he was obviously willing. Ian supposed Jules found many a wealthy man at the theater who was looking for companionship and willing to pay well for it.

He thought about the feel of a smooth, lithe body under his, and arousal immediately blossomed in his blood. He savored it a moment, tasting it, then shook it off. He was well sated from last evening, and he never took home a partner just for sex. That way led to affection, feelings, longing, and ruin, but then Jules didn't strike him as the type to form emotional commitments that weren't tied to gold coins.

It was just as well. As far as Ian was concerned, beds were no longer for the making of love or sharing of emotions; they were for "eating" in. He'd keep Jules in mind when the play was over.

Caught up in the sudden flow of patrons, Ian let the tide carry him into the hall where he took a seat off to one side. The chair was partially hidden in the shadows of the room, but with a clear view of the stage. His looks and unaccompanied state tended to draw attention in public places. Everyone seemed to have an unattached daughter or niece they wanted to introduce him to. Tonight he simply wanted to watch, not be watched.

Before long, the small orchestra signaled the start of the entertainment and Ian lost himself in the tragedy and farce of Frankenstein's creation. As compelling as the story was for him from a personal viewpoint, the play took on a new attraction when the character of Felix DeLacey walked on stage.

Felix was the son of one of the principal characters, and though not a major part of the production, Ian was instantly taken by the young man playing the role. He was young and beautiful, with luminous blond hair that framed his lean, pale face like a halo, the lamplight glistening through the nearly white strands. He was of average height, slender and lithe, but Ian could see the lines of firm muscle under the tight-fitting breeches and form-fitted vest buttoned over a stark white shirt with billowing sleeves.

When the young man clasped his hands behind his back, the puffy sleeves looked like angel's wings on his back. His voice was throaty and slightly raw, as if his words had been lightly sanded before they were spoken aloud. His diction was crisp, but Ian's vampire hearing detected the undertone of a cockney accent the man tried very hard to hide to lend credence to his role as a gentleman's son. High cheekbones and a tapered, masculine jawline completed the package.

Ian was smitten from the first moment the actor glanced at him and seemed to hold his mesmerized gaze during a pause in the action. Play forgotten, Ian stared at the man through the entire performance, his attraction and need growing through each successive scene. During the first intermission, he signaled an attendant and sent his calling card off to be delivered to the actor, and in the process learned the actor's name was Trevor Sheffield. Entranced, Ian started when the cue caller announced the end of the play.

Walking backstage to the dressing area, Ian was surprised to discover he was nervous about meeting this young man, a mere human a half a foot shorter than he was and easily forty pounds lighter. Yet with all his age, supernatural powers, and strength, he was suddenly nervous as a lad at the thought of being rebuffed by this man. It irritated and thrilled him, making his arousal soar. The air around him nearly crackled with energy. These two feelings, irritation and unbridled desire, Trevor would always instill in him.

He waited by the closed door the attendant had indicated, accepting his cloak and hat from the man moments later. He tipped the man generously and ignored the knowing wink and leering smile the man let slide across his face just before he walked away. Ian inhaled deeply, noticing the man's scent, cataloging it should he have to correct the man's lurid impression for Trevor's sake at a later date and time. Humans always seemed to need to think the worst of their fellow man. Ian supposed it made them feel better about their own lot in life.

As he waited, Jules appeared out of the throng of milling actors, stagehands, and backstage patrons. He rushed headlong at Ian, a smile on his lips and saucy sway to his slim hips that suggested a practiced air of unspoken seduction. Ian had no doubts Jules made his extra income bedding patrons and street cads alike. It was of no matter any more; Jules paled in comparison to Trevor's beauty and grace. Ian had lost interest in anyone else.

He caught Jules's gaze and returned only an unwelcoming, stony stare that made the young man falter in his confident steps. Ten feet away, Jules slowed as Trevor emerged from a curtained-off alcove, traces of the harsh stage makeup still on his neck and cheek. Jules came to an abrupt halt when Trevor stepped between them, locked eyes on Ian, and shyly smiled. Thoughts of Jules faded away, despite that young man's continued, angry presence.

Unable to resist the hesitant twist to Trevor's naturally rose-colored lips, Ian smiled back, feeling the urge to take and claim the man surging through his entire body. He had thought his soul had been destroyed with his turning, but if it had, he knew it had been reborn at this moment. His still heart ached and his stirring groin pulsed with need unlike any he had experienced before. His mouth watered with the scent of him and the thought of this man's taste—his blood, his seed, even the bead of sweat on his temple—all called to him. And he had yet to say hello.

"Good evening." Ian walked up to Trevor, towering over him by several inches. His smile widened and he extended his hand to the surprisingly shy man. "Ian Flynn, shameless admirer of your talents."

The young man huffed a nervous sound and flashed Ian a nervous smile, saying, "Evening, sir." Trevor shifted awkwardly from one foot to the other, his uncertain gaze darting between Ian's face and the floor then back again before settling on the vampire's still extended hand. "Oh, sorry, sir, wasn't thinking!" He clasped his hand into Ian's and firmly shook it.

The vampire savored the warmth, barely suppressing the shudder it chased down his spine. Trevor's skin was a combination of rough and soft, his fingertips and lower hand lightly callused, but his palms were soft and smooth. It delighted Ian just to touch it, a sensual caress against his own sensitive flesh. He lingered over the texture before allowing Trevor to reclaim his hand. He noticed the way Trevor immediately rubbed his fingers together, but Ian didn't know if the man was wiping off his touch or trying to re-experience it.

"Why don't you just call me Ian?"

Trevor ran one hand through his blond hair, running the tip of his tongue over his upper lip. "My name's Trevor. Ah, Trevor Sheffield, actor."

"I know that part." They both laughed lightly and Trevor licked at his lip again.

The tongue was pink and wet as it danced over the plump fullness of upper lip. Ian's gaze followed every nervous wiggle and thrust. He wondered what it would feel like dancing over the head of his cock or into his ass. He wanted to taste it and feel it battle against his own before he tamed it and swallowed it whole. He could consume every inch of this man and still need more of him.

The scent of harsh soap and lime invaded his nostrils and he had to push it aside to detect the slightly salty, musky smell of Trevor's body. It reminded him of almonds and chestnuts, slightly bitter and heavy, tempting him.

"So very pleased to make your acquaintance, Trevor." The tang of masculine arousal struck him like a blow as Ian bent nearer to Trevor over the pretext of more intimate conversation, and inhaled, nostrils flaring, cock hard and needy in the confines of his trousers. He shifted his cloak over his arm to hide his response from Trevor's shy glances. He needed to taste his man soon.

"I admired your grace and talent on the stage tonight, though seeing you without the trappings of your profession—" He boldly reached out and wiped a smear of paint from Trevor's blushing cheek with his thumb. "—enhances my opinion of your attributes, both of the flesh and the mind, even more." He let his touch linger a second longer than publicly acceptable.

Ian let an appreciative smile light his eyes as he studied Trevor's surprised, but pleased, reaction to his compliments.

"I was hoping you'd be free to share a late meal with me." Ian didn't make it a question. He quietly waited, watching desire, uncertainty, excitement, and attraction all battle for dominance on Trevor's expressive face. Ian knew why the man was so well suited for acting. His emotions played freely across his fine-boned face and flowed over his audience, even an audience of one. He could read every thought that crossed Trevor's mind.

Much to Ian's relief, attraction and desire won. Trevor dropped his gaze, pausing before hesitantly confessing, "Don't usually go out this late." A flush of pink bloomed at the top of his high-boned cheeks as he stumbled over an almost whispered explanation. "Got me mum to look after." He licked his upper lip and his voice grew firmer, his own gaze darting longingly over Ian's face and broad, muscular body. "But her sister's come to visit with her for a time." He stood a bit taller and returned Ian's smile. "Warm meal'd be nice. Be honored to join you, sir."

"Ian. I'd like you to call me Ian. An accepted dinner invitation allows us the indulgence of this one, tiny intimacy, don't you think?"

Trevor ducked his head, nervously fingered the edge of his cloak, and then looked Ian in the eye. "Would be all right, I think." He paused then added, "Ian."

Liking the way Trevor's throaty voice and soft cockney accent made his name sound, Ian moved closer and took Trevor's cloak from the man's arm. He held it out and indicated the young man should put it on. Trevor instantly obeyed and Ian enjoyed the feel of his warm, firm body close to his own as he shrugged the cloak over and around Trevor's lean shoulders. Slipping into his own cloak and hat, Ian guided Trevor out the side exit to a line of waiting cabs, not sparing the fuming, dismissed Jules a second glance.

§ § §

"Let me take those things for you." Ian hung up his own cloak and hat, then expertly divested Trevor of his soaked outerwear.

The snow and wind had picked up volumes during the time

the two of them had spent dining at a posh hotel. The thin fabric of the young man's cloak had not weathered the wet and wind well on the short walk from the hotel to Ian's townhouse flat. Trevor was left chilled and shivering, his shirt collar soaked and his worn but serviceable boots dull and squeaky from icy puddles.

Flinging the offending garment over the back of a chair, Ian guided Trevor through the dim sitting area to stand in front of the flickering hearth.

"I keep the fire banked while I'm out. It makes starting a blaze easier. And besides—" Ian knelt at the grate and began stirring the flames to life, adding more logs and a few lumps of coal to the embers. "—I like a room bathed in fire light."

"It's romantic." He stood and brushed off his hands, then reached up and grabbed Trevor's shivering arm. "I like romance." Gaze searching Trevor's face for some sign of resistance, he slowly drew the man nearer the fire and his partially open lips. "I like you."

"I...I-I like you, too." Trevor swallowed hard and softly, shyly added, "Immensely."

Trevor came like a moth to the flame, gaze locked on the vampire's intense and questioning stare, attraction and desire easily read on his open face. He moved into Ian's arms, hesitant but willing, uncertainty in his eyes and an awkwardness in his too-rigid stance.

"You're safe. I've got you." Ian wrapped his arms around Trevor and soothed his shivers with long sweeping strokes of his square hands and strong arms down Trevor's back and arms. He tucked the young man in close to his chest, delighted at the press of Trevor's firm arousal that branded his inner thigh.

Trevor gasped at the intimate contact, but Ian merely slid his hand down to Trevor's taut buttocks and gently, but insistently, pulled him closer. Trevor's breathing increased, but so did his hold on Ian's waist.

When the chills tapered off to a fine, occasional shudder, Ian nuzzled at the side of Trevor's neck, inhaling the sweet elixir of his scent and feeling the warm flow of Trevor's blood as it erratically pounded through the artery under Ian's cheek. He could smell the wine they had drunk during dinner on Trevor's skin and in his blood. It was a very good wine that left Trevor talkative and sleepy-eyed, though still quick to flash his shy, twisty smile, a combination Ian had instantly liked on the man.

Dinner had been exhilarating. Trevor's companionship had proved to be both physically arousing and mentally stimulating. While Ian found the young actor to be modest and relatively inexperienced in the ways of the world and its sexual pleasures, he discovered Trevor was well-read, inventive, amusing, and quick-witted. The hour had passed quickly, and Ian knew he needed more than just release and nourishment from Trevor. For the first time in centuries, he began to want more.

He brushed his lips over Trevor's ear and felt him shudder with excitement. He took the reaction as permission to do more and slowly worked his lips over Trevor's neck and cheek to run a line of moist kisses around Trevor's trembling jaw and up to his other ear.

Ian breathed into the shell and nipped at the small lobe before whispering, "You're a beautiful man, Trevor. And as striking as you look by firelight, you feel even better."

He pulled Trevor's ass in tight and ground his own trapped, swollen erection against Trevor's, pleased by the answering jump and urgent answering press of flesh under his restraining hand. "I want to feel your flesh against mine."

He felt Trevor tense, then relax in his arms. He kissed over Trevor's ear, thrusting his tongue into the narrow channel twice before nipping and licking his way down the offered neck and back up to Trevor's now panting, parted mouth. "Want to share the need in my loins, satisfy our desires. Let me do that for you, Trevor. Let me pleasure you like you've never been pleasured before, by man or woman. I'll make you feel things you didn't know you could."

Sliding a hand through Trevor's thick blond hair, Ian coaxed the man's head back and sealed his hungry lips to Trevor's. He devoured the willing mouth, opening his own wider and thrusting his tongue deep into the hot, wet cavern. He bathed the smoothly ridged palette, then stroked over each tooth, memorizing the contours and savoring the flavor of his lover. He teased the sensitive silky skin between lip and gum and drew Trevor's eager tongue into a battle for dominance he quickly won.

Vampire senses buzzing, the smell, sight, and feel of this man invaded every corner of his mind and newly rediscovered soul. Ian struggled briefly to gain control over the rising vampire impulses trying to break free to experience Trevor as well, but centuries of practice kept the ancient monster in chains, much like Mary Shelley's Frankenstein's monster earlier tonight.

Breathless and dazed, Trevor jerked back from the kiss far enough to gasp, "Never met anyone quite like you before, Ian. You make me want to do things I never have."

"There is no one else like me, Trevor." Ian rained a flood of frenzied kisses over Trevor's upturned face, then kissed him hard, whispering into his lover's waiting mouth. "Do those things with me. You'll never regret them. I promise." He licked up Trevor's arched throat and bit gently behind his ear, a spot Ian knew was tender and vulnerable and connected directly to Trevor's cock. He felt the man's shaft jump and surge against his own. He bit down harder, forcing a needy groan and then a whimper out of Trevor.

Voice raspy and full of lustful need, Ian growled. "Good. You agree."

Ian scooped Trevor up into his arms, ignored the throaty yelp of surprise, and strode out of the living area and into an upstairs bedroom. The room was colder than the other one, but the large, lavishly made bed was heaped with duvets and down comforters, and the smoldering fire was only a few logs away from being revived.

Planting Trevor on the edge of the bed, Ian disrobed with an amazing amount of speed and skill, then began working off Trevor's disheveled clothes. If he had any worries that the need to be naked was one-sided, they were banished each time his fingers collided with Trevor's less nimble, shaky hands over a buttonhole or a belt buckle. Within seconds, Ian had Trevor gloriously naked and stretched out full-length on the bed. He slid his own body alongside Trevor's slender, smooth form, letting the silky hairs of his chest tease the sensitive ribcage and underarm of his lover. His hands worked over every inch of flesh he could reach, while his lips and tongue re-explored the depths of Trevor's mouth again.

Moans and groans, dotted with whimpers and stuttered gasps, filled the air, raising the tension between them to higher levels. Trevor was already squirming and whimpering with need, hips thrusting and legs unsure whether to be bent or splayed wide. Ian slid his lower torso between them and Trevor instinctively wrapped his legs around the vampire's hips. The restless squirming became an urgent thrusting of pelvis against unyielding pelvis.

"You need a bit of release so we can make the evening last, my beauty." Ian pushed his muscular body down over Trevor's trim hips and grabbed hold of his waist. He grinned and locked gazes with Trevor's confused, desperate stare, then expertly swallowed Trevor's cock to the root in one stroke.

"Ian!"

Arched off the bed, Trevor nearly bowed in half at the sudden movement, a sharp cry of surprise and amazement twisting his face into a mask of intense pleasure that appeared to border on pain. Ian held on to the slim hips that bucked and heaved under him by pinning Trevor down with the weight of his own solid body on the young man's legs. He lapped and sucked at the swollen shaft in an unrelenting rhythm meant to bring Trevor the most pleasure in the quickest amount of time.

Ian had plans for the entire night, and making Trevor come as often and as hard as physically possible was among them. He intended to experience every inch of this beautiful, shy creature from his satiny, pale skin right down to the taste and smell of the golden strands of hair on his head. But first he thought he'd start with the taste of his cum, the smell of his musky opening, and the sight of Trevor's face, eyes closed in rapture, hair tousled and cheeks flushed with passion, fists tightly entwined in the bed sheets.

Unable to drag his mouth or his eyes away from the man, Ian stared up at Trevor's lusciously sprawled body while he suckled the man's cock. Every hollow corner of his ancient, empty soul was being filled with the essence of the delightful, hesitant being he now possessed body, mind, and hopefully, by morning, heart. He refused to give up this ray of sunshine that had unexpectedly entered his dark existence. In one short evening, this responsive, shy, and tender man had shown Ian he still had a soul buried deep within him. The soul with which Ian intended to capture Trevor's heart, along with his lean, passionate body.

Swallowing Trevor's cock to the base again, Ian worked his throat and sucked hard, one hand moving to fondle and tug the tight, wrinkled sac beneath. As he rolled the sac, he slid one long, thick finger between Trevor's ass cheeks and stroked the tip firmly over the tiny opening to Trevor's body, loving the way the ring of muscle spasmed and puckered under his touch. The exotic and unexpected stimulation seemed to drive Trevor to new heights of excitement and responsiveness, his body writhing under Ian's hold.

The air in the bedroom was cool, but Trevor's body was flushed pink and his cheeks burned red as he arched up and gave a hoarse cry, climaxing into Ian's eager mouth, giving over his seed as well as his liberated passions.

As the last droplet of cum touched his tongue, Ian swiftly moved his lips to the thin strip of flesh between Trevor's thigh and groin and sucked hard on the satin-like skin. Blood rose to the surface over the pounding pulse of the artery buried there, coloring the small circle of flesh a deep crimson. He used the sharp edge of a pointed canine to scratch the blood-filled surface and then feasted on the trickle of blood that oozed out.

The blood was rich and sweet, musky and pure, a sip of heaven on his tongue. Ian's senses reeled and his chest ached as visions of sunlight and blue skies entwined around feelings of joy and immeasurable arousal. Trevor was the taste of blatant lust and sweet victory to Ian. Trevor was bliss. Trevor was his for the taking. His forever. He could taste it, he could feel it, now he needed to proclaim it.

Still riding the crest of his climax, Trevor moaned and instinctively pulled away from the slight pain of the scratch, but Ian coaxed him into submissiveness by alternately massaging the root of his shaft under his sac and exploring the fluttering opening to Trevor's eager body.

Trevor whimpered, his groping hands reaching blindly for Ian, his over-stimulated cock never softening, despite his climax.

Capturing the most recent blood droplets on his tongue, Ian reluctantly moved away from Trevor's groin, abandoning the heady mix of rich, innocent blood and freshly spilled cum. He climbed up over Trevor and settled slightly off to one side so as not to crush his lover.

"Don't know what to do, Ian. Don't know how…"

The wild, uncertain look of desperate need and escalating desire on Trevor's beautiful face made Ian release a throaty, almost demonic rumble to the passionate gasps and moans that filled the room.

"I'll take you there, beauty. Don't worry. I know the way."

He reclaimed Trevor's mouth and this time got as good as he gave. Trevor returned his ravenous attack of lips, tongue, and grasping, groping, stroking hands over flesh and bone. They both appeared lost in the urgent impulse to consume each other whole.

Ian trailed his sensitive fingertips over Trevor's skin, mapping its texture with his callused but gentle hands, tracing the curve of Trevor's trim muscles, the shape of his spine, the swell of his firm, round ass, and the taut cords of his thigh wrapped over Ian's hip. Ian wove a hand through Trevor's hair, marveling at the fine, soft strands that caught the dim firelight and turned themselves into threads of pure gold before his eyes.

The sound of Trevor's heartbeat called to him and the lingering taste of the man invaded his soul. Ian pulled Trevor over on his side along with him as he turned, putting them chest to chest. He pulled Trevor's leg up over his waist and nestled their groins together, cocks aligned head to head and dripping. He engulfed both shafts in one large hand and began a slow stroking up and down, occasionally running his thumb over the heads and under the tip, making sure Trevor got the majority of the stimulation.

Seasoned and older, Ian could maintain an erection for hours, but he was sure Trevor was close again. It was obvious the young man had little experience or practice in bed. Ian liked that, but he planned on changing it, as well.

He worked his hand over the twin shafts of swollen flesh, ignoring the sharp bite of discomfort from Trevor's nails as his writhing lover scratched at his shoulders and chest, his arousal fueled by the combined scents of his own blood mixed with the remaining blood from the small wound he had given Trevor. When he felt Trevor's cock thicken and his balls tighten, Ian released their cocks and slipped his hand lower, finding the entrance to Trevor's quivering body.

"I-I was…so…I need…I—" Trevor's eyes were glazed over with lust, embarrassment burning high in his cheeks as his eyelids shyly fluttered with the obvious uncertainty of how to ask for something he didn't even know he wanted.

"Ssshh. I know." Ian quickly kissed Trevor's lips, then his sweaty brow. "Soon. I'll make you feel even better." He tipped Trevor's chin up so that their gazes met. Ian knew his own heavy-lidded gaze carried the full heat of his desires and he was pleased when Trevor didn't shrink from it. "Trust me?"

A trembled nod and Ian reclaimed Trevor's lips, pulling the man tightly to him, ravishing his mouth, hands everywhere on his slim, tense body until Trevor moaned and whimpered, limp and pliant in his strong arms.

Still devouring his lover, Ian reached across Trevor to a nightstand. He impatiently knocked the lid from a small earthen jar sitting on top and dipped his fingers into the container, coating his fingers with a thick, oily balm that smelt faintly of fish and herbs.

He turned them both slightly on the bed, then tucked Trevor under his side and coaxed his lover's knees apart with his elbow, exposing the rosebud entrance to Trevor's body. His slick fingertips found the fluttering ring of muscle and teased it, stroked it, and cajoled it open.

Trevor jumped, instinctively closing his legs at first; then he splayed them wider, hips thrusting up and in time to the muffled grunts and gasps coming out of his mouth, which Ian simply swallowed down with a kiss.

Tongue moving in a sensual rhythm along with his fingers, Ian rubbed the tip of his middle finger over Trevor's hole, soothing it and inflaming it with each stroke, while his tongue did the same to the soft recesses of Trevor's mouth. He drew Trevor's tongue into his own mouth and sucked on it, bobbing his head in time to the thrusts of his hand. Pinning Trevor's squirming torso to the bed with his own, Ian wrapped his free hand in Trevor's hair to hold him still against his lips and nudged two slick fingers into Trevor's ass.

All movement beneath him froze for a split second; then Trevor pressed down onto his hand, forcing his fingers deeper, the tight muscles clinging and grasping at him. Ian obliged them and slowly explored with his fingers until they could touch the small nub of hidden ecstasy buried inside his naïve lover. Ian was sure Trevor had never been touched this way and reveled in the fact that he would be the first and only man to see the passion and fire in the beautiful man's face when he stroked the virgin nub to life.

He pulled out of the fierce kiss and held Trevor's face inches from his own, gaze locked on the man's face, his intense stare taking in every nuance and flicker of emotion that flashed across the young actor's expression.

To Ian, Trevor looked dazed, his eyes wide and his jerky movements near frantic. He grunted a sound of distress as Ian abruptly ended the kiss, then arched and cried out, panting and gasping when Ian flicked at the virgin nub deep inside him and swirled long, thick fingers over the swollen gland.

"Bollocks!" Trevor cried out, twisting his hips and grinding his ass down on the thick invading digits up his ass.

Ian began slowly pumping his fingers in and out, striking the little sweet spot with each jab, gradually building the rhythm until he had a steady, deep stroke stretching and coaxing Trevor into a state of lust-dazed euphoria.

Impulsively, he bowed his head and licked at one erect nipple on Trevor's chest. Encouraged by the way Trevor grabbed his head and pressed it more tightly to his breast, Ian suckled the tit, biting and tugging it with his teeth until a bead of red blossomed on one side.

The fresh taste of Trevor's essence carried the spice of his arousal and Ian felt dizzy and drunk with the strength of it. He could read Trevor's deepest desires in his blood and Ian was shocked and thrilled to find that he was one of them.

Elated, he removed his fingers from Trevor's opening and wiped them off on his own straining cock, smearing the head with the balm and his own flowing juices. Moving quickly to silence the croaked murmur of discontent from his startled lover, Ian rolled Trevor over on his side again and slipped in close behind him, cock nudging the cheeks of Trevor's ass. He pulled Trevor's leg up and hooked his arm under the knee, then slid his arm high enough to rub his palm over Trevor's taut belly while holding the leg up high to expose Trevor's rosy, wet hole.

"Trust me, Trevor." Ian kissed Trevor's neck and then mouthed the lobe of his ear, whispering, "I'll never hurt you."

Pushing pillows to the floor, he wormed his other arm under Trevor's head, and then dropped his arm down to embrace the young man's torso and pressed Trevor's back to his chest. With little effort, his cock found the slick hole and the head pressed past the now lax guardian ring of nerves and muscle. With one smooth, unending thrust he eased into Trevor, all the while gauging his speed and force by the shudders and moans escaping his partner. Once the length of his shaft was fully encased in Trevor's sweet heat, Ian coaxed Trevor's face to tilt up with his chin.

"I want you, now, tomorrow, forever. I have to have you. Say you'll stay."

Not waiting for an answer, Ian gently kissed the parted, swollen lips again and again until Trevor returned his attention in kind, letting the kiss build their passions to a raging fervor once more.

Satisfied Trevor was fully aroused and ready, his flesh craving fulfillment and his gold-speckled, dark eyes brimming with need and desire, Ian began to move his hips. He thrust deep inside Trevor, then slowly withdrew, over and over again, until his movements morphed into snapping strokes and Trevor's throaty groans turned into blissful cries begging for release.

Ian took Trevor's shaft in his hand. He tugged and pressed the velvety, iron-hard flesh until the young man bucked and heaved, impaled on Ian's swollen, thrusting cock, and cum splattered his hand, filling the room with the tangible scent of unbridled passion.

Ian groaned, losing himself in the bliss of having his shaft milked by the spasming muscles in Trevor's ass, the press and release of hot flesh like a wanton embrace to his soul. Releasing Trevor's mouth, Ian rained rough kisses and sharp nips along Trevor's collarbone, sucking the warm flesh until it glowed a dark pink and bore his teeth marks in multiple places.

Trevor pressed his shoulder hard against Ian's lips, startling the vampire by breathing a husky whisper, begging, "Do it, mark me. I want you to."

The raw request spiked Ian's already burning desire higher and he felt his climax barrel down on him. He slammed his hips forward and plunged deeper into Trevor's tight channel at the same time as his teeth lightly pierced the first few layers of skin on Trevor's shoulder. Having just fed the evening before, Ian wouldn't need blood again for weeks, but he wanted the taste of his lover on his lips as he came. It would make his climax sweeter and more intense, bonding them together on a level others couldn't understand without experiencing. He didn't understand it himself, but he knew it existed. He'd never let it happen since he realized he could control it, but this time, he wanted that bond with Trevor. No one made him feel the way Trevor did.

Cock buried to the root, Ian froze in place, his body spasming, his seed pouring forth into his lover as Trevor's blood flowed into his mouth. Sensations of joy, bliss, fear, shame, want, and even love coursed through him like a hit of lightning, setting him on fire.

His mind reached out and touched Trevor's, capturing the man's essence, learning his keen mind, and invading Trevor's very soul. He felt the soundless cry of surprise and pain from Trevor's soul, and he withdrew slightly, only to be pulled back around as the feeling turned to despair and longing at his sudden retreat. Grabbing the thread of tentative welcome, Ian's essence flowed into Trevor's being, claiming him, washing over his soul and binding it to his own. They would be forever tied until the ravages of old age stole Trevor from him.

He planned to never show Trevor his true nature.

Riding a tide of euphoria like he had never known, Ian emptied himself into Trevor, clasping the man tightly to his chest. His lips released the smooth, warm shoulder, giving up the trickle of heady elixir that was Trevor's life force, and sought out Trevor's warm, willing mouth.

During the kiss, Ian eased out of Trevor's ass and rolled his lover over onto his back. Ian settled his own weight beside and partially on top of Trevor and wrapped the panting, dazed man in his arms. The chill of room began to register again, and Ian pulled up a rumpled duvet from the tangled heap on the foot of the bed and covered them both. Trevor shivered and cuddled closer. Ian tucked both the comforter and his lover to his side.

"Never done that before. I feel...like I can't...can't live without you now. It's so strange."

The words were soft and throaty, raw with a dazed, sleepy quality to them. If Ian had been human, he knew he would have had to strain to hear them. He tilted Trevor's downcast face up to look at him and gently stroked the side of his lover's flushed face with his thumb, reassuring and coaxing. After a moment, gold-flecked brown eyes met his waiting gaze. Ian smiled.

"I want you, too, Trevor. I don't ever want to spend another night without you by my side."

The emotions playing on Trevor's face were the same as when he was considering being Ian's lover—joy, uncertainty, fear, and desire; this time they were about their future together. The veil of shadow fell over Trevor's beautiful face and panic edged out the joy in his eyes. "I'm scared, Ian. What do we do?"

"Sshh, ssh. I'll handle everything. I'll take care of things, no worry." Ian gently kissed Trevor's mouth and petted his hand down Trevor's side, soothing away any worries and fears. "Sleep, beauty. I have you and nothing will take you from me."

"Promise?" Trevor's eyelids fluttered and fell and his breathing turned shallow. Ian savored the hot puffs of sweet breath that ghosted across his cheek.

"Promise. Now sleep."

Laying his head down on the pillow next to Trevor's, Ian vowed to make this last, make this work, make this be the only moment of pure joy in his long, lonely, pointless existence. They would be one together for whatever years Trevor lived and Ian would make each one a day of love and joy. There was no point to life without love.

And he knew right then, after Trevor passed, he would walk into the sun himself.

§ § §

Instead of waiting in the confines of the playhouse among the perfumed ladies and their cigar-smoking escorts, all packed into too small a space for Ian's comfort, the vampire elected to wander outside. The night was filled with the scents of the Christmas season. The enticing aroma of roasted chestnuts mingled with the heavy scent of pine from the fresh boughs that decorated the doors and several carriages that stood waiting for fares.

A light dusting of snow had begun to fall, covering the dirty cobblestone houses with a graceful, white mantle of innocence. Ian turned to watch a group of bundled carolers stop to serenade the playhouse patrons, hoping for a bit of coin or a kind word. Ian gave them both and was rewarded with a fresh chorus of song. The festive trappings and good cheer around him stirred something indefinable in his chest and he wished Trevor were standing with him to enjoy it, too. When the carolers passed on to new territory, so did Ian.

Unnoticed, he naturally gravitated to the gray shadows of the building's edges where lamplight and pedestrians refused to go, seeking solitude to enjoy the sights and sounds before him.

A long, debris-littered alley ran down beside the playhouse. He was no stranger to alleyways. Ian tucked himself around the corner and leaned against the building to wait, his keen hearing picking up the faint sounds of rats scurrying over the uneven cobblestones.

Even with his soul reborn, Ian took comfort in the darkness, enjoyed the cool hands of the shadows that wrapped around him and comforted him from the masses of humans milling around him. He longed to take Trevor away from this town to a more secluded, peaceful place where they could explore the land and each other in more detail. After the holidays maybe he would talk Trevor into exploring the Italian countryside with him.

As Ian watched the Christmas snow fall from the sky in spits and starts, contemplating his blissful future with Trevor, a gang of young street thugs moved down the lane, shouting and nipping between patrons, undoubtedly nicking purses and pockets as they worked their way toward the alleyway. So well hidden was he in the concealing shadows, the young men passed within a few feet of where Ian stood and never noticed him. Ian was used to blending into the night.

One scruffy, carrot-topped young man lagged behind the group, glancing impatiently back out into the street. Two others from their gang still mingled with the departing patrons of the playhouse.

A fellow street grub, short and stocky, with a round face and a festering sore on the point of his chin, broke away from the first two headed down the darkness toward the back of the playhouse. He turned back down the alley to grab the redhead and tugged on his arm, insistent and exasperated.

"Gawd, Mickey, you're lagging 'ahind! We gots work ta get done. Hurry up!"

Mickey's bright gaze shifted from the two out in the street to his companion and back, his movements restless and jerky. He glanced at the retreating back of the two that had already entered the alley, then gave the stocky man an almost desperate, pleading look.

"Know that, Todd. Just thought we should all be together on this." Fidgeting with the hem of his tattered scarf, Mickey shivered in the cold air and glanced at the street again. "Nigel and Pern ain't keeping up!"

From the shadows, Ian focused on Mickey's hammering heartbeat, curiously studying the nervous shift of his shoulders and the uneasy expression on his dirt-streaked face. He wanted to go back inside and snatch his lover from his impromptu celebrations, but some instinct he couldn't ignore kept him still and watchful.

Gripping Mickey's arm, Todd pulled him down the alley. He brushed a layer of snow off his hair and out of his eyes, scoffing, "No never mind 'bout those two. They're keeping the finery busy watching them so as no one's watching us. Come on!"

"Shouldn't it be all six of us? I mean…" Mickey paused, swallowing hard. "…he might fight back." He reluctantly stumbled along, drawn more by Todd's strong arm than his own willpower.

"Don't be daft! He's an actor! The poof'll never know what done him in." Todd pulled out a gleaming knife and proudly flashed it in Mickey's face. "It'll be so easy, I could do it meselfs. Wouldn't that be something?"

All of Ian's senses were immediately directed toward the

two, the puzzle of what they were up to piquing his curiosity. He expanded his hearing, pushing aside the muffling effects of the snowfall, the cheerful, holiday-inspired chatter outside the playhouse, and the rattle of horse-drawn carriages on cobblestone. He tracked their fading conversation, losing nothing to the sharp wind.

Reaching the end of the alley, Todd and Mickey paused to glance suspiciously at their surroundings, never seeing Ian's tall shadow and hooded, now yellow eyes. Todd yanked Mickey out in front of him, urging the nervous young man along with a shove to his back. Their movements became more fugitive as they edged off to Ian's left toward the playhouse stage door.

Before they disappeared, a knife suddenly appeared in Mickey's hand as well.

"Then why don't you?" Mickey's hand wavered, his grip on the knife overly tight and shaking. "Do it yourself, I mean."

Ian could read the panic on his thin face and hear it thundering through his blood vessels.

"This one don't feel right, Todd."

"You're crazy, just edgy 'cause it's Christmas Eve, you are. What better night for a bloke to meet his maker than tonight, eh? Kinda religious experience." Todd laughed, a hushed, ugly sound, and slapped Mickey upside of his bowed head. "'Sides, need all of us to be sure it gets done right. Jules's got a rich patron's pockets to pick and this nuisance is in his way."

Ian was stunned, the pieces of the tiny puzzle falling into place.

The sounds of a scuffle grabbed his attention and Todd started. He slapped Mickey's shoulder, forcing him to move faster. "Let's go! Arty and Reg have already got him!" Todd ran down the side alley into the darkness. Mickey skittered behind him, obviously torn between running forward and running backward.

A muffled, garbled shout and the sudden scent of familiar blood galvanized Ian into action. Even with all his vampire speed and agility, it took too long for him to reach the huddled group of filthy street rabble. It had already found its prey.

The four men beat and stabbed at a figure pressed up against one wall of the old playhouse. An occasional flash of pale blond caught in the bright moonlight between the dark heads of ragged caps and dull, dirty hair. As Ian descended on them, the blond head slid out of sight to the filth of the snow-covered ground while the grunting huddle of pounding arms and hunched shoulders finally stepped back.

The scent of Trevor's blood overwhelmed Ian. He logically knew what to expect—the sounds of the brief struggle, the dull thud of flesh hitting flesh and cries of pain and disbelief all too familiar and brutal to his ears. The sight of his beautiful beloved lying, unmoving, in a bloody heap in a dark, desolate alley like so much human waste was unbearable to the vampire.

Outrage, pain, and horror overtook centuries of control and discipline. Ian let his inner power burst free in a surge of unforgiving rage. He descended on the flailing mass of unsuspecting assailants like the night he existed in, silent, unmerciful and unstoppable, throwing the entire group back with one sweeping blow.

He ended Mickey's startled cry of surprise quickly by breaking his neck. Todd was torn limb from limb, his own wetly gleaming knife finding a new home in his own black heart.

Art and Reg, the first to grab their prey and begin the assault, were less charitably dealt with. Their eyes were torn from their sockets, their grasping arms shattered, and their throats ripped open. Then their writhing, mangled, and broken bodies were thrown against a wall where they dropped to the slushy cobblestone, left in the filth and waste to slowly bleed to death, dinner for the ever-present scavenging rats.

It had taken Ian seconds to turn the alley into a death house, but he was still too late. Free of his assailants. Trevor lay at Ian's feet, unmoving, unnaturally pale in the dim moonlight, a layer of glistening white captured in his hair and eyelashes. Ian could barely hear the stuttering rhythm of his lover's heartbeat and only the movement of snowflakes drifting off his chest signaled the occasional shallow breath. From the street, Ian could hear the faint sound of the joyous carolers as they sang. While Shepherds Watched would forever take on a new and dark meaning for Ian.

Dropping to his knees, Ian scooped Trevor into his arms, cradling his lover's rapidly cooling body to his chest. He smoothed Trevor's snow-dampened hair off his face, surprised to see his own hand trembling. It had been so very long since he had experienced genuine terror. Loving Trevor had awakened so many long-forgotten feelings in the vampire. He had been so bewitched by the joy in the good emotions, he had not remembered the agony of the bad until now.

All his dreams and plans of a bright and happy future with his lover until Trevor's natural final days were lived out dissolved and blew away with the cold wind. His reason for continuing in his dark, empty existence was slipping away with each draining pulse of Trevor's wounded heart. Ian's heart felt the same pain; each thrust of the knife had entered his chest as well.

But while Trevor's pain would be brief, like his young life, Ian's pain would be eternal. He couldn't face the specter of life without Trevor in it. He wouldn't. He had waited hundreds of long, lonely years to find his love and now that he had, he wasn't leaving him. This night, this hallowed, blessed eve, they would face judgment in the afterlife as one and die together in this accursed alleyway.

Ian heard Trevor's faint heartbeat flutter and stop. He clutched his lover to him, heart-to-heart, and let out a silent, anguished cry of indescribable pain. Tears streamed down his face as his pain transformed into rage. He held Trevor in a brutal grip, looked down into his lover's beautiful face, quivering fingertips gently tracing the delicate curve of Trevor's eyelids to feel the soft feathery brush of his long lashes one more time against his skin.

A flicker of movement under his touch stilled his hand. He bowed his head and stared at Trevor's pale face, straining to hear his heartbeat again. A faint, barely audible thump-thud touched the edges of his keen senses and Ian's firm vow to end both their lives crumbled to dust.

Ian had never created a new vampire; not in all the years of his existence had he inflicted his curse on another; never had he committed what he considered to be a vampire's greatest sin. Killed, as he had tonight, for protection or revenge, yes, but never to feed and never to damn another to the dark loneliness of vampirism.

But it wouldn't be lonely for Trevor or him if they had each other in the darkness.

When Trevor woke to his new existence and hated Ian for turning him, Ian would destroy them both. It was that simple, and yet, so complex.

A single, shallow breath of air escaped Trevor's lips, ghosting over Ian's face. The fear that it may have been Trevor's last pulled Ian from his internal debate and let his heart decide the matter.

Panicked, Ian tightly clasped Trevor to him, and sunk his now-extended fangs into the soft, smooth skin of his lover's exposed neck, the move brutal and primal, the wound horrific and deep.

§ § §

Nausea rolled through Trevor's stomach and a flash of pain made him jump and gasp. He opened his eyes to the lamplight of Ian's bedroom and a flood of disjointed, horrific memories embroiled him in their chaotic rush, stealing his air and his voice.

He ran his hand over his smooth, hairless chest, noting the coolness of his flesh and the ivory tone of skin. Panic shot down his limbs, exploding in his chest, the sharp stabbing pain of his attackers' weapons suddenly remembered by his body in vivid detail. More detail than he had been aware of at the time of the assault. Enough detail that Trevor knew he should not be lying comfortably in Ian's bed, naked, aware, and unmarked. Enough detail that his hand slid to his left breast and lay there searching for the familiar thump of his own heartbeat.

His chest was still and cold.

As terror rose up in his lifeless heart, but before it could burst out, a hand slid along his arm and his fingers were firmly laced together with larger, blunt ones. Trevor stared at the interwoven hands for a moment, then turned his eyes up to meet Ian's waiting brown ones.

Ian had been lying beside him, still and silent as the dead. As Trevor stared at his lover, a yellow cast gave his warm brown eyes a luminescent glow. Trevor thought he should be frightened or repulsed, but Ian's eyes remained warm and loving, his face open and concerned. Trevor couldn't help but be reassured and beguiled by the small tentative smile on the large man's usually firm mouth. It was the first time he had seen Ian anything but supremely confident in his action.

Trevor wet his dry, cool lips, his gaze searching Ian's face for answers, dreading an explanation, but needing to hear his lover's soft, commanding voice.

"Am I dead, Ian? Are you?" Trevor's gaze flickered around the confines of the luxurious room and soft bedding. "Are we dead, together, in heaven, then?"

He heard his own voice waver. Trevor clamped his jaw shut to keep in the whimper that rose in his throat. Maybe it was the set of Ian's mouth or the odd color of his eyes, but something told him it wasn't going to be that easy.

"Not heaven, my beauty, but not hell, either." Ian squeezed their entwined hands, the touch firm, gentle, and real, anchoring Trevor. "Not as long as we are together."

Despite the stillness in his chest, Trevor didn't feel "dead." Indeed, he felt strangely energized and hyperaware. The threads of the fine linens were like rough twigs under his back and the snowflakes hitting the window sounded as if pebbles were being pelted against the rippled glass.

Suddenly, the light of the smoking lamp was too bright and the weight of the down comforter too heavy. Trevor flung the blanket off his naked body, shielding his eyes from the light with his free hand, panic and confusion fueling his jerky movements.

"Then what am I? What's been done to me? Why am I not dead?" Trevor's voice rose, his eyes burning bright. "I was killed in the alleyway, I know it. I remember the knife in my chest and the slowing of my heart. I know I died!"

He tried to fight his way free from Ian's hold, but the bigger man slipped behind him and pinned Trevor's back to his broad chest. Holding Trevor's arms crossed over his own heaving chest, Ian wrapped his arms around him and gently held him. The feel of Ian's naked flesh against his own sensitive skin was like lying on the finest satin draped tightly over iron. Trevor had never felt so much power and strength in a man before. It was thrilling and frightening all at once. Before tonight, he thought he had known everything about this man.

Trevor gradually stopped tugging and pulling as the urge to flee subsided, with Ian's softly murmured words finally breaking through the haze of terror in his mind.

"Hush, my beauty, sshhh. I'm here. I'll guide you." Ian nuzzled his face into Trevor's hair and breathed warm air against his skin and scalp.

The warmth was sweet and welcome. Trevor pushed his head back into it, allowing Ian to soothe him.

"You'll not face this alone, Trevor. I swear." Ian tightened his embrace. "Never alone."

Calmer, Trevor focused on his body and the demands of his overwrought senses. He felt things more keenly, heard things clearer, and even his sight, always slightly short-sighted, was now crisp. Colors were more vibrant and smells were almost overwhelming if he focused on them. He could hear the mice scurrying through the walls and the snow falling on the window ledge outside the room. He knew he was dead, but he had never felt so alive before.

Trevor slid his hand over his cool, naked abdomen, then ran his other over Ian's marble-hard arm where it held him pinned in place with a gentle but firm embrace. They felt exactly the same. He wasn't as brawny as Ian naturally was, but now, his once pink skin was a shade paler, firmer, and cool, just like Ian's.

"I-I feel strange, Ian. Unnatural." Trevor's whole body shook this time, not just his voice. "I should be dead." He concentrated on what his body and mind were telling him and he grew more confused. "And I'm not."

He clasped Ian's large hands tighter to his left breast and hung on to them like they were his only hope of remaining sane. "My heart doesn't beat and I feel a hunger unlike any I have ever known."

Trevor twisted in Ian's grip so that he could see his lover's face. The yellow cast to Ian's eyes was almost hypnotic. It held his gaze captive, focused on Ian's face. He started for a brief instant when he noticed Ian's eyeteeth looked longer and sharper than they normally did.

A flash of sudden insight, absurd and outlandish, surged through him, an innate, primal knowledge that was a part of him now. His stomach fluttered and his breathing became shallow.

Even instinctively knowing the answer, he had to hear it from Ian. He faltered, then breathlessly asked, "Why am I like this, Ian? What's happened to me?"

Ian buried his face in Trevor's hair and gasped into the blond strands, voice ragged and possessive, a raw hunger to them Trevor had never heard before. It made his cock stir and his blood race even as he fought back a tinge of horror.

"I couldn't lose you."

Trevor's voice caught in his throat. He partially turned in Ian's embrace to face him. He watched as guilt and stubborn defiance battled for dominance on Ian's face, neither winning, but both inexplicably touching Trevor's heart.

"You did this to me?"

It was only a whisper, but Ian flinched as if shouted at. His eyes pleaded with Trevor for understanding, but his voice was as strong and unyielding as his continued grip on Trevor's body.

"You were dying in my arms." He took a deep breath. His voice wavered slightly. "I couldn't lose you." The light in Ian's eyes burned brighter. One hand caressed Trevor's shoulders, back, belly and beyond, soothing, begging, arousing Trevor with its bold touch. "Please forgive me. I couldn't lose you or I'd lose myself, as well."

Looking into Trevor's eyes, Ian softly vowed, "We were as one before this, and now that's true more so than ever. We are inseparable for all time." He swallowed hard, guilt winning over confidence for a moment. "If you choose to stay with me."

His gaze darted over Trevor's face, obviously seeking some sort of clue to Trevor's thoughts. As much as the new, overwhelming voice in Trevor's head screamed for him to accept and indulge in this unnatural existence, a tiny part of his old self resisted, frightened and unsure of this shadowy future. His Christian upbringing was well ingrained, defiant even in the face of the dark, insurmountable changes Trevor knew his body and world had undergone.

A sharp stab of pain rippled through his mouth. Trevor felt the budding, elongated points of new fangs emerge from his upper jaws, the razor-fine edge of one slicing his own lip as he grimaced in surprise. He smeared the blood away with his fingers, but the smell pulled a dark thirst up from deep inside him.

It coursed through his body like boiling water, scalding his senses and heightening them. His arousal stood tall and aching, pressed against Ian's hard abdomen. He felt powerful and raw, sinfully base and suddenly tainted. Air left his lungs and his throat constricted with fear as the need to be free crashed in on him.

"At what cost, Ian? My soul?" Trevor struggled against Ian's hold, repulsion and terror temporarily overpowering his desire to be at Ian's side. He grunted and twisted in Ian's grip, but the larger, stronger man couldn't be budged. "Am I one of the accursed undead, a servant of the devil now?"

"Do you think I am? Did you fall in love with a devil, Trevor? An evil man?"

"No." A mere whisper of sound, Trevor licked his lips and answered Ian again, this time with more conviction, and more uncertainty. "No, you're not, Ian. You're not."

"We are shunned by the light, and all things holy, but that doesn't make us Satan's minions. We need to feed from other living creatures just as we did before, but we need not kill to do it. We need not harm or damage, take a life or change a life, if we choose not to do so. I have been in this form for hundreds of years and I have not killed a single being in the quest for nourishment."

Ian brushed the tousled hair from Trevor's hopeful face and reverently rubbed a callused thumb over the fine line of his lover's cheekbone and down his jaw. "I can teach you. Show you how."

He slid his hand to Trevor's hair and worked his fingers over the scalp beneath them, relaxing and calming Trevor's skittishness with just his touch. "I do not murder for food and neither will you." Tightening his grip, Ian lightly shook Trevor's head, then pressed their foreheads together and quietly vowed, "I'll see us both perish before I'll let that happen."

The hold on his arms lessened as Ian's hands found other places on Trevor's now unresisting body to touch and hold. Desire surged again, forcing aside the fear. Trevor whimpered and arched into Ian's hands, hungry for his touch.

"What are we, Ian?" Trevor's arms wound around his lover's neck, clinging to Ian's powerful shoulders, fingers digging into them. His tear-filled gaze searched his lover's face for answers and reassurance. "What will others call us now?"

"Others?" Ian kissed Trevor's mouth, the brief caress of lips chaste and fleeting, less than Trevor wanted, but almost more than he could stand. Ian's answer ghosted over his face. "Others will call us demons." Ian said the word in a detached, nonjudgmental way, as if he had just called them carpenters. It oddly reassured Trevor.

"What name do we give ourselves?"

"The ancient one." Once again Ian kissed him, light and teasing, a taste of things to come. "The one belonging to the first of our kind, the true masters of the dark." This time he breathed the word into Trevor's mouth, warming his lips and setting his darkened soul on fire with its heated, airy caress. "Vampye."

Ian pronounced it with the lilt of his native northern accent, giving the word a sensual, powerful sound that vibrated through to Trevor's very core. His cock jerked and his blood raced faster through his veins. He arched and ground his erection against Ian's bare flesh, wanting release from at least one of his hungers.

A gust of icy wind rattled the window, its mighty swirls of air carrying the faint sound of carolers up to them. Both glanced at the frost-edged panes that separated them from the rest of the world, a sudden reminder of the masses of humanity they had left behind.

Trevor lowered his gaze, a pang of guilt striking through him, as he remembered what night this still was. He shrugged, uncomfortable with his own thoughts, and darted a beseeching look at Ian. His cockney accent became prominent, strong and thick, as it always did when he felt deeply about something. "Seems blasphemous for this to happen on Christmas Eve, don't it? Mean, it's a holy day, and all."

Shaking his head, Ian stroked Trevor's side, long, firm caresses that calmed his mental turmoil and excited the rest of his body. Trevor knew he could never face this new existence without Ian at his side. No one did the things this lover did with just the mere touch of his hand. His words were even more soothing to Trevor, each word passionate and strong.

"It's the perfect time, Trevor. The night of the Savior's birth is exactly right for the night of my savior's birth. It couldn't be more perfect. Salvation comes in many forms, Trevor, and you're mine. Without you, I would gladly perish."

Ian swooped down and kissed Trevor passionately. Lips sealed together, he rolled them so that Ian was on top.

"You have just fears, beauty—" He kissed Trevor's eyelids and lips softly between words. "—but let me show you some of the pleasures of your new life." He lifted Trevor's arm, holding the soft inner arm against his cheek. Ian ran his lips and fangs down the delicate flesh, wrist to elbow, slicing a shallow furrow. When the blood welled rich and full from the wound, he followed the red trail back up Trevor's arm, licking and sucking the bright red flow off the skin to Trevor's wrist.

Trevor gasped at the burning pain that came with the wound, but his hips bucked and he squirmed with need, as a bolt of arousal shot through his veins and rocketed to his cock. His shaft was hard and full, trapped between them, poking uselessly at Ian's stomach, a smear of his own pre-cum lubricating the patch of flesh he rubbed against.

His gasp was captured by Ian's lips again and swallowed as Ian invaded his mouth, exploring and bathing his entire being with his power. The weight of Ian's body was solid and firm, iron hard, his skin luxuriously silky. The hair on his chest was darker than on his head, but fine and thick under Trevor's palms. Trevor's fingers blindly searched until they found the taut buds of nipples. He flicked and rubbed at them, loving the way his efforts fanned Ian's passion higher.

A strange hunger mixed with his lust. It rolled through Trevor until he couldn't control the impulse to bite at Ian's lips, his newly emerged fangs tender, but sharp. A droplet of blood touched his tongue and the hunger exploded in his gut like oil thrown on a fire.

He lunged upward trying to gain a better biting hold on Ian. An unearthly power rippled through him, and he twisted and fought to find the nourishment he needed, but he was no match for Ian's ancient strength. Trevor bucked and jerked, but his wrists were calmly pinned to the mattress over his head and his bucking hips held firmly in place by the vampire's weight.

Flinging his head from side to side, Trevor growled out his frustration inches from Ian's calm face. "I need!"

He didn't recognize his own voice, the tone raw and dangerous. It shocked him and he dropped his head back on the pillow and stared up at his lover. "I-I…need…" He was at a loss to verbalize exactly what it was he did need. "Ian?" He heard the pleading tone to his own voice. Tears welled in his eyes as they searched Ian's face for some kind of understanding.

"Hush, beauty. I know, I know." Still holding Trevor's wrist tightly, Ian moved their hands so he could gently brush Trevor's cheek with his thumb, artfully avoiding teeth as Trevor twisted and strained against him. "The taste of my blood has awakened the first hunger in you."

He pressed Trevor's head into the feather pillow, forehead pressed to forehead, and whispered, the sound faint and breathy, but easily heard by another vampire's ears. "This will be the strongest of the urges to feed. After this is properly sated, I'll teach you how to control it, hide it, turn it to your advantage." He teasingly nipped the tip of Trevor's nose, easily avoiding Trevor's unrelenting, eager fangs. "You're an intelligent man; you'll do well."

Thwarted, Trevor settled back, emotions in turmoil, but still aroused and oddly thrilled by Ian's restraining hold and powerful presence. Hopeful, he locked gazes with Ian. "I won't have to kill?"

As soon as he said the word, the urge to destroy something living flashed through him and he panicked. Frantic with fear and confusion, he cried out. "Ian! I feel like I could kill!" Trevor renewed his struggle for a moment while Ian hurried to patiently calm him again. "I'll kill, I will!"

"You won't! I swear it." He shook Trevor until the young vampire's teeth clattered and his hair flew into his eyes. Trevor gasped and shuddered, then calmed, a sob escaping his lips with his words.

"Never?"

Ian pushed the stray blond strands off Trevor's face with his chin and gently said, "Not to feed."

The brush of Ian's beard stubble blazed along his skin and relief flowed in Trevor's veins. He believed Ian with all his being, dark and unfamiliar as it was to him now. Ian was still his anchor in life, the past one and this new, shadow-filled, stormy one. He was its originator and Trevor's only source of guidance and understanding, as well as his one true love. He put his trust in

Ian, despite the vampire being the reason for his distress and predicament. Ian had done it for love, Trevor knew that.

The hold on his wrists loosened and Trevor turned questioning eyes on his lover as Ian firmly tilted Trevor's face up to meet his steely gaze. "But maybe for self-protection, if you have to." Trevor blinked rapidly to keep the panic at bay and Ian gently added, "but never for nourishment, never because of starvation. I swear it."

"Cross your heart and hope to—" Trevor huffed a tiny, embarrassed chuckle and averted his gaze. "Guess that doesn't mean too much now, eh?"

Letting out a loud laugh, Ian tilted Trevor's face back to meet his stare. He smiled, seductive and teasing. Heated gazes locked together, Ian licked across Trevor's mouth, then sucked on his lower lip, tugging it before letting it slip away, wet and slick, to whisper, "How about we make it a blood oath?"

The hunger rose again.

Without moving from on top of Trevor, Ian seductively tilted his head to one side, exposing his throat. Trevor instinctively lunged, driven by a new, indefinable need to taste the vampire's rich, aged blood a second time. His fangs pierced Ian's flesh, making a soft pop as they penetrated.

New and inexperienced, Trevor made to brutally shake his head and widen the wounds, but a massive, firm fist clamped onto his hair and held him still, preventing him from inflicting more damage than necessary.

"That's my beauty. Bold and fierce. You'll learn to use finesse over time. For now just slay the hunger." Ian gasped and pressed Trevor's mouth more tightly against his neck, a moan of pleasure rumbling from deep inside his throat. "Feast from me."

The blood rolled over Trevor's tongue, thick and silky smooth like liquid satin. It tasted of berries, hickory, and lime, rich and intoxicating. Flashes of emotions washed through him, love, lust, desire, and guilt, and it was some time before he realized they were Ian's feelings, not his. The realization he was sharing his lover's most intimate emotions made them all the more intense. Trevor's ever-present arousal slowly began to overwhelm his ebbing hunger for blood. Now his body craved to be satisfied in other ways.

As if Ian was aware of the change in Trevor's needs, the grip on Trevor's hair lessened and he was able to pull back. As Ian broke away, Trevor smeared the last droplets of Ian's blood from the healing wounds over his lips.

Ian's face appeared inches from his own. They locked yellow gazes for a brief, intense moment, then Ian's tongue darted out and began to lick the blood from Trevor's ruby red lips, slowly and thoroughly. Each languid lap of wet muscle was erotic and arousing to Trevor, his lips hypersensitive and his sexual need beyond explosive.

Ian's hips began to move in concert with his attentions to Trevor's mouth, sliding their cocks together in a delicious dance. The licks turned to sucking kisses as Ian worked his lips from Trevor's mouth, over his cheek, down his neck and across his chest.

He raised one of Trevor's arms and slowly worked his kisses up the inner aspect, grazing the soft flesh with his fangs, never breaking the skin but leaving a trail of teeth marks in his wake. When he reached Trevor's wrist, Ian suckled at the pulse point, teasing it, until Trevor was squirming with need and anticipation.

"Ian! Please!"

"Not yet, beauty." Ian dropped Trevor's arm and returned his attention to Trevor's mouth while his hands slid under Trevor's ass and kneaded the firm globes of flesh, spreading them.

His fingers were in constant motion, edging their way closer and closer until they touched the puckered entrance to Trevor's body. Once there, Ian began to stroke and rub at the tight ring of muscle, relenting only when it fluttered and relaxed under his fingertips.

Trevor groaned and arched his hips, then pushed down on the blunt fingertip pressing into his ass. The need to be filled, to have more than just a touch raced through him and Trevor bucked his lower half, spreading his legs wide and wrapping them high around Ian's waist.

"More. Want more." Trevor twisted and tossed his head and shoulders, pinned in place, exposed and open, at Ian's loving mercy, desperate to feel Ian inside of him.

Ian's cock rubbed at his balls and the blunt head of the vampire's shaft replaced his finger. He reached for Trevor's abandoned arm, licking over the smooth flesh as he inched his cock into the tight, fluttering opening.

Moaning at the thrill of the familiar, delightful burn and pressure of the large shaft, Trevor met each small thrust of Ian's hips with one of his own, trying to pull Ian's cock in deeper and faster.

The sensation of Ian's veined and bulging cock sliding against his channel walls, spreading his asshole wider with each inch that was buried in him, made Trevor gasp and moan, his thoughts jumbled as the room spun.

Making love as a hyperaware vampire was different than before, more intense, more exotic, and more satisfying. He felt every emotion Ian felt and understood his desires and needs like never before. Trevor knew why Ian had not been able to face the future without him and he understood the decision to bring him across to the dark. He knew Ian would willingly die without him. Ian's love for him was that strong.

He nearly screamed when Ian's slow, tiny thrusts unexpectedly turned into faster, smoother, longer strokes that rubbed slickly along his channel and bumped relentlessly over his prostate with each pass. His climax built way too soon and too fast. Trevor wanted this to go on forever.

Making love with Ian had been amazing and wondrous before this, but now it was indescribable. They seemed linked on a level that transcended the rest of the world's existence. Blood lust and vampirism be damned, Trevor wanted a lifetime of this and Ian.

His climax teetered on the edge, waiting for one last touch

or sensation to push him over the brink. Trevor's frustration mounted and his body cried out for release as the sensation intensified but no relief came. Trevor's pleading gaze locked on Ian's lust-filled stare.

Never pulling away his gaze, Ian drew Trevor's wrist to his lips and kissed the soft vulnerable inner strip of pale flesh. He thrust hard and deep once, biting into the wrist at the same time, cock buried to the root, and lusting gaze riveted on Trevor's face.

Trevor screamed, his body spasming, and then came, the burn of the hard thrust and the sheer ecstasy of the bite too much to bear together. It was exactly what he needed to fall over the razor-sharp edge he had been teetering on. His climax was explosive. His skin sizzled and his senses reeled. Sweat broke out over his body and his mind became dazed and clouded. His cock jerked and erupted, coating his abdomen and Ian's chest, the scent of the cum intoxicating.

Flesh was pressed to his lips and Trevor opened his eyes. He grabbed onto Ian's arm and licked over the same spot on his lover's wrist that Ian had feasted at on his own body. He felt Ian grip his hip in a bruising hold and then arch, plunging deep into his ass and staying there. Trevor understood his lover's desire and bit into Ian's wrist, losing himself in the joy and pleasure he found in Ian's blood.

A roar of triumph shook the walls and Ian's hips thrust in rapid, staccato rhythm, the vampire emptying his load deep inside of Trevor. When he was spent, Ian withdrew and collapsed in a heap beside Trevor, panting. He turned on the mattress to give Trevor a sated smile.

Trevor met Ian's sultry gaze with one of his own and leisurely licked the last trickle of blood from Ian's arm as his lover watched. The look of feral want that sparked in Ian's eyes fueled his own arousal to stir again. He felt his cock burst to life when Ian returned the gesture and began to lick and suckle the open wounds of Trevor's wrist, too.

Ian leaned over Trevor, bringing the wrist up with him. He alternated between kissing Trevor's lips and sucking on his wrist, occasionally licking a droplet of his own blood off Trevor's lips as well.

"Now do you believe me, beauty?" Ian's hand wandered to Trevor's rising cock and lightly stroked it.

Gasping softly, Trevor arched his hips. "Not sure I'm a hundred percent convinced." Trevor shoved his straining shaft into Ian's playful hand and turned a hot, sultry stare on his lover and breathlessly asked, "Can you explain it to me again?"

§ § §

Ian stared at the night sky, lost in the memories of his and Trevor's first Christmas. It had been the only Christmas Eve the two of them had spent together. They had kept their oath and Trevor had never killed for food, but he had used his vampire skills and abilities to kill for revenge.

As much as Ian wanted Trevor with him for this one night, he never interfered. In all his centuries as a vampire, he considered turning Trevor to be his greatest sin. His own guilt kept him silent about his lover's absences, but modern times and police methods were making Trevor's yearly haunt more and more dangerous.

Ian noticed a small patch of sky where the clouds had parted. His breath caught when one star caught his eyes, its brilliant light twinkling solitary and bright through the falling snowflakes.

He couldn't resist. Even if heaven didn't listen to a demon's prayers, that didn't mean he couldn't say one. Maybe the star would understand and carry it to the heavens anyway.

Fixing his gaze on the tiny pinpoint of light, obvious to the cold and snow, Ian pictured his love in his mind and softly spoke to the still night air.

"Please take care of him and protect him from harm."

The only prayer that came to mind was an ancient Irish poem he thought fit their situation in an oddly perfect way, although he was pretty sure the creator hadn't been talking about the undead when it was written.

"Do not stand at my grave and weep,

I am not there…I do not sleep.

I am the thousand winds that blow…

I am the diamond glints on snow…"

Pausing to remember all the words, Ian took a deep breath. The snow silently drifted around, clinging to his eyelashes, hair, and clothing. Trevor filled his thoughts and his senses. He knew it was all of his lover he would be able to have this night and he cherished each one of the memories, holding them close to his heart, childishly hoping his Christmas prayer would be carried in the star's light.

§ § §

Christmas Eve was only one day away and the streets were jammed with shoppers, carolers, hooligans, and school kids. Even late into the evening, the London streets were overrun with people window shopping, coming home from work, and just out enjoying the festive holiday season. A smattering of pickpockets and petty thieves wandered among the strollers, but every corner seemed to have two police bobbies stationed on it.

Even the alleyways, dirty and foreboding places on the best of days, now wore a thin cloak of clean, glittering snow, a rarity for London. But despite their illusion of purity, they were still the playground of the disreputable and immoral, traveled by the city's most undesirables.

Here was where Trevor came to re-enact his last night on earth as a mortal. It was his chance to alter the outcome, to pay back his attackers and to soothe his conscience.

And his conscience needed to be soothed. His guilt over enjoying his present life, loving an existence that enabled him to spend all eternity with the one man who made his every moment on earth worth the price he had paid for the gift. His guilt over loving Ian more than he hated his unholy existence as a dark creature banished to the night for all time. Love of a greater power could not transcend his love for Ian. For that, he paid tribute every anniversary of the Savior's birth and his own rebirth.

Trevor leisurely strolled past a small side alley that he knew led to a maze of dozens of other poorly lit, filthy back streets between the stores and workshops that populated this seedier section of town. He waited until the tall police officer a few feet away was looking in the other direction, then moved silently into the alley. He was swiftly swallowed by the shadows of the closely packed buildings.

Following the faint but familiar sounds of a scuffle he had heard from the mouth of the alley, Trevor sidled down the dark pathway, back pressed to the cold damp brick walls, feet soundless as only a vampire's could be. It took only three turns to put him in the heart of the confrontation.

In the light of the single bare bulb hanging from a warehouse iron rod twenty feet up the side of the building to his right, he could see four men entwined a battle of fists and bats. The occasional glitter of metal shone in the dim light as arms and legs twisted around each other and under bodies so rapidly, Trevor wasn't sure who was battling whom.

Not that it mattered to him. In these secluded paths where the underbelly of society basked in the grime, anyone here had nothing but evil on their mind and they deserved whatever happened to them. He felt no pity for any of them and knew he would grant them no mercy.

Trevor cocked his head, listening, to be sure there wasn't anyone else in the nearby alleys or shadowed doorways to witness his actions or creep up on him, whether they be more scum or a wandering policeman. A faint fluttering heartbeat that didn't belong to the group of men in front of him touched his hearing, but it was too fast to be a man's. He shrugged it off as a stray cat and turned his attention to the business at hand.

Allowing the change to happen, Trevor ran his tongue delicately over his fangs as they descended in his mouth, and marveled at how clear his vision became despite the sudden yellow tint to it.

Soundlessly, he swooped down on the men as three of them forced the fourth to the ground and they all rolled around in the gray slush of the alley floor, grunting and swearing. Trevor found it telling that no one called out for help, reinforcing his conviction that none of the men were innocent bystanders.

Baring his teeth and gleefully anticipating the fight, Trevor swooped down on the most aggressive man in the huddle of flying arms and weapons. He snapped the man's neck with a satisfying crunch that only his hearing could detect. He tossed the useless body aside and grabbed a second attacker, the remaining men still unaware of his presence.

The blood lust rose and Trevor battled it down, refusing to feed fully from the likes of this human trash. He did allow them to feel the terror and pain of his vengeful power during the last moment of their lives. He was forced to make it faster than he would have liked, needing to dispatch them quickly before the ever-vigilant police force was alerted to his presence.

By the time he had coldly finished off the top three assailants, his face was contorted in rage and covered in the blood. Moonlight had broken through the clouded night sky and he could see his pale hands shine with an almost luminescent quality. Trevor imagined his face and blond hair looked much the same in the eerie light, unearthly and bright.

The final brawler was sprawled in a heap, wet and gritty from the alley's debris and slush, alive, but nearly senseless from the blows he'd received. Trevor felt no compassion for him. He was no better than the others, just unfortunate enough to be on the wrong side of the numbers. Reaching down to grasp the shirtfront of the man, Trevor paused, body bathed in a ray of moonlight, his fist wrapped in the man's torn, bloodied shirt. His mouth was open, fangs ready to deliver one more round of dark, symbolic justice, when a tiny sound scratched at the edges of his hearing, drawing his attention.

His head snapped up and his keen eyes picked out a small figure near a barred cellar window, jammed into the small shadows of the brick-patterned overhang. As he watched, frozen in place by the presence of an unexpected witness, a young girl crawled out into the moonlight and slowly approached him.

She was just as tattered and grimy as the men, her dark curls tangled and matted, and her soiled clothing inadequate for the season.

Trevor knew he was a terrifying sight, bloodied and fanged, eyes bright yellow and pale skin glowing, but the child slowly walked closer to him, eyes wide and a look of awe on her lean, dirt-smudged face.

"Are you an angel?" She looked and sounded about eight years old, but her sad eyes told of decades beyond that.

"You look like an angel. One of those avenger angels the minister talks about. From the big church daddy takes me to sometimes." She reached for Trevor with one shaking, tiny hand, but halted as the man in Trevor's grip stirred and moaned. "Daddy?"

The man groaned again and slumped. Wordlessly, Trevor let him fall from his grasp, gaze still riveted to the child's tear-streaked face and dark, expressive eyes.

"Thank you for saving my daddy." She gave Trevor a solemn nod and knelt down in the alley slime, gently cradling the man's head in her barely-there lap. Stunned, Trevor let her. "Daddy said we needed to stay away from all the policemen so they wouldn't take me away, but it's awfully dangerous back here."

"I'll be sure to thank you when I say my prayers tonight." She didn't try to shake his hand, but he knew she thought about it by the way her gaze danced over his bloody fists. "My name's Becca. What's yours?"

Trevor stared at her and thought about what to tell her. He decided the less she knew, the better for her. "Gabriel."

He glanced around at the seedy street and was suddenly overwhelmed by the desolate scene of a homeless child and father fighting off villains and leeches for what little they owned. He had miscalculated his victim for the first time in all his years of seeking vengeance. It unsettled him, made his response harsh and clipped.

"You going to sleep here? In the alleys?"

He softened his voice at the child's fearful, startled expression. "This how you're spending Christmas?" Glancing over his shoulder to make sure they were still alone and unheard, Trevor gestured at the gloom surrounding them, his gaze lingering on the bodies of the dead men. "What kinda holiday is this for a little bit like you, eh?"

"It doesn't matter where you spend Christmas as long as you're with someone you love, Gabriel. Daddy says so."

Her words ate at Trevor's heart and he thought about Ian, alone and far away. He knew where he should truly be on this night. But revenge was so hard to let go of.

Becca rubbed the blood off her father's forehead with the cuff of her thin jacket, gaze still locked on Trevor's face. The man was slowly coming around. He hadn't suffered any serious damage that Trevor could see, and his heart sounded strong and regular.

Rage fading, he allowed the change to slip away, self-consciously rubbing the blood off his hands onto his pant legs. "Don't you want presents? Warm food? A safe place to sleep?"

"Uh-huh. I'll get some." She sounded amazingly convinced, considering her present circumstances.

"And just how do you know that, niblet?" Trevor almost laughed at her innocence. It had been so long since he had been exposed to a child's simple, pure reasoning.

Becca looked over her shoulder at the cellar window where she had been hiding, then looked up at Trevor, awe back in her gaze. "Before, when they were fighting? Before you came?"

Uncertain, Trevor nodded to encourage her when she appeared to expect an answer from him.

"I prayed for someone to come and help." She shrugged and a small, solemn smile creased her red-cheeked face. "And then you were here. A Christmas angel." She patted her father's cheek. "And then the bad men were…" She glanced at the nearby corpses from the corner of her eye and quickly looked down at her hands. "…gone."

Becca turned a bright stare on Trevor. "I know prayers get answered now." She leaned into Trevor's personal space and whispered, "I know I'm not supposed to pray for 'things,' but I'm going to ask for a Christmas dinner and a warmer coat for daddy."

The child looked Trevor over from head to toe and then glanced curiously behind him. "Nobody should be alone on Christmas." Reaching out, Becca slipped her hand into one of Trevor's and hesitantly invited, "You can spend it with us if you don't have to go back to heaven right away."

Something sharp lanced through Trevor's chest, and a strange pressure expanded under his ribcage, making it hard for him to draw a breath. His tightly held desire for revenge suddenly dissolved away into the cold night air, leaving the taste of burnt ashes on his lips where traces of the dead men's blood still lingered.

There was someplace he needed to be, someone he needed to be with, this Christmas Eve and every night after that. Someone who loved him despite his selfish, foolhardy quest for unobtainable justice.

Trevor looked at Becca's open, trusting face, her injured father who had only been trying to protect her, and her outstretched hand. He slipped his own hand into hers, marveling at the strength in the tiny fingers that curled around his.

The sound of footsteps hastened his decision, a faint conversation between two bobbies carrying clearly on the crisp night air. He fished in his pants pocket with his free hand as he shook his head at Becca.

"Thanks anyway, but I can't stay, sweetpea." He disengaged his hand and replaced it with a roll of bills. "There's a bit to help get your da fixed up and buy him that coat and such. There enough to keep the coppers from nicking you away from him, too." He stood and darted a glance at the still empty alleyway, waiting to be sure that Becca wouldn't be left prey to some new menace.

"Do you have to go?"

He leaned down, tapped Becca on the nose with a clean knuckle, and winked. "Heaven's waiting for me. Gotta go."

Two officers came into view as they rounded a corner one building away. Trevor leapt into the air, grabbed the fire escape ladder overhead, and scaled the side of the warehouse in under two seconds. He was long gone before the bobbies' eyesight picked him out of the shadows. Shouts and whistles filled the night.

§ § §

The single bright star glittered and pulsed, its brilliant light stark against the black sky, surrounded by the feathery gray wisps of slow moving snow clouds.

Ian stared at the star, snowflakes catching in his long, dark eyelashes. The captured snowflakes glistened, distorting his vision as it melted into his eyes. He blinked the moisture away, uncomfortably aware that some of the wetness escaping his eyes wasn't only melted snow.

For the first time in a very long while, Ian let down his guard and allowed his love, loneliness, and the nagging anxiety over Trevor's uncertain safety have free rein. He'd never let anyone else see it, but even a being as self-confident and controlled as he was had doubts and fears. Tonight, these seemed especially strong. He sighed and picked up on the verse where he had left off, speaking softly to the waiting starlight.

"I am the sunlight on ripened grain…

I am the gentle autumn rain.

When you waken in the morning rush

I am the swift uplifting rush…"

Pausing for breath, Ian started and turned when another voice took up the poem and finished it for him.

"Of gentle birds in circling flight…

I am the soft star that shines at night.

Do not stand at my grave and cy -

I am not there…I did not die…"

Silhouetted by the cheerful Christmas lights and decorations Stuart had hung in the living room, Trevor stood in the open doorway to the patio. The sight took Ian's breath away. His chest ached and his stomach fluttered. Trevor was home.

"I'm sort of glad not to be buried in some cold, wet grave with a load of dirt sitting on my chest." Trevor slowly walked out onto the patio and stood in front of Ian just out of arm's reach. "I did not die." He sniffed and glanced away, then met Ian's expectant gaze. "Kinda glad of that."

The mellow tunes of Nat King Cole drifted on the stream of warm air that escaped the apartment and muted light filtered out from behind Trevor. It shimmered in the pale strands of his blond hair while the crisp, clean snow that still clung to his clothing glimmered in the starlight. He was bathed in the combined rays, front and back, and the effect was glorious. There was a slight pink to his cheeks, marking him as well fed, and a shy smile on his lips. To Ian, he looked like an angel with a burnished halo.

"You're home." Ian swallowed hard and resisted the urge to grab Trevor and drag him into a crushing embrace. He took in a deep breath to steady the flutter in his chest.

"Back early, aren't you?" The thought that Trevor had returned for some darker reason than wanting to be with Ian on Christmas darted across Ian's mind and made him uncharacteristically hesitant.

"Running late, actually." Trevor scuffed his toe in the snow then locked gazes with Ian's uncertain stare. He took another step closer, entering Ian's personal space. He slowly edged forward, closing the gap between them until their bodies brushed.

"Met a Christmas angel last night. Little bitty one named Becca." He ran his hands up the front of Ian's chest, and then slipped his fingers under the edges of Ian's open collar to rub at the carotid pulse points on the vampire's sensitive neck.

"A Christmas angel?" Ian stood very still so not to dislodge

Trevor's tenuous hold. He couldn't keep a skeptical smile from tugging at his lips. "Named Becca."

"Uh huh. A real, live angel. Too skinny, but a sweet bit of fluff." Trevor smirked at Ian's expression, but Ian could tell Trevor was uneasy, maybe even nervous about Ian's reaction to him being home. "She told me Christmas was to be spent with someone you loved."

"Smart bit of fluff." Ian shifted closer and let his hands find the man's slender hips. There was a skittishness in Trevor's approach that made Ian cautious. Instead of pulling Trevor to him, he swayed his own body forward and let their groins touch.

"She was that." Trevor's hands traced the curve of Ian's jaw, his thumbs brushing lightly over Ian's parted lips. His gaze followed his fingertips, then bounced up to meet Ian's appraising stare. "Smarter than me, apparently." Trevor sighed and moistened his bottom lip before admitting, "As bad as it was, she was where she belonged and I wasn't." Trevor pressed his length against Ian.

Ian's arousal burst to life and he felt Trevor's body answer in kind, but he stopped himself from pushing the moment. Instead, he smiled down at Trevor's upturned face and studied his uncertain expression for clues to what his lover was thinking. He saw lust and attraction in Trevor's eyes, along with a new mix of embarrassment and guilt. Puzzled, Ian moved one hand to the small of Trevor's back and massaged the tense muscles there.

"You're sure about being here? After all these decades, you're suddenly done handing out punishment? You're ready to stay with me instead?"

Trevor wordlessly nodded, but the embarrassment in his eyes grew.

Ian cradled Trevor's face between his hands and softly kissed his lips before drawing back. His tone was soft but the look in his eyes was steely. "Why now, Trevor?"

"Realized I was punishing you right along with the thugs that did me in. Didn't mean to, but I was." He dropped his gaze for several seconds. "Might've even meant to. A little."

His own buried guilt surfaced, and Ian felt a rush of forgiveness and understanding wash over him. He'd never known Trevor harbored any guilt over that fateful night. He hadn't objected to Trevor's Christmas activities because he felt he deserved to be punished just as much as Trevor obviously had.

When Ian gently raised Trevor's chin, the starlight glistened in the twin streams of wetness trailing down his face. Snowflakes stuck to the moisture and instantly melted. Ian brushed the tears and flakes away with his thumbs then moved them to brush over Trevor's mouth.

"And now, beauty?"

Trevor leaned into Ian's caress and closed his eyes, his hips slowly grinding against Ian's thigh and cock, a tremulous sigh escaping his lips. "Don't want revenge anymore."

Ian kissed each closed eyelid, first one side then the next, and then back again. "What do you want?" He kissed his way down the side of Trevor's face and nuzzled his neck.

"You. Just you. Best gift I ever got. You and me forever." Trevor craned his head to one side, encouraging Ian to explore further. "You and me on Christmas Eve, just like the first one."

"You remember that one, do you?" Ian nipped the thin skin between neck and shoulder, then licked off the resulting ooze of blood.

Trevor gasped and pressed Ian's face closer. "Can't forget one of the best nights I ever had. You made me go blind for a while that night."

"Blind? Really?" Preening, Ian smirked with delight at the revelation.

Trevor smacked Ian's broad shoulder, unimpressed when the solid bulk didn't budge. "Big-headed bastard, aren't you now! Should never have told you!"

Ian laughed and wiggled his eyebrows at his lover. "Maybe we could try for mute this time." He grabbed Trevor and wrestled him into a crushing embrace, kissing and exploring his lover's mouth and neck until Trevor was breathless and squirming in his arms. His cock was hard and ready, but Ian wanted this to be a seduction unlike any Trevor could remember before this.

An unexpected, overly loud, and dramatic clearing of a dry throat momentarily broke them apart. Still entwined in each other's arms, both vampires glanced guiltily toward the source of the untimely interruption.

"I was going to bring out the mistletoe to set the mood, but I see it isn't necessary." Tossing the festive twig and berries in the air, Stuart turned on his heel and headed back into the apartment, droning tonelessly, "Possibly you would like to tie it around Master Trevor's waist instead?"

Ian instinctively lunged for the object, snatching it out of the air in mid-arc as it sailed overhead. He looked at the mistletoe and then arched one eyebrow at Trevor. He pulled Trevor close and held it up over their heads.

Trevor reached up and slowly pulled Ian's hand back down, mistletoe included. He softly kissed his lover's mouth, breathing his words into Ian's parted lips. "I like Stuart's idea better."

A wicked glint in his eyes, Ian grinned and dropped to his knees. This was going to be a very merry Christmas, indeed.

ENTHRALLED

"*That* is a very long way down."

Standing on the curved top of the thin railing of his apartment's balcony, the ground looked farther away than it had when Colin had been standing on the balcony itself. Ten floors *were* very high. High enough to make sure when he hit the street below, there wouldn't be any chance of a medical team having something to work with.

Colin shifted his weight slightly, his unbuttoned, white dress shirt billowing and flapping in the night breeze around his slender body. The cuff of one sleeve was edged in bright red, and a slow trickle of the same color dripped from one fingertip. His faded blue jeans hugged his hips and thighs, following the curve of his small, firm ass like a well-worn glove.

He looked down at the parked cars and faint white lines on the street below. They swirled dizzily as the half bottle of sleeping pills battled with the two inches of whiskey he had washed them down with ten minutes ago. He averted his gaze to take in the heavens above him, but the night was black and starless, as void and dark as his tired soul. At twenty-five, Colin Dobson felt the weight of an entire lifetime on his shoulders.

A slight wind blew through his dark hair, ruffling his curls and making his unfocused eyes water. The sound of paper rustling nearby eventually grabbed his attention and he glanced down to see the letter he had dropped earlier, the final straw in a long string of unpleasant happenings in his short, chaotic life. It was such a small thing, really, being left alone for his birthday once again, but it was just the final snapping thread to unravel his tenuous self-control.

The paper was trapped in the intricate ironwork of the patio set, captured between the biting wind and the table leg. As he watched, the breeze shifted and the paper skittered away, like so much in his life had done lately, disappearing into the night.

Half lidded, his teal eyes followed the letter, then drifted closed. He opened them to find himself staring at his sock-covered feet. His black-clad toes were curled around the polished iron banister to keep what little balance he still possessed. He studied the weave of the knit fabric for a moment, fascinated by the tiny line of golden thread that ran across his toes. The thread moved with each flex and wiggle of his foot and Colin suddenly imagined it symbolized the delicate rope of sanity he was holding onto at the moment -- thin, wavering and surrounded by darkness.

A bright spot of color made his gaze dart to his left. He stood mesmerized by the tiny dot of red that spattered onto the railing, and then dripped off the edge to splash down into the street a hundred feet below. Colin cursed himself for his cowardice. He hadn't been able to cut through his wrist deep enough to end his problems in a neater fashion, but a lifetime fear of sharp objects took control and his attempt stopped almost as soon as it began. All he had to show for it was a superficial three inch cut that was more scratch than laceration and another blow to his dwindling ego. He sighed at the thought that he wasn't even man enough to take control of his life long enough to end it in a decent, respectable manner. Instead, he'd had to turn to drugs and alcohol, with an impending grand finale of blunt body trauma in the middle of a public thoroughfare ten stories away.

Another splotch of color joined the first, and Colin forced his gaze up as bright red layered over the now darker, lifeless rusty brown. A wave of dizziness floated around him, invading his thoughts and clouding his mind. Now that he was on top of the three-foot tall railing, he was suddenly confused about his plan of action.

Should he fling himself off the building, taking temporary flight like some comic book superman, pretending to be the hero for once in his life, if only for a brief second? Or should he just step off his balcony into the clear night air like he was walking off a city curb?

Did it really matter which one he picked? He knew no one would know what he was thinking. No one else could understand how he felt right now. Colin had a vast, aching emptiness that had shoved aside the constant pain in his chest until he was little more than an empty, useless shell. No one was left to care how he died or what his last thoughts would be. His life had been nothing more than a small hiccup in the timeline of the world anyway. A tiny blemish that would be forgotten before the spectators gawking over his broken and mangled body faded away.

Throwing his head back, Colin turned his handsome, still boyish face upward, tensed his legs for the jump, spread his arms wide, opened his glazed, watery eyes to meet his coming fate face-to-face like the man his father always wanted him to be, then slowly tipped over the edge into the welcoming night.

CHAPTER ONE

"Deceitful mongrels! I'll eat your hearts for this!"

Dodging to the left then making a sharp dive to his extreme right, Rowland Campbell managed to escape the crossbow's mark for a second time. With teeth bared, extended fangs showing, his normally pale blue eyes were now a fluorescent yellow with just a tinge of red in them. The millennia-old vampire snarled under his breath, letting a bit of his rage at being caught off guard by this trio of hunters fuel his instinctive sense of survival.

Since his human days as a Roman general, when he used a name even he had forgotten, Rowland had a knack for winning and surviving under the worst of conditions. That was undoubtedly one of the reasons he had weathered the many changes the centuries had brought down on him since being turned. Even now, trapped between an un-scalable glass building wall and three rabid hunters out to claim his head for a trophy, he was still sure he could make it out in one piece. He might not be able to kill the hunters this night, but he would live to fight them another day. And their day would definitely come. Rowland Campbell took no prisoners and left no unfriendly witnesses to tell the tale of his existence. Ever. At times, even identifying what species his victims were was occasionally a problem for the people finding the remains.

A series of faint hisses warned him the next assault had been fired, and he rolled to one side to escape a volley of wooden arrows shot from high-tech, rapid firing crossbows. He had an inkling these dramatic and gadget-loaded hunters fancied themselves cutting a romantic figure as they brandished their modern day versions of an ancient weapon that was as steeped in myth and lore as the vampire legend itself.

The few glimpses of them he had seen in between shots revealed them to be heavily leather clad and sporting more hand weapons than could possibly be legal to carry out in the open, making them look like futuristic warriors in a cheap space odyssey. One even wore a long, velvet cloak that swished and swayed, giving away his location with each movement. Luckily for Rowland, they seemed to like to stay grouped together, so pinpointing them was only a matter of filtering out the night sounds and listening.

Even though they had several opportunities to rush him, the trio of men remained on the low roof to the right of the glass building Rowland crouched beside, pinning their vampire prey in the short alley between the two structures. All Rowland needed to do was make it to either the end of the alley or up to the rooftop unscathed, and he would be able to leave these foolhardy, but persistent, hunters behind. Then he in turn would track them down and they would become the unsuspecting prey.

Slipping soundlessly behind a large dumpster, Rowland turned to face the building, mentally calculating the jump he would need to make the leap to the seven-story rooftop. His keen eyesight picked out a rusted, unused flagpole brace still attached to the side of the building, and his decision on which escape route to take was made.

He let one corner of his thin lips quirk up in what he knew to be a mirthless, unattractive smirk and casually allowed the full force of the beast that dwelt within him to have free rein, feeling the massive, ancient energy and strength course through his already powerful frame.

Looking back down the building, he caught sight of himself in the blackened glass, a perfect reflecting surface in the dim light provided by the streetlights at each end of the alley. A tall, proud man stared back at him, with naturally platinum, brush-cropped hair, golden eyes flecked with splinters of red, with a handsome if square-jawed face set on a body that was broad, taut and muscular.

He had been turned at the time of his thirty-eighth year, his body honed and toned by years in the military and the battlefield. Even before he became a supernatural creature with awe-inspiring powers, he had been an intimidating man and a fierce, unforgiving warrior. Any shred of mercy he had ever possessed was long gone, along with the centuries that had passed while he hunted his fellow man for food.

The crisp, clean lines of his black suit and black dress shirt showed the cut of his well-muscled body and accentuated the pale color of his nearly flawless skin. Only a small scar on the tip of his chin marred the smooth surface of his face, a lasting testimony to the temper and insanity of the last conquered woman he had taken during what was to be his final campaign.

Rowland casually straightened the lines of his jacket and moved out from behind the dumpster. Combining a distraction with his ultimate goal, he suddenly moved more rapidly than the men could possibly track with their human eyes. He jumped into the air and zigzagged up the side of the building using the force of his initial leap to propel himself up to the flagpole brace. Pushing off the short piece of jutting metal, he rocketed up the remainder of the slick glass wall. Arrows pinged and bounced all around him, ricocheting off the smooth surface and falling harmlessly to the alleyway below.

Just before he reached the rooftop, the smell of unwashed human male struck him, and he immediately knew why the three men below hadn't rushed him. They had wanted him to make a break for the rooftop where a fourth hunter waited patiently for him. Knowing they would expect him to panic and retreat at the last minute, Rowland continued up to land on the gritty asphalt roof, his shoes making a heavy, ominous thud as he paused a split second to target his lone opponent.

In a blink of an eye he was on the surprised man, dragging the hunter to his chest, pinning the cocked and ready crossbow between them. His fangs tore into the hunter's face and shoulders, blinding his prey with the man's own blood as his massive fingertips tightened on the thick leather collar the man wore protectively around his neck. Locking eyes with his victim's, he tightened his grip, watching the light fade from his prey's startled gaze.

When this moment occurred, he always felt the power of

his victim's life energy drain away, usually mixed with massive elements of desire, hope, terror and pain. It was like a drug he was addicted to. It reaffirmed his cursed existence, fortified his conviction that evil had found a home within his heart, replacing his soul and devouring his spirit. He was death and deserved nothing more than the centuries of pain and loneliness that was his entire existence. He was unredeemable by anyone's standards. A small smile creased his face, and he squeezed until he heard cartilage break.

He didn't need to feed, it was early and there was more suitable prey walking the street for later. Now, Rowland was content with making a statement, forewarning the other hunters what they could look forward to when he tracked them down one by one.

He released his hold on the dead man, pushing off the falling body to take flight for his final escape. When he was ten feet straight up into the air, the hunter's body hit the rooftop. The faint, but telling click of the crossbow striking the ground and firing met his ear a second too late. A sudden, sharp pain knocked him upright in the air and fire spread through his chest, racing down his limbs and torturing every cell in his body. His hands flew to his chest and wrapped around the protruding end of the wooden shaft lodged deep within his ribcage. Moving the shaft he felt the barrel rub against his heart and the fire consuming his body became a roaring inferno of agony.

Still suspended in air, Rowland hovered over the rooftop, momentarily stunned, until the sounds of the other three hunters hurriedly approaching snapped him back into action.

Blood poured from around the arrow and his strength flowed away with it. Pressing his hands to the wound, Rowland resumed his flight, keeping his path straightforward, conserving his energy. He needed shelter and to feed, preferably in the same place and he needed it soon. Within a few blocks he was in a high-priced apartment district in the heart of the semi-sleeping city.

Numerous lights dotted the surrounding apartment buildings, but few, if any, had open doors on such a brisk, chilly night. He heard the sound of a woman's laughter from an apartment balcony on the twelfth floor. She was talking on the phone to a friend, murmuring snide remarks and cutting comments about co-workers and lamenting her evening alone at home. Rowland felt that familiar smirk of delighted evil twist his lips when he killed the hunter, and he strained to obtain enough lift to gain access to the welcoming sound of the harsh, feminine laughter.

Fifty feet before the woman's balcony, the arrow shifted and a spasm of pain shot through the vampire's chest. With a roar of agony, he tumbled out of the air, dropping two floors. With a final surge of flagging strength, Rowland propelled himself forward. With a sudden thud and deep, soul-shattering bellow of pain, he struck a soft object, plunging the arrow into his chest until it protruded out his back. The world twisted and went black.

At a loss for anything meaningful to say at the end of his life, Colin sighed and murmured, "Forgive me."

As his feet left the firm surface of the railing, Colin looked out into the night, determined to meet his fate with his eyes wide open. Instead of gracefully tipping over to see the gray asphalt rising up to meet him, Colin was greeted by Death himself. He only had a split second before Death embraced him with a roar of triumph.

Colliding chest to chest, Colin was thrown back over his patio railing. The sound of air rushing by him made his ears pound and his skin prickle. Sailing through the air into his open bedroom terrace doors, he landed heavily on his back beside his bed, his head making a dull thud as it bounced off the carpet. The room swam and his stomach churned at the sudden movement and abrupt stop. Swallowing down nausea, Colin blinked back the moisture from his bleary eyes and looked up.

A terrifying face, twisted in a harsh grimace of defiance and anger, hovered above him. The eyes were golden yellow, flecked with blood red. The bristled white hair cropped close to the creature's head was splattered with dots of reddish brown. Its mouth was open, lips pulled back to reveal sharp white fangs that glistened in the faint light from the table lamp beside Colin's bed. The teeth were stained the same blood red as the creature's eyes.

Colin knew his fate had finally found him, but his moment of final peace was snatched away as Death groaned, closed his eyes and slumped unconscious over Colin's small, thin body. Somewhere in the back of his drugged and drunken mind drifted the message that his attacker, this creature, was a vampire, and in his current mental state Colin accepted this as fact without needing to explore it further.

The vampire's barrel chest pressed him to the plush floor, a frame defined by unyielding, rock-hard muscles. Colin groggily tried to regain the breath forced out from his own chest. A thick thigh rested between his faded blue jean clad legs, his sock-covered toes barely reaching to below the bend in the creature's knees. Something poked at his right armpit, causing his white linen shirt to cling to his chest and side, a wet, coolness seeping through to his own chilled flesh.

"What the hell?" Wiggling his hand out from under his own body where it had been trapped in the fall, Colin's fingertips found the end of a smooth, thin stick wedged firmly against his arm. Following the slick shaft, his hand slid up to the creature's chest where it was lodged. Colin shifted his shoulder to free his skewed shirt from under the shaft's end, his actions nudging the vampire's arm and tugging on the arrow.

The vampire's golden and red eyelids flew open. Colin instantly froze in place, his hand pressed against the platinum haired man's bleeding body. The vampire's eyes actually glowed in the dim light as they raked over his face, seemingly memorizing every pore of his pale skin.

"Move again and I'll kill you." The thin, sneering lips had barely moved, but the cultured voice was deep and commanding, the tone harsh and unmistakably deadly, even to Colin's temporarily impaired hearing.

Despite the genuine intent behind the threat, the vampire's words brought a small smile to Colin's own full, dry mouth. He drowsily batted his eyelashes at his attacker and slowly moistened his lips with the tip of his tongue before trying to speak. Even then his words were slurred and hesitant, the drugs and alcohol firmly in control of his abilities.

"Promise?" Colin fluttered his eyelids in an attempt to keep his gaze focused on the intense stare burning into his. "Like this?"

Colin lifted his only free shoulder a fraction of an inch. A massive square hand slammed it back down onto the floor so hard Colin gasped and blinked through the drug-muted stab of pain. His hand was pried from around the slick, blood-coated shaft and both his wrists were pinned to the floor above his head, held easily in one of the vampire's hands in a move so fast, Colin didn't see it happen.

That deep, cultured, faintly British voice purred in his ear again, making his numb nerve endings tingle all the way down to his crushed groin.

"A pretty little one with a death wish. How fortunate. We can both have what we crave." The vampire nuzzled his chin over Colin's face, rasping the edge of his prominent jaw along Colin's light five o'clock shadow. "But first, the arrow must be pulled out. You'll have to help me with that." A wet, rough tongue licked the soft flesh under Colin's jaw, the slight scrape and burn of teeth marking the skin over his pulse. "Then I'll grant you what you desire, my pretty little one."

Colin found himself mesmerized by the sound of the vampire's sultry voice, and his cock stirred wantonly in its confined prison. Colin panted a little for air, the weight of the man and the stench of blood mixing with the alcohol in his stomach until it churned and burned at the back of his throat.

Suddenly the vampire heaved himself up to land on his side with a thud and a muffled groan of pain.

Colin breathed a sigh of relief and pulled in the first deep breath he'd been able to draw since falling. He could see both of the large man's hands wrapped tightly around the feathered end still sticking out of the front of his body. A three-pronged metal arrowhead glistened on Colin's side, along with several inches of the wooden shaft.

The creature's deep, commanding voice carried bitingly in the still bedroom air, demanding and sure, even now. "Break off the tip."

"Okay. I help you live then you help me die. Seems fair to me." Colin tried to roll over and push himself up off the floor, but his body wouldn't cooperate even if his mouth couldn't seem to stop working, silly childhood questions finally finding a voice. "Are vampires actually alive?"

The room swayed and tilted with the slightest move of his head. "And if they are, why do you need blood to live if you're already dead?"

A harsh growl was the only answer his questions received. It didn't matter, they were rhetorical anyway. Something to distract him from the nausea rolling in his stomach.

Colin fingered the sharp tip and finally slurred, "Can't. Can't get up. Downers finally hitting. Another twenty minutes," he yawned and patted the vampire's back soothingly, "and I won't need you after all."

A guttural, primal roar shook the room and the arrow shaft under his fingers suddenly disappeared. Colin blinked and twisted to get a better look at the creature beside him, but the vampire was no longer lying there. In his place were the blood-coated, mangled remains of what was once a wooden arrow.

The air in the room seemed to rush by him in a swirling blaze of darkness and muted lights. Colin felt his body lifted and turned, whirled and dangled, before his cotton-filled head stopped spinning and his body flopped boneless and naked down onto his sheets. Pinned down, wrists held at his lean shoulders, Colin's eyes watered as strong, unforgiving fingers laced through his dark curls and tightly gripped his hair.

The weight of the vampire settled abruptly on his chest once more, the blood-soaked shirt cold against his exposed flesh. Colin's legs were flung wide and one clothed, thickly-muscled thigh buried itself between them. Colin could feel the vampire's fully erect cock pressing demandingly against the length of his own fluttering shaft. He couldn't think of a reason to resist the sensation so he didn't, arching his hips up and savored the rush of pleasure that sizzled through his body. This was more intimate physical contact than his body had experienced in his entire lifetime and now he actually had something that he would miss about life when he died. How ironic. He could feel hot tears slip down his face as the drugged stupor ate away the last of his self-control.

Opening his heavy eyelids, Colin met the same terrifying creature that had swept him off the railing, but this time the vampire had added hunger to the look of anger and murderous intent. Completely unfazed, Colin merely nodded, struggling to keep his eyes open. "If I were sober, I bet you'd be really scary looking."

One of the vampire's thumbs uncurled from his hair and began to stroke across Colin's full lower lip, caressing the moist inner lining then using the wetness to paint over the sensitive outer flesh. The expression of impending death barely affected Colin, but the delicate touch sent a shiver straight through him.

"Do it. Do it now." Colin fought to keep his body still, surprised at the arousal the deadly creature's touch coaxed from his body. He was amazed at how excited he was at being pinned down by this beast. His body grew warm and he panted with each new shallow breath he managed to pull in despite the heavy weight on his chest. He found it faintly amusing that what amounted to his "first time" with another man would be when he was on the brink of having his death wish granted.

He locked his bleary gaze on the golden-eyed monster's fanged mouth then slowly turned his head to one side and arched his neck, silently offering everything he had. The pressure on his scratched wrist increased and Colin felt the warm blood ooze from the still raw wound. He watched the vampire raise the injured wrist to his lips and delicately lap at the trickle of fresh blood. Colin relaxed back against the mattress and studied the expression of bliss and hunger that replaced the creature's grimace of pain and rage, oddly fascinated by the erotic look in the vampire's eyes.

It was the first time he had ever been the cause of someone, anyone, looking like that. A burst of pride and desire blossomed in his hollow chest. The desire flared out from his ribcage and traveled to his groin where his cock jerked and strained against the weight of the thigh holding it immobile. Colin was about to throw caution and reason to the wind and hump the vampire's leg when the creature's eyes glowed a deep gold, the red flecks expanding.

"I can taste your youth and your untried passions. A virgin in so many ways."

The vampire purred softly, his deep voice like melted chocolate, smooth, rich and addicting. Even the undertone of raw need and hunger excited Colin. His wrist was lapped and suckled, talented lips encouraging the tiny flow of blood, widening the shallow wound by forcing the edges apart.

Colin hissed at the slight burn his numb senses could still detect, but his toes curled and his hips jerked at the same time as a low groan escaped his lips. A soft chuckle teased near his ear and cool lips nipped at the tip of his chin before returning to his bleeding wrist. A blunt hand found a nipple and a single fingernail raked over its swollen, erect nub. Colin gasped and squirmed, never taking his eyes off his smiling companion.

"You're so needy, so ready for my every touch." The vampire flicked his nail over Colin's now aching nipple again. "I think I've changed my mind."

Colin blanched and whimpered, confused and exhausted.

"Oh, don't worry, my pretty little one, I plan on feeding from you. I just don't plan on killing you. At least, not right away. I think after I feed and heal a bit, I'll spend the next few days teaching you what it's like to have a vampire for a lover." He sucked hard on Colin's wrist, working the wound open even wider. "And as I hate to deny myself anything worth having, if you are an exceptionally good learner, I might even make you my thrall."

"Thrall? What...?" Speech slow and his words indistinct, Colin barely managed to hang on to consciousness.

"A vampire's human companion. Their lover, slave, and source of occasional nourishment."

Colin felt the vampire stroke one finger slowly up his chest from his ribcage to his carotid artery, letting a finger rest against the pounding, slightly irregular beat Colin could feel hammering in his neck.

"The relationship can last for centuries," he whispered near Colin's ear, low and seductive with just a touch of deadly intent, "or hours, depending on the vampire's mood."

"So do it." Colin licked his lips and gave the vampire a sleepy-eyed, sultry look. "Make me your thrall. Bite me."

"Remember you begged for this later, pretty." His lips brushed the shell of Colin's ear.

"Yeah, sure, later."

Immediately, the highly erotic, sucking sensation was back at Colin's wrist, but only for a moment before a spike of true agony flashed up his arm. The vampire's fangs were embedded deep into his flesh and blood poured down his arm before the creature clamped his lips over the gaping hole and began to feed. Once the searing pain from being bitten lessened, a strange euphoria mingled with the nauseating effect of the downers and whiskey. Colin knew the last threads of his life were slipping away. A satisfied smile tugged at his mouth and a small breathless chuckle escaped from between his dry, numb lips.

Abruptly the sucking stopped. The vampire froze in place, then licked at the wound. Surprise evident in his voice, he hissed, "Tell me what you are."

Colin huffed out an amused, unintelligible murmur and fought to keep his eyes open, just to see the creature's expression. Blood ran down his wrist and the vampire lapped and sucked at the open wound again, a frown marring his handsome, harsh face.

As the blood flowed unchecked, the vampire held Colin's wrist closed and yanked Colin up to within a few inches of his snarling face. "Why doesn't this stop?" He jerked Colin until the young man's eyes fluttered open wider and demanded, "Tell. Me. *Why.*"

A mildly triumphant note mixed in with Colin's stuttered reply. "Sorry to disappoint you, big guy," Colin's fingers curved and he laid them on the vampire's cheek. "But it's not going to stop, not now, not until I'm dead."

Colin smiled and his eyes slid shut, but a sharp shake and low growl in his ear snapped him back to awareness.

"I said, tell me *why!*"

Body melting into a boneless heap, Colin still managed to look the enraged vampire in the eye. He noticed for the first time the man's eyes were now a pale shade of icy blue, cool and startling. As the last thing he would ever see, Colin decided they were a very nice sight to leave this world with.

Ground out between gritted teeth and fangs, came the low, urgent demand of "Why?"

"Uh? Oh… hemophiliac… born to bleed." Colin snickered, then hiccupped. "Guess I get my death wish after all. Thanks for helping."

Colin's teeth rattled and his head spun as he was thrown back down on the bed. He trailed his blood-covered hand across the vampire's cheek and murmured just before passing out, "Nice eyes. Even when they do that… glowy… thing."

The touch to Rowland's cheek was like an electric caress that set his body and mind on fire. His face actually burned where the thin streak of blood trailed across his flesh.

Stunned into inactivity, Rowland stared at the limp, pale man under him. He jerked upright and straddled the slim, naked body, letting out an enraged bellow that echoed eerily in the large bedroom. Doves resting on the balcony railing outside the still open door cooed and scattered into a flurry of wings and lost feathers at the sound.

Clamping the hemorrhaging wrist to his lips, he drank down as much of the sweet nectar as he safely could, then forced mouthful after mouthful of his own saliva into the blood vessels and flesh surrounding the wound. Over an hour later the clotting factors from his own body began to seal the wound and the bleeding tapered off to a mere dribble. With the first sigh of relief he could remember exhaling in centuries, he lay down beside his young conquest. Nothing would keep this sweetness from being his for the taking and the keeping, least of all a petty bleeding disorder.

The moment Rowland had sunk his fangs into the young man's flesh he knew this one was different. Under the bitter taint of tranquilizers and alcohol, and the familiar smell of blood and rising bile, there was a sweet, bright current of purity, like sunlight. Granted, it had a cord of dark despair twisted around it, but the thread was thin and could be easily broken. Rowland had no desire to release the man from it, it served his purposes as well, but it was interesting to know how dark a place the young man was in at this moment.

Expecting to experience the inevitable surge of power and delicious energy he received with the first deep taste of warm, pulsing blood, Rowland had gulped down a mouthful and then another. Letting the third linger in his mouth, he was forced to freeze his actions. When his eyes darted to his victim's, he was unexpectedly horrified and perplexed. As the light began to dim in the human's eyes, there was no rush of energy, no kick of adrenaline, no thrill of draining away part of the young man's life force. Instead, Rowland felt a surge of panic flush through his body at the thought of losing this man. This one was indeed different.

Rowland had long ago lost a sexual preference. This one, this pretty little one, was a perfect choice for a thrall. Too perfect to waste and too important to rush. This one needed to be seduced and possibly even cherished.

Leaving the unconscious man outstretched on the sheets of the large bed, Rowland stripped off his own soiled clothing and began planning his young, inexperienced thrall's seduction.

The shadow-shrouded room slowly came into focus. After a few lethargic blinks and a slow turn of his head, Colin recognized it as his own bedroom. The furniture wavered slightly at first then settled into firm surfaces and familiar lines. The lamp on his bedside table was lit, casting a golden wash of warm color that didn't extend past the foot of his bed. A thick comforter lay draped over him, his body beneath naked and sore.

Colin raised his right hand to rub the sleep from his eyes, wincing at the burning pain that tingled at his wrist. Holding his arm in mid-air, he stared at the neat, professional-looking dressing wrapped snuggly over the painful area, confused about how the injury had occurred. In fact, he couldn't remember how he came to be in bed, naked and exhausted beyond any memory in time. A slight movement at the end of the bed brought a tall, regal figure into the hazy light and Colin's last quarter hour of consciousness came rushing back to him.

His lungs seemed to lose the ability to move and his breath stilled, trapped in place, until the need for air became too urgent for his body to deny. Dropping his bandaged arm to the bed, Colin pulled in a shaky, shallow gasp, forcing his eyes to track the large, broad-chested figure as it sauntered around the bed and moved to stand beside him.

"Good evening, Colin. The night is just beginning. I'm pleased you'll be able to join me."

Drained, barely able to move, Colin still responded to the rich, deep voice. The seed of fear that had taken root in his chest at the sight of the vampire died away. Even his earlier despair and intense loneliness seemed a pointless waste of precious energy.

After clearing his parched throat to ease the passage of his words, they still tumbled out in a hushed whisper. "How do you know my name?"

Clad in a dark red, silk robe Colin didn't recognize, the vampire sat down next to him and leaned forward into Colin's personal space, arms outstretched and braced on either side of Colin. "By looking through your private correspondence. I know your name, age, profession, and checking account balance." He tugged the comforter down several inches to reveal Colin's chest and flat stomach, a leering gaze wandering over the exposed, quivering, pale flesh. He ran one long, blunt finger down the comforter to Colin's groin. "I know your waist size, inseam, approximate weight, and how long your cock is when it's partially erect." The vampire winked at him. "I am Rowland Campbell."

Despite the faint blush he could feel heat his cheeks, Colin ignored the taunting and the introduction. "How long have I been out?"

"Two days. Long enough for me to heal, rest and feed -- benefit of the acid-tongued woman who used to live on the twelfth floor." Rowland fingered the open edges of the red robe he was wearing. "At least her lovers had good taste in bed jackets. She, on the other hand, tasted appalling. Too much recreational cocaine and no fat in her diet, I suspect."

Faintly horrified, Colin pressed his lips shut and tried not to think about the woman. Gently tracing the edges of the gauze wrapped around his injured wrist Colin asked, "How...?" Squeezing shut his eyes to stop the sudden burn of tears only made them burst free and stream down his cheeks. Unwilling to look his savior/tormentor in the face, he clenched his eyelids tighter. "*Why* am I still alive?"

Lifted from the bed to a near sitting position by a bruising grip on his upper arms, Colin's head bobbed on his shoulders, his entire body shaken in a harsh grip. Snapping his eyelids open he stared at the now familiar face of the vampire's full wrath and fury.

Rowland seethed, words spitting out at a furious rate, his tone threatening and decisive. "Because I desired it!" He raised one arm to deliver a backhanded blow, but stilled at the last moment. He gripped Colin's jaw in his massive palm and forced the young man's face up to meet his icy blue stare.

"You agreed to be my thrall, and my thrall you *shall* be." His voice, first low and sultry, shifted to a seductive purr of promise and pleasure. He lessened his biting grip and ran his hands up Colin's arms, gently laying him back down on the mattress. "Now I need only to teach you *how* to be my pleasure."

Trying not to shudder under the vampire's arousing touch and hungry stare, Colin pressed himself deeper against the bed.

Rowland stood and slowly slipped the robe off his body, revealing the muscular, hardened body of a sword-wielding warrior of forgotten days long past. Colin noticed an array of battle scars crisscrossing his broad, heavily-muscled torso, making him look even deadlier than before. The vampire's skin was a pale shade of alabaster, defined as well as any of Michelangelo's proud statues. His thick, full erection jutted out from a thicket of pale golden hair, the uncircumcised hood engulfing its blunt tip like a shield of armor.

A flash of fear and desire flooded through Colin's weakened body and his cock stirred beneath the silky covers. Despite his confusion and anxiety, he longed to feel the touch of a lover. If he was going to die at the hands of this creature, falling into the arms of a temporary lover sounded far better than falling off a ten-story balcony.

Longing to reach out and touch the vision of mythic manhood before him, but too depleted and depressed to move anything other than his eyelids, Colin returned the vampire's seductive glance and wet his lips. He knew he should be screaming, running for the nearest church, but all he could do was stare back at the man's hypnotic blue eyes and murmur, "Okay. Teach me."

He watched Rowland's eyebrow quirk up and a small smile tugged at one corner of his mouth. "Aren't we the brave little one?" the vampire hissed.

Rowland approached the bed, slid under the single comforter, and rolled on top of Colin's unresisting body. Instantly reacting to the cool, smooth slide of flesh on flesh, Colin whimpered as the creature's firm cock stroked over his own heated groin. A tremor of excitement and fear shot through him. He continued to tremble, mouth open and panting, eyes glued to the amused stare hovering above him.

"The trembling form of a virgin in my bed, how lovely. I'd almost forgotten what it felt like." Rowland supported his weight on his forearms and forced his legs between Colin's lax thighs. "Why have you never had a lover, Colin? A young man as attractive as you should have dozens of suitors."

Unable to force words out of his tightening throat, Colin shook his head. It wasn't enough for his captor. The vampire gripped his dark curls and tilted Colin's head back in a gentle, but immobilizing hold. "I asked you a question, pretty." The grip eased and Rowland's tone softened, as did his glare. "Tell me."

Swallowing hard past a dry lump in his throat, Colin stuttered, "Home schooling, private tutors, online college courses, private trust fund, over protective, never-there parents, all meant to keep me from getting hurt." He sighed, worrying at his lip. "Never had the opportunity to meet anyone. My entire life's been about living safely and avoiding injury." A wry smile twisted his lips and a tiny twinkle managed to light his tired eyes. "I think meeting you has kind of blown the last twenty-five years of caution all to hell though."

He felt a huff of laughter shake the vampire's chest and his smile quivered on his own lips. A flat broad thumb gently rubbed over his mouth.

Rowland's deep voice was a gentle mix of sarcasm and wonder. "Saving yourself for me, no doubt."

Growing serious at the thought, Colin froze for a moment. He found himself searching the vampire's face, looking for some sign of need or desire in the man, some clue that he, Colin Dobson, was actually wanted by another. A spark of something Colin couldn't define suddenly crossed the vampire's face, and his own body responded to it. His skin flushed, his cock filled, his breathing increased, and a queasy, fluttering feeling in his stomach threatened to send him into a bout of dry heaves.

He turned his head into the grip Rowland had on his hair and rubbed his head over the vampire's curled fingertips. "Maybe I was." He let his lips part invitingly, darting the tip of his tongue out to wet his lower lip. "Let's… find out."

The soft, glistening pink of Colin's tongue drew Rowland's eyes to the young man's full, parted lips. Desire surged through his body and he dipped his head down to greedily accept the tentative invitation. His hands clenched in the silky curls on Colin's head and he drew his young lover tightly to him. The heady scent of Colin's arousal made Rowland hungry for the taste of the young man's flesh.

Starting with the offered kiss, the vampire devoured and explored, caressing and stroking his tongue over Colin's soft palate and hesitant tongue. Refusing to allow Colin to back away from his advances, he pressed his weight onto the slender form beneath him and rubbed his thigh enticingly over Colin's erect cock, delighting in the wetness that leaked from the tip and smeared over his skin.

One flick of his long arm and the comforter floated to the floor, exposing both of their naked bodies to the pale light and warmth of the room. Pulling back from the embrace, Rowland slowly released his hold on the soft curls and studied the expression on Colin's face. The young man's eyes were closed, his lids nearly translucent in the golden stream of light from the lamp, and his full, bow-shaped lips were swollen, dusky pink and slick from the kiss.

Colin's eyelids fluttered and Rowland leaned in to brush a delicate, chaste kiss on each one. He mouthed a trail of light caresses down his lover's face, outlining the cut of Colin's high cheek bones. He nuzzled the jaw line next, adding a sliver of tongue to his eager lips, tasting and teasing the sensitive underside of Colin's chin and throat, slowly easing his way past the thundering pulse calling to him, to nip lightly at the curve where slender neck met shoulder.

Colin moaned and panted in Rowland's ear, the sweet sound of blossoming need and hunger fueling the ancient man's own long neglected desires. He pressed his nose against Colin's warm, fragrant flesh and inhaled deeply. At the same time, he licked at the fine sheen of sweat forming on the young man's skin.

This little one smelled like the spring rain, and tasted of ginger, sharp and slightly biting on the vampire's sensitive tongue.

The memory of Colin's blood, light and sweet like wisps of whiskey-flavored smoke, constantly invaded his thoughts, inflaming all his senses. A surging wave of primal need washed over the vampire. Rowland allowed it to take partial control of his actions. He licked, mouthed, tasted, suckled and explored every inch of smooth, pale flesh he could find on Colin's face, neck and chest. Working his way down Colin's flat, quivering belly, he teased at the young man's sensitive groin crease, laving his tongue over and over the thin strip of flesh to savor the pulsing beat laying shallow and vulnerable under his lips.

Small, fidgety hands alternately grabbed, then pushed at his shoulders. The hands trembled, their heated surface like a branding iron against his own cool flesh, igniting a fire of ravenous desire in the pit of his stomach unlike anything he had delighted in since before his change.

Reining in the fierce urge to ravage and abuse in his usual, self-serving matter, he gently nuzzled the sparse patch of dark hair between Colin's legs, breathing in the rich, musky, masculine scent of the young man's arousal. He slid his hands up Colin's slender torso, lightly massaging and stroking the tense abdominal muscles under his palms, delighting in the tremors that rippled against his skin. Deliciously panted moans, intermixed with breathless gasps from above him rewarded his tender touch.

Careful not to scratch the delicate flesh between himself and the sweet nectar flowing through Colin's femoral vessels, Rowland grazed the surface of one of his fangs along the thin crease that divided thigh from pelvis. Hands continuing to stroke and pleasure his now writhing lover, Rowland nudged Colin's spread legs further apart and trailed his teeth into the triangular nest of crisp curls at the base of Colin's cock. The stiff shaft bobbed and quivered, straining upward, its hot, flushed head jutting against the side of the vampire's face, marking him with its heat. Turning his head, Rowland ran his lips up the shaft, stroking it with his tongue, as he lavished it with wet kisses and slow, teasing sucks.

The hands weakly clinging to his shoulders spasmed and jerked up into his hair, scratching at his scalp. Unhurriedly, he captured their wrists and pinned them to the bed, never missing a stroke of his tongue on the silky-smooth length of wanton, jutting flesh.

He swirled his tongue around the underside of the head, then brushed the flat of the slick muscle over the tip, bathing it with a slick sheen of moisture. Spurring Rowland on were Colin's garbled, weakly shouted cries of need as the young man begged to be taken over the edge into climax.

His own cock full and heavy, Rowland released Colin's wrists to palm his cock. One hand came to rest on Colin's stomach, massaging and smoothing his nervous, anxious first-time lover, his mouth still methodically stimulating and teasing the straining shaft at his lips. Without breaking his rhythm, the vampire tucked his long body into a crouch between Colin's wide-spread thighs, raising Colin's lower half into the air slightly, so that he could tuck his bent knees under the man's firm, rounded ass.

Working his rough palm over the smooth, taut skin of Colin's abdomen, Rowland brought his other hand to his mouth to nick the end of a finger with his fang. Thick blood pooled in his cupped hand. Before he lowered it, he added a generous mouthful of saliva to the mix. Bring his hand to his cock, he coated the flesh with his body fluids, hissing at the delicious sliding sensation of the slick, viscous gel the mixture had become. He licked the last smear from his fingers and surged up and over Colin's body to rest his forehead on his lover's sweat-covered brow.

Voice deep and sultry, his stare hypnotic and seductive, Rowland placed a soft, gentle kiss on each of Colin's clenched eyes and commanded, "Let me in, Colin. Relax, listen to my voice and let me in."

The blunt tip of his shaft nestled against the untried entrance to Colin's body, pressing the tight rosebud of nerve endings and muscles until they spasmed and trembled.

Colin gasped and balled his hands into white-knuckled fists on the bed, but didn't open his eyes. A spastic nod signaled his intent to comply, but his body remained tightly coiled.

Sliding his arms under Colin's bent knees, Rowland patiently raised Colin's hips higher, aligning his shaft for easier, more comfortable access. The tight muscles fluttered and grasped at the tip of his cock and he inhaled, deep and long to maintain his iron control. Whatever it was about this young man that drew the vampire in him -- his taste, his scent, or maybe his purity of soul -- it also attracted the man in him. He almost felt bewitched.

Rowland lowered his voice to a bare whisper, letting his lips brush over Colin's open, panting mouth. "Open your eyes and look at me, pretty. Look at me and see your master, your pleasure, your need and desire. See your own heated passion and hunger in my eyes. Look at me and see your future."

A strangled sound whimpered from Colin's throat and his need-glazed eyes opened to stare Rowland in the face. Locking his commanding gaze to Colin's frightened, but lust-filled one, Rowland used his formidable powers to nudge at the walls of resistance still remaining in Colin's mind. Within seconds, he felt the final barriers to him crumble and Colin relaxed in his embrace, the taut tremors fading.

Their gazes locked, Rowland pressed forcefully against Colin's now slick opening, burrowing past the slight resistance and sheathing his shaft deep into the constricted heat of his lover's lithe body. He instantly sealed his mouth to Colin's lips, swallowing down the guttural cry of wanton passion that erupted from his young lover. It took him a moment to realize it had been his name, screamed in ecstasy and primal need.

"Rowland!"

Colin bucked and twisted, his mouth taken in a ravenous kiss, his words swallowed and the air devoured from his very lungs. Sensations bombarded every system in his body. Bright lights exploded behind his eyes, his lids falling shut as his body literally gave itself over to his domineering new lover. The smell of the vampire's cool flesh had a rich, earthy scent to it that faintly reminded Colin of strong European coffee, heady and rich. The taste of his mouth was coppery and slick, his commanding possessive kiss smooth, seductive and addicting. The constant soothing caresses that Rowland lavished over his body, brought goose flesh to the surface and caused his skin to flush and quiver.

Colin's muscles melted at the vampire's command and his body clung and formed to his lover's demands. Even his newly breached entrance welcomed the intrusion, opening to receive the vampire's iron-hard shaft, then gripping and clinging to it with every slow, slick stroke.

Exhausted and weak beyond anything he had ever experienced before, Colin still couldn't keep his hands from rising off the bed. He gripped Rowland's shoulder, instinctively arched his back, forcing the cock buried in his tight channel to plunge deeper. Every stroke of Rowland's wide cock set his nerves on fire, the burn a heated pleasure.

The unfamiliar pressure in his ass was strange and thrilling, giving Colin a feeling of completeness he had never felt before. His own cock jerked and tingled, pinned between their rubbing abdomens. A flame burst to life deep in his pelvis and his scrotum pulled up, tight and heavy, against the thin strip of sensitive flesh that led to his stretched, stuffed opening.

Suddenly the angle of Rowland's thrusts changed, the tip of his long cock striking one vulnerable spot inside of Colin again and again, the stroking caress merciless in its pleasurable attack. The demanding tongue in his mouth ravaged every millimeter of his soft, willing flesh, conquering his body and mind with its sensuous explorations and relentless caresses. His breath was stolen and replaced with the vampire's own, its warm, moist offering thick with oxygen and seductive whiffs of the vampire's own scent.

Colin felt possessed, owned and claimed, and he reveled in it. He belonged. He had found someone who wanted him and desired him. This lover was unafraid of bruising him, breaking him, or letting him experience life, desire, or passion.

A bolt of energy shot through Colin's sweat-slick body, a

sizzling nearly blinding heat that invaded every cell. His massive climax broke free, erupting from every pore, every breath, every nerve, taking Colin to a plateau of mind-dizzying ecstasy he had never experienced. His cock pulsed and sprayed a small offering of creamy white that coated his shaft. It added a slick warmth to the slip-slide of Rowland's belly over its overly sensitive surface, extending his climax and heightening his response.

The room dissolved in fireworks. His sight disappeared, his hearing muted, words strangled in the back of his throat and caught on his busy tongue, but his flesh burned and his nerves sizzled, the input to his system overwhelming. A series of rapid, harsh jabs hammered over his prostate, the blunt head of Rowland's cock burying itself deeper and deeper in his ass. His mouth was suddenly released, the lips that had captured his own now free to roar a primal, unintelligible growl into the bedroom air.

Colin bucked and gasped, his lungs finally under his own control, as a fierce blast of heat sprayed his insides, the liquid slick and hot. He could feel it clinging to him, coating his channel. The heat grew and spread throughout his body, absorbed and welcomed by his flesh. The fire it caused grew more intense, an inferno of passionate release, consuming him piece by piece until even his mind was ablaze in an unfamiliar mix of satiated desire and fulfillment.

Just as he blacked out, Colin knew he had found something to live for in the arms of death.

For the first time in Rowland's memory, his climax rushed over him before he was prepared. The tight, hot flesh wrapped around his shaft milked his cock, spasming and clenching his length in a continuous bombardment of sensation. Colin's unbridled moans and cries of need sent shocks of electric-like energy through Rowland's thrusting body, heating his desire and fanning the already raging inferno of passion burning in him to new levels of want.

His mind fed on every gasped sigh and strangled whimper his virginal lover uttered and his flesh ached for the feel of the young man under him. Rowland couldn't stop his own hands from exploring every inch of the delicate skin under his touch. Every stroke of his cock was matched by a caress of his fingertips until the sensations became too much for him to bear. His seed erupted in a fierce, convulsive stream, a tangible testament to the convoluted feelings churning and infusing his mind and body.

He would never let this one go, not for all time. But this lover was more fragile than all the others, and he knew he would need to take precious care of him -- body, mind and soul -- or Colin would break and crumble to dust under the vampire's usual demanding control. For this one, Rowland would have to make concessions, starting now.

Instead of pushing off his lover and moving away, Rowland gently pulled out and lowered Colin's lax legs to the bed. Still crouched between his lover's legs, he slowly licked and lapped at the spent fluids on Colin's belly, enticing his thrall back to consciousness and arousal.

Colin stirred at the same time his cock did, his dazed eyes opening to meet Rowland's intent stare as the vampire continued to clean off the limp, but rallying shaft. Colin gasped and shifted his hips, arching up into the moist heat as Rowland swallowed his lover's cock to the root, coaxing it to full engorgement with each bob of his head and swirl of his tongue. Sliding his fingers under Colin's tight sac, he massaged the root of the man's cock buried under the sensitive strip of perineum. He plunged two fingers into the fluttering, slick opening he had just pulled out of, dragging a choked scream from Colin at the same moment he sucked the sudden orgasm from his shaft.

Releasing Colin's cock, he kissed his way up the panting, heaving body to lay beside his lover, rough hands soothing away the chill and muscle tremors that vibrated through Colin's slender frame. Lying on his back, Rowland pulled Colin to him, draping the human over his side and embracing him with one arm. Reaching down with his free arm, he plucked the discarded comforter off the floor to cover them.

Neither spoke for several minutes then Colin tilted his head up to stare Rowland in the face and asked, "How did you stop the bleeding? Before, when you bit me, when I thought I was finally going to die?"

Rowland studied his lover's face and decided it was a question he would answer. His thrall would need to understand in order to accept his new life.

"Like this." The vampire pulled Colin's hand off his chest and sliced the tip of one finger with a suddenly evident fang. It welled with blood, what would be a tiny trickle in most people was an unchecked stream of red in Colin. He immediately popped the finger into his mouth and sucked, then bit at the tender flesh.

Colin winced and tried to jerk his hand way, but Rowland held on securely and when he removed it from his lips seconds later, the wound had sealed. It had taken him far less effort than last time.

"When I feed, I sometimes inject my saliva into my victim's bloodstream. It contains various elements that either clot or thin blood according to my needs. The first time, I simply had to overwhelm your system until the disorder that taints your blood was temporarily subdued." He licked at the finger once more, and then pulled it down to hold Colin's hand firmly against his chest.

"Subdued?" Colin yawned then fidgeted at his side, trying unsuccessfully to twist around so he could lift his upper body. "You mean I'm cured? You cured me?"

He yawned again, exhaustion showing in his every uncoordinated movement, but the bright gleam of amazement on Colin's attractive, young face touched a part of Rowland he thought had writhed and died. He had given hope to another person.

"Yes and no." He gently coaxed Colin back down to lay at his side. Wrapping the covers more completely around his lover's shoulders, Rowland added the weight of his embrace to keep the young man down. He watched Colin's eyelids flutter while he talked, long dark lashes fanning out across his unmarked cheeks. "As long as I feed from you daily, the effects will stay in your body and your disorder will be kept at bay. If I stop, you will once again be plagued by its symptoms."

A sleepy murmur mumbled against his chest, soft, innocent lips brushing tantalizingly over his ribcage. "You're saying, as long as I'm with you, your thrall, then I can live a normal life?"

One hand threaded through Colin's dark curls and Rowland rubbed soothing circles with his fingertips over the scalp beneath them. "As normal as the life of a vampire's thrall ever is, yes." He blinked in amazement when Colin snuggled closer, releasing a deep sigh of satisfaction to blow its warmth over his cool skin.

"You've saved my life, given me a reason to keep it. I think I can live with this." Colin burrowed closer and squeezed Rowland's hand. "And you." His breathing became slow and shallow as his boneless, sleeping body melted into the vampire's side.

Staring off into the dark of the bedroom, Rowland gently explored the exposed skin of his lover, examining the changes of the last few days. Speaking only to himself and the beam of pale moonlight streaming through the balcony doors, he mused, "This is the first time since becoming a vampire that I have saved a human life rather than destroyed it." He kissed the top of Colin's head then blustered with a bit of his natural harshness, "I'll have to make sure this doesn't become a trend." He ran his hands lovingly over Colin's back and whispered, "But then, there will never be another like you."

§ § §

When Rowland returned from a trip to the kitchen to find food and drink for Colin, he found his young thrall missing from their bed. He grabbed the comforter and followed the distinctive scent of his new lover out the open doors to the balcony. There, at the railing where he had first seen him, Colin stood, silhouetted against the night sky, his small, slender form wrapped in the pale blue sheet from the bed.

Rowland approached silently, knowing Colin could now sense his presence. Draping the thicker comforter over his shivering lover, he wrapped his arms around Colin and hugged him to his chest, hands possessively holding the young man's crossed arms.

Colin immediately leaned back into his embrace and Rowland felt a stirring in his chest that gave him pause.

This man brought to life feelings he had never thought it possible to experience. Colin was the missing element of his long, harsh existence, he knew that now. He realized that from this point on, without his thrall, without this responsive, passionate, fragile human in his life, he would experience loneliness for the first time in over two thousand years. This was not something Rowland was willing to let happen.

Tilting his head down, he rested his cheek on the side of Colin's head, inhaling the man's scent in the soft curls over his ear.

Colin nuzzled his head against the pressure and murmured, "Do you think we were meant to find each other like this?" He turned his head and looked up at Rowland.

Rowland saw the confusion and need in the pleading, teal eyes and he couldn't fight the desire to soothe his trembling lover's worries. "Our own needs collided here just two nights ago. We have since turned both of our impending deaths on this balcony into one, new life." He kissed Colin's temple and pulled him tighter to his chest. "I think that miraculous, don't you?"

Colin sighed audibly and looked back at the dark void of night beyond the balcony. One hand freed itself from the comforter and gripped the back of one of Rowland's hands. "You have to admit the chances of me jumping off my balcony at the same moment in time as you fell from the sky is pretty outrageous."

Overcome with the need to confide his own thoughts to this new part of his soul, Rowland leaned closer and whispered in Colin's ear. "As I descended through the air that night, wounded and near death, I thought for a brief second that you were an angel cast out of heaven and sent into my arms."

"An angel?" Colin's voice sounded hushed and disbelieving.

Mouthing the rim of the tiny ear under his lips, Rowland blew a stream of warm breath over the wet flesh, delighting in the small squirming action it produced as his lover's firm, rounded ass wiggled against his groin. "Yes, an angel. Your white shirt billowed around you like a pair of wings and your cherub curls framed your sweet face like a halo of darkness. It deceived me, taking me back to the legends and myths of my childhood from so long ago." He exhaled long and hard before quietly adding, "For a moment, I believed."

"Believed what?" Colin had stilled his movements.

Rowland could tell the young man was intently focused on his answer, truly interested in Rowland's feelings and needs.

"That there would be forgiveness. Understand, my love, this is a life that was forced upon me, not one I asked for. But it is also one I have embraced in all its forms and deeds. I have survived at the expense of countless human lives. One day, either forgiveness or restitution will be due." He tightened his grip, savoring the feel of Colin's warmth and sharp gingery scent. "I believed I didn't care, until now that is. Now, I prefer to think forgiveness will be granted when my final time comes." He rained a trail of chaste kisses down Colin's neck, licking lightly over the warm pulse point before sucking a tiny earlobe into his mouth and nibbling it. He released the plump treasure to whisper seductively, "If not, then why have I been granted a living angel for a lover?"

"Lover? Or just a thrall, a temporary plaything?" Hurt and fear rolled over the words and touched Rowland's mind.

"It is true, you are now a vampire's thrall, Colin, *my* thrall. But, I am enraptured and possessed, trapped by your beauty, your delicate spirit and soul, your passion and desire. Although I am your master and your lover, you have become my soul. It is I who am *enthralled*."

Colin turned in his arms and burrowed against his body, returning the tight embrace. A faint, muffled "love you" brushed by his sensitive hearing and something cold and hard in his chest burst, the sensation both painful and pleasurable.

In that one moment, Rowland Campbell, millennia-old vampire and harbinger of death, realized he had already been granted forgiveness. He had his arms, and his dry, still heart, wrapped around it.

After all, hadn't he heard the words "I forgive thee" when this angel appeared in his arms?

BREATHING

"This is where you wanted to take me? A New Orleans tattoo parlor?" A shiver of ingrained fear ran down Colin's slender back, a lifetime of avoiding sharp objects inducing an automatic, horrified response from him. He no longer had to fear bleeding to death from a simple laceration, not since becoming lover to a vampire who healed him, temporarily, of his genetic bleeding disorder, but twenty-five years of conditioning was hard to overcome. "One with needles? Dirty, sharp needles?"

"Right now there are other things that need be feared more than this." Rowland Campbell put a fraction more pressure on the small of Colin's back, urging him off the crowded square filled with rambunctious partygoers sampling the sights and sounds of the picturesque French Quarter.

Colin watched with mounting trepidation as the tall, burly vampire glanced up and down the street warily before he shut the door behind them, then turned the heavy lock, sealing the shop off from any new customers. "This needs to be done now."

Despite the massive degree of lingering devastation from Hurricane Katrina, this part of the city was untouched, still attracting the annual hordes of people for the string of weekly festivals and parties New Orleans was famous for. The sector was teeming with life and chaos. Colin found it exciting, but Rowland appeared distracted and on guard. If one as powerful and cautious as his lover was worried, Colin had reason to be terrified. Almost as terrified as being told he was going to spend the entire night being tattooed.

Outside the window, the homeless mingled with the drunken revelers, the smell of human sweat and grime mixed with the scent of spicy foods and flowing liquor. The uneven streets, dark corners, above-ground graveyards, and miles and miles of abandoned houses and businesses gave birth to a bevy of unwatched places to find shelter and a variety of senseless or impaired humans to feast on. This was an environment rich for the taking from a vampire's point of view. So why wasn't Rowland out looking for his evening meal instead of barricading doors and window to shut them out?

"Is something wrong? You're... tense."

"We're being followed." Rowland drew down the shade covering the glass panel in the door and pulled Colin deeper into the shadows of the candlelit storefront.

"Who? Why?" Edging closer to Rowland, Colin took comfort in his lover's solid presence.

"The remaining hunters who attacked me the first night we met. The why is obvious. They hunt vampires. They have been trailing us for several days. That's why we're here. This trip is necessary." Rowland ran both hands up Colin's arms to his shoulders, where he caressed Colin's breastbone with his callused thumbs, icy blue gaze bathing Colin in a reassuring glint of confidence and power. "You, my tiny pleasure, will always be safe. I will assure that."

Colin couldn't help but smile and nod, his expression mirroring the adoring look on Rowland's handsome, square-jawed face. He stepped closer until their bodies touched. The scent of the rich, strong European coffee Rowland liked to sip reached his senses and ignited a spark of arousal. He loved that heady scent — rich, masculine, and bold. His gaze flickered to the small scar on the vampire's chin, and Colin had to fight down the urge to taste the white line with his tongue. It was difficult to resist, but his lover's strong hands turned him around and propelled him forward a few more steps.

Rowland had been turned centuries ago, at the height of his physical prowess, a massive, burly leader of a ruthless, yet honorable, warrior clan from an age so long ago Colin had trouble imagining it existing. Like a mighty draft horse dwarfed a sleek thoroughbred, Rowland dwarfed most other men. Broad-shouldered, massively muscled arms, and legs like tree trunks attached to an iron hard torso sculpted out of a mountain of flesh and bone. Colin couldn't help but feel secure and protected at his lover's side, even with the idea of men hunting them.

A thin, dark-skinned man appeared suddenly from an alcove at the back of the tiny shop. The man had come from a doorway closed off by a blood red curtain, but the fabric hung limp and still, no sway or flutter showing any sign of the man having moved it aside to enter the cluttered room.

The man's half-lidded gaze instantly locked with Rowland's. The vampire's arm slipped around Colin's waist, drawing him nearer, surprising Colin.

Frowning slightly, Colin slid a hand under Rowland's suit jacket to twist his fingers into the silky gray shirt beneath. Colin's heart rate shot up and his throat tightened. Although Rowland wasn't one for casual displays of affection, and definitely not in public, he didn't push his hand away. Gooseflesh rose on Colin's arms, and the room grew stuffy, the air heavy with the smell of ink, and other things Colin didn't recognize.

Just as suddenly, an almost overwhelming wave of power rolled over Colin. Rowland's presence intensified in his mind and body until Colin knew it literally radiated from him as well as the vampire. He could feel Rowland in his limbs, taste him on his tongue. The vampire's scent filled Colin's lungs. Every breath he exhaled would tell the stranger he belonged to Rowland. He was cocooned in an invisible, protective blanket, a force field that embodied the aura of great power, and death. It would have been suffocating had Colin not been so unnerved by Rowland's show of power to this lone man.

Colin's grip on Rowland's shirt tightened, his knuckles pressing against the rock hard muscles of the vampire's side, the coolness of Rowland's flesh a comfort where it touched Colin's through the thin, fine fabric.

It *was* comforting, even if the lack of all movement under the shirt was noticeable to Colin. It bothered him that the gentle sway and dip of breathing wasn't there, was never there, when Colin touched his lover.

Oddly, this was the first time Rowland had let his full power wash through Colin. Colin found it possessive, sexy, and a disturbing display of ownership. Why was this stranger important to impress?

The dark man shuddered, physically recoiled from them, stopping dead in his tracks, the creaking of his leather pants and heavy boots abruptly still in mid-stride.

His skin was covered in colorful tattoos, all amply displayed on his bare torso, his pale coffee-colored flesh like an ancient parchment for the complex drawings. Dragons, snakes, and creatures Colin didn't even recognize fought, played, and made love across the man's body. He was fascinating to look at, but Colin was too interested in watching the man's expression to concentrate on the body art.

The lazy, arrogant glint in the man's eyes mellowed instantly to humbled deference. His gaze flickered over Colin for the briefest of moments before turning to meet Rowland's hard stare. The undisguised look of surprise on the man's face coupled with a flash of panic made Colin's palms sweat. The man recovered and straightened his stance.

"I am Armand, Master." Armand bowed his bald head a fraction of an inch, respectful but not groveling. "Forgive me for not recognizing you immediately. Your ability to shield your true self is flawless." This time he bowed from the waist, still a wisp of a gesture, but Colin got the impression it was a large concession on the dark man's part.

Armand let his gaze dart over Colin again, taking in his grip on Rowland's shirt. "Your…" his nostrils flared as he retested the air surrounding them before finding what he obviously thought was an appropriate word, "… companion is as ill at ease as he is attractive, Master. Perhaps a drink of something," he flashed just a hint of fanged teeth, "to calm him?"

"That will not be necessary." Rowland's blunt, cold voice sounded as if he was commanding a servant. "There are hunters not far behind."

"He is treasured?" Armand didn't wait for an answer. "Not

good. Hunters are not kind to thralls when they... *acquire* them."

A small gasp of protest escaped Colin's lips before he could stop it. He knew hunters looked for vampires, but why would they want him as well?

"There is no need for discussion. Begin work on the tattoo immediately, and very carefully." Rowland reached under his jacket and disengaged Colin's hand from his shirt. The vampire engulfed Colin's sweaty palm in his own, and held onto it rather than dropping away. There was a now familiar, slight pressure right over his radial pulse, a signal wordlessly telling him to remain silent. Although it was a possessive and commanding touch, it was also intimate and reassuring. Colin delighted in any physical affection from Rowland. He felt pleasure flush across his cheeks as Rowland smoothly continued talking.

"He is fully human, but with a rare affliction. You may have to stop now and then if he bleeds too much, but I want the entire job completed well before dawn. These hunters are experienced. They will not wait for dawn. It is highly likely they will rush the shop well before that."

Without asking for more explanations, Armand latched the inside window shutters and double bolted the door. He dropped a bar across the entry, mumbling a few broken phrases Colin couldn't quite hear. The words were spoken in a singsong voice that made him think of a wizard's spell casting from a child's movie.

"A challenge, then." Armand's gaze lingered over Colin this time, scrutinizing him, searching for some hint of his mysterious "affliction." Colin could see him scent the air, and suddenly realized this was the only time he had seen the dark man take a breath. He knew by the way panic edged back into the man's features that all he had sensed was Rowland's powerful presence. "It will be as you wish, Master."

"Here are the designs you are to use." Rowland slipped two sheets of folded paper from his jacket's breast pocket and handed them to Armand. "The arch is complex, but I want all the elements included exactly as you see them. The other design is to be centered in front."

Armand smiled and accepted the paper. Unfolding the designs, his smile slipped off his face and the earlier hint of panic was replaced by an open stare of horror. "All these in one marking? The power these symbols will invoke would be…" Armand gasped, studying Colin with a new respect and interest. "Such a mark on a mere human, even a thrall, even a delicious one…"

A low growl from Rowland cut Armand short. He flinched and took a step back. "No disrespect intended, Master. But the cost of these spells —"

Rowland pulled a black velvet pouch from his jacket pocket and tossed it at Armand, its solid weight clear by the way it thudded heavily against Armand's lean, bare chest. Colin heard the clatter of what sounded like glass marbles.

Dark chocolate eyes darting from Rowland to Colin and back again, Armand reluctantly caught the sack and yanked it open. Gazing into the bag, he grew very still, then poured its contents over the countertop, the clatter of glass marbles turning into the clink of diamonds, rubies, and emerald as they cascaded over the inked designs. A glint of greed pushed back the hesitation and panic in Armand's eyes as he scooped the gems up and pocketed them.

"Good. We understand each other." Rowland recovered the step Armand had taken backward and gained two more, until they were nearly touching. "There will be no errors. You will use full binding curses in every drop of ink in this design." Armand was neither as tall as Rowland nor as broad, and nowhere near as muscled and toned. He was no match for the ancient, and the look on his face said Armand knew it. "Every single drop. Do I make myself clear?"

Nodding, the tattooed man seemed to shrink in the shadow of Rowland's presence. Colin felt the wave of power from the ancient vampire expand until it dominated the entire room.

"How many hunters? I'll need to prepare death chants for

them."

Colin shot a startled glance between the vampires. He had a dozen questions to ask, but he had learned quickly that Rowland was not one to discuss things in length, and certainly not in the presence of others.

"Two left of the original three. Their scents were distinct."

"They seek revenge, then. Come. Time grows short." Armand walked backwards, seemingly pushed toward his workroom behind the curtain by the unseen force of Rowland's aura. Or maybe it was the brutal, deadly glare on the older vampire's face.

Rowland followed with Colin's hand held tightly in his own.

Colin rubbed his cheek across Rowland's lap, the fold of the black trousers soft and silky on his flaming skin. He pressed his forehead against Rowland's side, feeling the coolness of his body seep through the fine fabric of the shirt, soothing the heat of his own flesh.

Rowland sat perfectly still. No movement from the passage of air through lungs that did not need to breathe, no twitch of stiff muscles locked in the same position after hours without shifting, no need to relieve a bladder that didn't fill, or rumblings from a stomach that didn't demand or digest food. Colin thought it was much like resting on a park bench with his cheek against a stone statue, its cold marble gratefully leeching away the heat of his embarrassment, lessening the crimson flush he knew colored every inch of his exposed body.

The absence of breathing from Rowland truly disturbed Colin, the one reminder it was a creature he loved, and not a man. Not a man anymore. Not a living, breathing man, anyway.

He lay chest down on a padded table, bent at the waist so his knees rested on lower braces, feet in padded metal stirrups, a sort of reverse pelvic exam table, one he imagined a proctologist might own. Naked from the waist down, his legs were spread only enough to allow Armand to work on the area of extremely tender flesh that ran from the crease under his cheeks to the entrance of his body, which was where the tattooed vampire was now working.

Armand had spent the last few hours creating an archway of entwined vines and thorned brambles, an intricate design of overlapping, never-ending cords that reached from the crease below one ass cheek and up his buttock to emerge as a long, complex collection of animals and twisted symbols that filled the small of his back. Armand then did a mirror image on his other buttock around to the crease under his second butt cheek.

Colin sighed, trying not to move. "You never mentioned you'd like to see a tattoo on me before."

"And I do not wish it now, pretty." One thumb traveled down from Colin's hair to rub affectionately over his temple. Colin could feel his pulse pound against Rowland's touch, increasing in intensity from just the mere stroking. "To mar your perfect skin without reason would be a violation."

"Then why?" Colin's arms were bent and tucked to his sides, his fingers curled and stiff against his palms, shoulder high. He slid his hands forward half an inch to press his knuckles into Rowland's thigh where his head rested.

"This tattoo is a talisman. The chants the spellbinder is calling forth will weave the power of the individual symbols into your flesh. You will be well protected from certain attacks."

"Attacks? What kind of attacks?"

"Under other circumstances, I would have years to prepare you, but these hunters are persistent and give me no choice. You need protection for the times that I am away from your side."

"Why would they kill me? I'm not a vampire."

"But you are my thrall. When hunters capture a vampire's thrall, even after they have destroyed the vampire, they take great pains to soil and sully the thrall so that the vampire's scent is... displaced."

"Sully?"

"Sexually."

"Rape?"

"Yes, and worse."

"What if it isn't hunters?"

"The only others would be other vampires."

"Not a better choice?"

"Most vampires see humans only as food. They tend to dine first, and check ownership later. These marks claim you as mine for all but the most inexperienced and newly awakened. They tend to be undisciplined, and arrogant. Full of their newfound power, and drunk on the glory of it. New vampires tend to be brutal and harsh."

"Sounds like... my family." Pushing all thoughts of his cold, uncaring parents from his mind, Colin rolled his stiff shoulders slightly, careful to keep from wiggling his ass and disturbing Armand's work. The chanting had turned into a faint buzz in the background for now. "So if we meet other vampires they'll try to hurt me?"

"As a human, you will have no social standing among them. However, as my thrall you are above them. Remember that at all times. You belong to one of the most ancient and powerful warriors in existence. Use this knowledge to protect yourself."

"If they know, isn't that enough?"

"No. You'll find many of my kind are devious and cruel, as I was when I met you. As I still am." A shiver ran through Colin. Rowland used his fingers, still entwined in Colin's hair, to tap reprovingly on Colin's head. "Useful attributes at times." It was an offhand, casual remark that Colin thought bordered on amused. "But now you need to relax. Let the power of the symbols seep into your soul as well as your body." Colin sighed and buried his head deeper in Rowland's lap as his lover coaxed him into compliance. "Be still, and I will tell you about the forces of each ancient design that will be guarding you."

Rowland talked, low and soothingly, his voice hypnotizing, distracting Colin from the discomfort and embarrassment of this ordeal. The vampire's deep, rhythmic voice also served to block out the constant droning chants from Armand, which were in a sharp, clipped language Colin neither understood nor even recognized.

The chants were faint, bordering on being maddeningly irritating after a few hours had Rowland not been distracting Colin with touches to both his body and mind. The vampire's reassuring, commanding presence was the only thing keeping him calm. Colin didn't know precisely why, but he was aware this was an event of some magnitude. If Rowland's brooding demeanor before arriving wasn't enough, Armand's reaction to the complex tattoo and the cost was damning evidence. As the chanting continued, the air in the room became still and heavy, infused with energy Colin could feel but couldn't explain.

Rowland described each of the symbols and patterns of the tattoo in detail. When Colin stiffened at the description of a swirled butterfly Armand was embedding at the base of his spine, Rowland ran his thick, long fingers through Colin's hair and told him how it symbolized a rebirth, a transformation such as Colin had experienced since being claimed.

The feminine design still irritated Colin until Rowland informed him the butterfly was sitting on top of an arrow that symbolized a powerful warrior, just like the tattoo Rowland had on his right hip.

Rowland's tattoo was bold and darkly colored, but it reminded Colin more of the head of Rowland's hefty penis than of any arrow, making it both powerful and phallic. Both could be used as weapons to spear victims. Colin knew Rowland had used his cock to pierce Colin's heart and body. It was a comfort to know he would have a tattoo that matched his lover's.

He tried to relax, forget Armand was present, and let the erotic potential of the situation flow through his mind and over his body. After all, his face was in Rowland's lap, his cheek resting on a pillow of flesh that had become increasingly larger and harder as the tattooing had progressed.

Even so, Rowland never grew restless or antsy. Never a hint of breath born of frustration from him. Only Colin seemed adversely affected — aroused and exposed, handled and touched. He sighed and closed his eyes, concentrating on the feel of Rowland's fingers in his hair, and the smell of the vampire's earthy, aroused musk beneath his lips, ignoring the complete stillness of Rowland's body.

Colin twitched and squirmed slightly, a sting and pinch stabbing through the curtain of enforced relaxation in his mind. The area of Colin's ass that Armand was working on was more tender than any inked so far.

With a calming caress to his back, Rowland explained Armand was joining the free ends of the large tattoo that ran from where each of Colin's legs met his ass cheeks. He was extending the design across Colin's tender perineum so it formed an unbroken circle from below his asshole to the small of his back and down again. Despite Rowland's gently numbing influence in his mind, the discomfort from the constant stab and burn of the needle and dye increased.

Armand worked with the speed of a demon, accomplishing layer after layer of the intricate design on Colin's skin faster than any human could, but Colin tired of lying in one position for so long. He began to flinch with every needle piercing. He gasped and jumped just enough that Armand's chanting, though never faltering, grew slightly louder in warning.

The fingers in his hair gripped his skull, and Colin responded to the unspoken command, stilling his movements, allowing himself to be pinned back down on Rowland's lap. Colin could feel Rowland's unusual tension, and a flash of anger from him. He tried to look up at Rowland's expression without moving his head, but failed to see anything more than the weave of the vampire's gray silk shirt, smooth and still, unruffled by even the tiniest of breaths. Still as the dead.

Within seconds, Colin's mind became unfocused, his thoughts indistinct. His limbs went slack, the rigid tension in his thighs and back gone for the first time since he saw the spellbinder's intimidating, medieval-looking work table. Along with the clarity of thought went the burning pain. A warm tingle not unlike arousal replaced the fiery sting of the rapid, piercing needle.

Now the feel of Rowland's cock under his cheek was exotic, exciting. Colin forgot about Armand. He imagined the intimate touch of cool fingers on his ass and opening to be Rowland's, not a stranger's. Colin rubbed his jaw along Rowland's thick length, feeling it grow and stiffen, and delighting in the response he caused.

He turned his face into the fabric and inhaled. The distinctive scent of Rowland's body, bold and earthy, filled his nostrils, exciting him. A flood of warmth and anticipation spiked through him. His stomach fluttered. A tingle shot down his spine, starting at Rowland's fingers in his hair, and ending at his spasming hole, the ring of muscle trying vainly to capture the blunt touch near it and draw the fingers in.

Colin groaned and mouthed Rowland's cock through the trousers. His breath, captured in the fine threads, was hot and eager while his hands moved to wantonly knead the flesh of the vampire's thigh. Regardless of who was doing the handling, the sudden pressure of fingers rearranging his balls and expanding cock inflamed him. It was difficult not to hump the table to find more stimulation for his swollen cock.

The sound of a zipper purred in his ear, and Colin eagerly turned into the sound, his mouth pressing to the satin-over-steel cock now jutting up from Rowland's lap. Rowland's hand encouraged him to raise his head, and the uncircumcised tip of the vampire's stout cock kissed Colin's lips. Mindless of their audience, Colin sucked the hooded shaft in and began teasing the fold of sensitive flesh, running his tongue under it, using his lips to pull the foreskin up and down, as if it was a hand around the glorious rod of flesh it encased. A small hiss from above him rewarded his efforts.

In a corner of his mind, the unbroken flow of chants sounded strained and less distant than before. The image of Armand's hands on his cleft and opening, the tattoo artist's dark face inches from Colin's swollen cock and balls, brought heat to Colin's cheeks. The cool puffs of air carrying the ancient chants as they breathed spells of death and devastation into the symbols now embedded into his flesh made gooseflesh rise on the back of his neck and arms, and unexpectedly, panic burst to life in his chest.

Colin let Rowland's cock slip from his lips along with a whimper, his lungs immobilized with fear. Air trapped, his conscious mind grew dim as a dark heaviness invaded his entire being. Blood pounded through his temples, his vision blurred, and his power of speech left him.

"Breathe, pretty. Breathe. Do not fight it. Breathe for me."

Colin found it odd to think the vampire understood his need when Rowland never drew a single idle breath. Not in thousands of years. Not a sigh in frustration, not a gasp of pleasure or huff of disdain. Not even to smell a flower. Rowland had no use for air, no use for breathing. No use for human expression.

Colin wanted those things from a lover. He thought of sighs and groans as clues about feelings and thoughts. Their absence left him floundering emotionally at times. He'd led an isolated life until falling into Rowland's arms, but he'd had plenty of opportunity to learn how to read doctors, nurses, sitters, and even his parents by their body language. A whole paragraph could be said with one deep sigh.

In all fairness to Rowland, Colin assumed the ancient vampire had forgotten that breathing could be more than just sustenance to human life. Colin himself hadn't understood that until it was missing.

One subtle, but constant reminder of what his lover was. Or wasn't.

Both of Rowland's hands now cupped Colin's face, the vampire's callused thumbs rubbing soothing circles over his temples while the coolness of the large palms leeched the heat from his cheeks. "This part is almost complete, my pleasure. You'll be rewarded for your patience very soon."

The heaviness eased, allowing Colin to pull in several deep breaths. He nodded silently, enjoying the vampire's touch and the sound of his voice.

Another wave of sensual pleasure invaded Colin's mind, and the image of Armand faded, pushed away by arousal. Colin was still embarrassed, but he couldn't find the energy to let it be important. Content, he drew in another deep breath, and relaxed. All his focus shifted to the cock near his mouth, and the teasing, enticing, but now suddenly disembodied pressure around his anxious hole.

Rising up to rest his upper torso on his bent elbows and forearms, Colin reclaimed Rowland's weeping cock. He used his lips to pinch the foreskin closed over the tip, sucking the pearl-white droplet from the slit at the same time. Holding the foreskin over the tip, he wiggled his wet tongue under the loose fold of flesh, teasing the bulbous head with its rough, flattened surface. He swirled under the hood, then used his lips to retract the skin again, his head bobbing slowly, suction and spit alternating over the newly revealed dome.

Once the crown of Rowland's cock touched the back of his throat, Colin's lingering inhibitions dissolved. His own cock felt swollen to the point of splitting its skin, his balls already tightly drawn up against his cock's root, inches from the teasing press and probe he could only blindly feel.

Mimicking the touches on his ass and delicate opening, Colin pressed his tongue along the satiny skin of Rowland's cock, tracing veins and ridges, mapping out familiar paths to the vampire's more sensitive spots. Once there, Colin probed and licked, suckled and tapped, devouring the shaft in a slow dance of need and want, savoring the slight bucking of Rowland's hips, and the increasingly firm grip in his hair. Rowland might not sigh or gasp his pleasure, but his lover gave other clues to his desires. How had Colin forgotten that?

Lost in the fog of sensations at both his body's openings, Colin barely registered the change when the touches to his ass stopped and the chanting grew louder. It wasn't until Rowland gently forced Colin to release the cock in his mouth that he finally took notice of the shift in the mood of the room.

The calming effects of Rowland's influence in his mind faded slightly, allowing him to experience more of what was actually happening to him. His ass and his perineum were swollen, throbbing, and hot with the sting of what felt like a million ant bites.

The loss of physical contact with Rowland sent a jolt of fear through Colin, but the feeling vanished when he felt the familiar probe of his lover's large, blunt cock at his opening. A reassuring wave of coolness settled over his heated flesh as Rowland ran his hands up Colin's bare back.

Rowland pushed past the fluttering ring of muscle with such ease and power that Colin gasped and clenched his ass tightly around the welcome but massive invasion. More soothing hand strokes on his skin and murmured endearments in his mind relaxed him enough that he found himself bearing down on the thrusts and tightening up during the withdrawing strokes as Rowland buried his cock deep inside Colin's channel again and again.

His butt cheeks felt like flaming globes, heavy and hot. The delicate skin under his asshole screamed, ravaged and raw from the tattoo iron. Every rub of Rowland's palm or brush of his trousers and groin hair over the area notched up the burn. Each stroke sent jolts of ecstasy up his spine until Colin couldn't tell the pain from the pleasure. His cock ached, pinned between his own body and the soft leather of the table, sliding through the smears of his own pre-cum that marred the slick surface, eager for more.

"God, Rowland! For God's sake, please, I can't wait." Colin's voice came out a strained whisper, afraid of somehow disrupting the incessant chanting. Armand stood at his side now, close but no longer touching him. Glancing up over his shoulder, Colin could see the man's black eyes were closed, but his mouth still moved in an endless murmur of foreign words.

Rowland abruptly changed the angle of his thrust. Colin jerked and writhed as his prostate hummed to life, a blast of fire sizzling through his heavy groin and deep into his balls. Jolt after jolt racked his body — pleasure, pain, ecstasy, and fear all rolled into one tidal wave of ultimate bliss that made him convulse and cry out wordlessly, the sound frozen in the back of his throat, his own ability to breathe forsaking him. His scrotum tightened and his climax rippled up and out from the pit of his belly.

Passion flowed like lava through his veins, hot, blistering, all consuming, leaving him nothing but a glorious rapture, leaden limbs, and innate knowledge that this was an absolute bliss not to be found with any other lover.

His cock pulsed, emptying onto the table. The air filled with the scent of him. His heart skipped a beat when he felt Rowland slide one hand under him to run a palm through the silky come, and then leave. He knew from experience that he would taste himself in Rowland's next kiss.

Bearing down, Colin clenched his ass, trying to give Rowland a tight ride, knowing the vampire liked to come deep inside him and stay buried until Colin's body absorbed every last drop of his spent seed, a vampire's essence. A second wash of climax shuddered through his gut and left Colin breathless and dazed.

Colin closed his eyes and imagined what it looked like as inch after inch of the thick, slick cock left his opening. The flared head reached the ring of muscle at his entrance and he steadied himself for a hard thrust, expecting Rowland to plunge back in full force, heading toward climax.

His eyes flashed open and a gasp escaped his parched lips as the head popped out, his asshole winking in unexpected spasms at the sudden emptiness.

"What's — what's wrong? Rowland?" Colin struggled to find the strength to turn over and look at his lover, but a strong hand in the middle of his back stopped the effort.

"Shhh. Lie still. All is as it should be."

A slick, fat shaft slid up the cleft of his ass cheeks. Colin sighed and relaxed back onto the table as a familiar whisper in his brain lulled him into instant obedience. Within seconds, he felt cool strands of come on ass where it pooled in the small of his back and dripped across his sore, burning, newly tattooed cheeks.

"My cum will heal your flesh quickly and seal the spellbinder's words in the markings." Rowland's voice was ragged, drenched in lust, hoarse with pleasure from his climax. The sound of raw need ignited a new flame in Colin's gut.

The vampire's strong, beefy hands began to knead and massage Colin's ass. He could feel the fluids being worked into every line and piercing of the circular tattoo. "My scent will be locked into the ink along with the spells. There will be no question who you belong to."

Rowland's hands were gentle. The difference in temperature between the come and the abused flesh was dramatic, almost like having an ice pack dropped on his inflamed buttocks.

Colin gasped at the first touch, but the pain and soreness faded with each passing moment until the tattooed flesh was as malleable as the rest of his body.

Armand's chanting abruptly rose to a shout then, just as suddenly, ended. The spellbinder fell to his knees and stayed there, head bowed and hands at his sides, flexing and clenching at air. Both Colin and Rowland ignored him. The vampire continued his sensual massage.

Colin lost himself in the erotic bliss of the moment. "What's it look like?"

"This is a layered rope of knotted vines entwined with thorns. It runs across here..." Rowland lightly trailed his fingers over Colin's sensitive perineum from one side to the other. "... to here."

Colin squirmed, panting with fresh arousal. A blunt probing at his opening had him sighing in relief as Rowland plunged two slippery fingers into his ass. Colin pushed back, taking in more of the thick digits, clenching his cheeks and thrusting his hips in a wanton dance to entice Rowland to give him more.

A sudden swipe of fingertips over his prostate and Colin howled, his body jerking as sizzling ecstasy rippled up from his cock and traveled along his nerves until even his fingertips and toes tingled. When the jolt of pleasure receded, he realized the fingers had been traded for Rowland's still stiff cock. He was impaled on the hard shaft so deeply he could feel the slap of the vampire's thighs against his newly decorated ass with the first stroke.

The thrusts were slow and deep, gentle, teasing, nothing like what Colin wanted. He wanted to be taken and claimed.

Before he could complain, Armand's rough, dry, disembodied voice broke in. "We will need to finish soon for the spells to be at their height of power during the binding, Master. Midnight approaches."

"Then let us proceed, Armand." Back in control, Rowland's voice held a dangerous edge Colin recognized as the same tone he had used the first night Colin met him, and that meant Rowland had survival as his primary concern.

Colin felt a wave of fear wash through him. There was something going on that Rowland hadn't seen fit to tell him. He had learned in the months they had been together that Rowland was not the sharing type. Tonight was the first he had heard of the hunters on their trail. While Colin was usually content to allow the vampire to deal with the details of their day-to-day lives together in the unfamiliar, shadowy world of the night, there were times when Colin wished the vampire would prepare him more. Even this tattoo shop visit had been a surprise.

Without warning, an overwhelming thrill of pleasure shot though him, chasing away all thoughts except his lover. Rowland shoved in deep and hard. His massive hands closed around Colin's hips. Colin felt himself lifted off his stomach and turned, his legs grabbed and shoulders spun on the smooth leather table padding, until he lay on his back, ass still riding Rowland's long, hard cock, his legs now supported by the vampire's arms.

"Oh, shit, shit! Rowland!" Colin bucked, gasping at the sudden pressure and twisting in his gut, the pain turning to pleasure as Rowland's cock nudged at his prostate.

Armand rushed to adjust the table fittings and soon Colin's lower half was supported in a fashion he had only seen on medical shows about birthing babies. Rowland eased back, but his cock remained inside Colin's clenched channel. Colin blushed and squirmed as Armand moved in close, preparing to work on the tender flesh just above his erect, jutting cock.

Colin forgot his embarrassment as Rowland's hand shot out and gripped Armand by the wrist, stopping the spellbinder from touching Colin with the raised tattoo iron.

The tattoo artist had been nothing but compliant, but Colin still heard the blatant threat in Rowland's voice. "Do you know my proper name for the final spell?"

Armand's reply was a hushed murmur full of reverence and a glimmer of fear. "Everyone knows of your beginnings, Master. You are legend."

Colin raised his head from the table to look down the length of his shirt-covered chest at the two men clustered at his groin. He felt open and exposed, but wanton and more aroused than he had ever been, on display with Rowland still deep in his ass.

Rowland was now motionless, the strain of waiting evident only by the way the vampire's cock pulsed and twitched impatiently against the inside walls of Colin's ass. The movement made Colin pant, and clench his ass tighter.

"Say it so there is no mistake, Spellbinder."

The vampire's outward intensity was nearly overwhelming,

palpable, but the whisper in Colin's mind remained soothing, pushing away the pain and embarrassment. Still, Colin sensed a vaguely urgent unease in his lover, an unease that had little to do with the twitching, needy cock buried inside him.

"Ruaghnal Caedmon." Colin could feel the spellbinder breathe out as he spoke the foreign name. Armand's words were a mere whisper, hushed, awed.

After a nod from Rowland, Armand bent over, ink iron in hand, poised to begin the final tattoo just above Colin's leaking cock. He was so close he blocked Colin's view of himself, but Colin knew his shaft was almost touching the dark man's cheek.

"Finish. There is not much time."

Rowland's expression showed none of the tension Colin felt in his body and mind. His grip, back on Colin's hip, was bruisingly tight, while his other hand moved to capture Colin's cock and ease it away from Armand's face, the cool touch familiar and exciting.

Colin barely noticed when Armand began working again, the hum of the inking iron and the murmur of chants a faint buzz behind the roar of his barely contained arousal as spiderwebs of pleasure crawled over his flesh. With Rowland's cock deep inside his ass, the vibrations of the tattoo iron's humming motor traveled through his pelvis and shook Rowland's thick shaft, like a thousand ants dancing in his belly. The whole thing was erotic as hell.

"What does this tattoo look like?" Colin gasped and grabbed the hand on his hip, fingers digging into the icy flesh.

"Smaller. A ring of fire, along with my symbol, the arrowhead." Rowland looked at the emerging tattoo as he spoke, gaze never wavering from Armand's rapid design, as if he was ensuring that every dot of ink was as he had instructed. "It joins the other to make an unbroken ring."

"Putting my ass and cock inside? What's it mean?" Colin tried to move, needed to move, but the hand on his hip, and the pressure in his mind, held him still.

Suddenly Rowland's gaze met his over the top of Armand's

bowed head. The intensity of the vampire's expression made Colin's mouth go dry and his heart beat faster. It was pure possessive desire mixed with something Colin would have called confusion if he didn't know Rowland was never confused by anything.

"It means you are mine."

"Yours?" He wanted to squirm and buck, force Rowland to move, to make the buzz of pleasure into a storm of ecstasy. The only movement Colin was left with was the ability to breathe, the only one in the room with the need to do so.

"Mine. Until the end of time. Whether you remain human or become vampire. You are mine."

"Oh." The room had grown warm and stuffy, and the smell of sex and sweat was so strong he could taste it in the air. It lingered in his nostrils and made his cock harder. He was Rowland's. Until the end of time. Colin felt the burn and tingle of orgasm churning in his groin.

"I can do that." He forced himself to hold Rowland's gaze, returning the intensity, trying to let the vampire understand how much he needed what Rowland offered.

Without looking away from Colin, Rowland instructed Armand, "Finish. The hour approaches."

A grunt and nod answered him. Armand was blindingly fast, finishing the six inch square pattern before Colin had time to grow more restless, the pain kept at bay by Rowland's presence in Colin's mind.

Once the design was completed, the chanting ended swiftly, without ceremony. Rowland eased away his hold on Colin's mind and body. Fucking hard and fast, he allowed Colin to buck, grind, writhe and heave as much as his lover pleased, pushing Colin to a rapid, blistering climax. Rowland pulled out to spill his own cum over Colin's raw, reddened belly, soothing and healing the entire surface with the blood-tinged spurts of viscous fluids just as he had done before.

Rowland massaged the newly marked ink as it began to heal,

his touch loving, gentle and oh, so soothing.

Colin purred his satisfaction, limbs once again heavy, body and mind consumed by the peak of yet another climax. He reached out to cover Rowland's hands as they caressed his lower abdomen, but the sound of shattered glass and the sudden roar of an explosion rocked the room.

The door and half the wall it had been attached to blew inward. Smoke filled the room, billowing like a blanket of dirty fog, obscuring the room in seconds, bringing with it waves of heat and acid-tasting air. Colin choked, wiping tears from his eyes, hands flailing for the familiar touch of Rowland's cool skin. His fingers met air, but he had only a second to panic over that fact before he found himself flipped off the table to land on the floor. He immediately tried to stand.

"Rowland!" Nothing but the roar of the licking flames answered. He was alone. "Rowland! Rowland!"

Colin gagged and choked, strangled by the foul air. Rowland would never leave him like this. He was sure of it. Maybe the vampire had been injured in the explosion?

He dropped back down to the floor where he realized the air was cooler. It was also less toxic. Colin's head hurt, his throat was raw, and his stomach rolled with a gut-wrenching nausea from the fumes. All around him mini-explosions erupted as every bottle of ink on the table and shelves shattered, adding their chemical elements to the putrid air. The heat intensified, forcing Colin deeper into the inking room.

Colin crawled away from the flaming doorway, scrambling like a crab over the cold, sticky linoleum floor, naked from the waist down. He blindly searched the floor as he moved, searching for Rowland, but anxious to find either of the vampires at this point.

He banged into furniture every few feet, but found nothing more than broken glass and peeling flooring. His hands were bleeding from the glass. He could smell hair singeing, and his exposed skin felt tight and hot. His mouth and throat felt like he'd swallowed gasoline. His lungs ached with each new shallow breath. Panic settled into his chest. "Rowland!"

He couldn't remember seeing a window in the room. An impenetrable wall was at his back, and flames surrounded him on the three other sides. There would be no escape. Colin pressed his face to the floor, gasping for each lungful of air. He knew Rowland would never leave him willingly. So that only meant one thing — Rowland was dead. Didn't vampires turn to ashes if caught in a fire?

Colin curled into a tighter ball, marveling at how cool his tears felt on his cheeks. If Rowland was dead, there was no reason to escape this fire.

The room grew darker, and the last thing he remembered was a whoosh of air, and what smelled like charred flesh.

CHAPTER FIVE

"We're alive?" Colin's voice was husky, his throat dry and raw. He coughed, and worked to pushed up off of Rowland's chest where he lay sprawled. They were both naked, in a king-sized bed in a room Colin didn't recognize. He assumed it was a hotel. A very high-end hotel.

He briefly wondered how Rowland had gotten his unconscious body into the hotel, then dismissed the thought. Rowland could do anything. Obviously. The vampire had rescued Colin from an inescapable inferno. Naked, strange room, raw throat, sore aching skin from the waist down — none of it mattered. What did matter was that Rowland had come back for him, and they were both okay.

So he said it out loud again. "We're alive."

"Well, some of us are." Strong arms pulled him back down so he was stretched out atop Rowland's massive, perfect body.

Rowland's reply was amused, comfortingly droll. It told Colin everything was going to be fine. "You know what I mean."

"Yes, apparently we are 'alive'."

"How long have I been out?"

"A day. You have no lasting injures. Even your lungs have recuperated from the ordeal."

"What happened?" Colin shifted so he was more comfortable, dropping his legs to either side of Rowland's rib cage. The skin on his legs and feet felt tight and sensitive, but nothing appeared to be bruised or broken. He moved his hands under Rowland's armpits and raised his torso so he could see his lover's face better. His cock slid along the hard muscles of Rowland's belly, making it swell. Rowland's cool, strong hands absently rubbed up and down his arms.

"The hunters set fire to the shop."

"I couldn't find you." The paralyzing fear that had overwhelmed him during the fire surged up, making his words sound like an accusation instead of a statement.

"I had to remove the hunters."

Rowland clasped both palms to Colin's face and cradled it, pale blue eyes gazing intensely into Colin's. Colin knew the vampire could sense his fear and anger so he didn't bother to hide it.

"They were lying in wait for us in case we managed to escape the flames. I couldn't risk having them take you." Rowland's thumbs caressed Colin's lips, and Colin's tongue darted out to lap at them, returning the caress. "I knew them to be overly confident and reckless from the last attack. They were too eager for a kill. All I had to do was show myself to them and then return for you." He smiled a sardonic twist of his pale lips. "They eagerly followed me into the flames."

"Did you kill them?" Colin wasn't sure whether he was hopeful or distraught over the idea. Accepting the fact Rowland could be a killer when necessary was disturbing when he allowed himself to think about it at length.

"In a manner of speaking." Rowland gave a slight shrug of his broad shoulders. "The burning fumes from the inks and the spellbinder's charms were sufficient to do the job for me. They suffocated within seconds." He lowered his gaze, eyelids hooding the expression in his eyes. Colin didn't want to see it anyway. "Not as satisfying, but certainly less work."

Wanting to change the subject, Colin asked, "Armand?"

"Safe. He'll have a new shop open within a month." Rowland's hand dropped from Colin's face to trail across his shoulders and down his chest, the touch light and teasing. A shiver of arousal skittered down Colin's spine at the cool caress.

"The fumes were everywhere. I couldn't see, couldn't breathe. Not unless I stayed on the floor." One of the things Colin loved about Rowland was the man's physical prowess and amazing fortitude, but this was beyond imagining. The shop had been a hellhole of death. "How did you survive in that long enough to find me and carry me out?"

Rowland's expression gentled, a glimmer of understanding in his steady gaze. "As you have silently mourned so many times, my pleasure, *I* do not need to breathe."

Colin stared down into his lover's eyes, mesmerized by the tenderness in the vampire's tone, his body responding to the vampire's touch, while his heart responded to the loving look in Rowland's usually hard expression.

"I just... it's just hard... I don't know how to describe it." His heart raced, filled with pain that he might have hurt Rowland's feelings. "I just missed it. Missed little things that would make you seem human. I'm sorry." Colin dropped his gaze, embarrassed. He felt heat flush his face. He stammered when he found his voice again. "But it doesn't matter now because I don't miss it anymore." He sat up and placed his palms flat on Rowland's unmoving chest, fingers molded to the curve of the vampire's unmoving ribs. "I've learned to tell what you're feeling in other ways."

The full realization of what Rowland had risked for him this night hit him hard. His jaw trembled with the effort to keep his voice calm. "Like walking through a blazing wall of fire to save me."

He used one hand to touch the singed hair on his legs, feeling the coarse, crisp strands crinkle under his fingertips. He trailed his hand up to run it over the newly inked dark swirls and symbols on his lower abdomen, the light touch making his semi-firm cock stir.

Looking up at Rowland's bland, stoic expression, he almost faltered in his determination to bare his soul, but that oddly confused expression was back on the vampire's face, and Colin suddenly knew what it meant. The vampire was dismayed, and yes, confused, by his own emotions.

Rowland loved him, truly loved him.

Colin's chest ached and his throat tightened with the intensity of the revelation. He was finally loved the way he had always dreamed about being loved. "Or paying a king's ransom to protect me first…" he touched the tattoo lovingly, "… even with vampire hunters out to kill you."

He had to fight back the tears that threatened to fall. It was embarrassing enough that his voice was breaking like a prepubescent boy's. Drawing in a deep breath, he collected his emotions and reined them in. "That beats a fleeting satisfied sigh any day."

Cupping his face, Rowland ran his thumbs over Colin's quivering mouth. The gentle touch soothed the ache in Colin's chest. He fell forward, arms sliding around Rowland's neck, his head buried in the crook of the vampire's shoulder.

Rowland wrapped his arms around Colin and hugged him tightly. Colin sighed in contentment, his own warm breath flowing back around his face, trapped by the vampire's embrace. Lightly kissing the flesh under his lips, he whispered, "I love you."

"I like it best when *you* sigh." Rowland kissed the corner of Colin's mouth, tasting his lips, tugging at the pouting lower flesh with his teeth, then moving to part Colin's lips with his tongue, seeking entrance and gaining it.

After what felt like forever, Colin pulled back far enough to whisper, "I love you, Ruaghnal Caedmon."

As his answer, Rowland recaptured Colin's mouth in an urgent kiss that left Colin gasping and hard. Without ending, the mood of the kiss changed. Rowland's lips gentled, his tongue caressed the roof of Colin's mouth, searching and stroking.

Colin returned the lavish strokes with small licks and muffled moans of encouragement. He nipped at Rowland's tongue, purposely drawing blood, wanting to call forth the vampire's primal nature, but other than a slight stiffening of the vampire's entire body that faded as quickly as it came, Rowland's lovemaking remained tender and slow. So tender, Colin trembled under every touch of Rowland's strong, callused hands. Hands that kneaded and caressed his arms, then moved to his back and wrapped around him, holding him tightly to Rowland's rippling chest and torso.

Colin moaned and squirmed as Rowland leisurely moved his grasp down Colin's waist to his buttocks and eased his cheeks apart. The air in the bedroom teased at his opening until a blunt finger rubbed around the puckered hole, heating it and making it clench in anticipation.

Their mouths remained sealed together in a slow, passionate kiss unlike any they had shared before. It was demanding, forceful, but with a tenderness Colin couldn't ever remember Rowland showing quite like this before. It was a lazy exploration, thorough, lingering and appreciative. It wasn't just a kiss. It was a caress to Colin's very soul. It left Colin dazed and flushed, aroused and eager for more, for anything Rowland wanted from him.

Colin's gaze darted to Rowland's pale blue eyes, searching for a clue to what his lover was thinking. Rowland's hands came up to frame his face again. They shared a silent moment of communication before Colin buried his face in the crook of Rowland's neck, unnerved by the expression in the vampire's steady stare.

After a long pause, Colin sat back up, his ass resting comfortably on Rowland's hard, motionless lower torso. His cock curved out from his groin, swollen, eager and red. Sliding backward until he could feel the heat of Rowland's thick rod pressing along the crack of his cheeks, Colin leaned back. He relaxed into the support of Rowland's knees, the vampire's large square hands tracing over the symbols and creatures now embedded in the flesh of his groin.

The cool touch circled his cock and explored his sac, squeezing and tugging, rubbing and stroking at random intervals until Colin could barely tolerate it. Blood pounded through his veins, and his cock seemed ready to split out of his skin.

The world shifted as Rowland pinned Colin to the mattress. The only sound in the room was Colin's panted breaths as Rowland recaptured Colin's swollen lips in a gentle, undemanding kiss. Rowland wrapped his arms securely around Colin and rolled them over, Colin once again on top.

Surprised at being placed in the dominant position, Colin broke the kiss to study Rowland's face. He tilted his head, an uncertain smile on his lips. Rowland gently guided Colin's thighs apart, pulling his knees down on either side of Rowland's hips. Colin's wrists were captured in a familiar, hard grip, then his hands were raised until they came to rest on the vampire's chest. Rowland slid his hands down to lay them open-palmed on top of Colin's, pressing both pairs into the surface of the vampire's chest before dropping them down to the bed, fingertips passively stroking the tops of Colin's bent knees. Colin bent down and took his lover's mouth in a deep, lingering kiss.

Instinctively, a rhythm began. Colin's hips rocked against the smooth, hard planes of Rowland's lower abdomen, growing impatient for more stimulation. Usually Rowland's passion just carried Colin along, but leading had its own thrill.

Ending the kiss, Colin lavished attention on first one nipple, and then the other, trailing a wet path across Rowland's broad chest. Fine tremors vibrated through the hard body under him. Colin straightened and moved forward. He hesitated for a moment until Rowland bit his own hand and offered it to Colin. He gathered a palm full of the thick blood, reaching behind to anoint Rowland's cock. Lifting his hips into position, he slowly eased down, never pausing, never breathing, never taking his gaze off of Rowland's intense, possessive expression until he was fully seated on the vampire's shaft.

Colin was startled at the amount of penetration this position gave them. Never having made love like this before, he hadn't realized how different it would be, how full he would be, how thick Rowland would feel, how easily he could stimulate his own prostate with just an arch of his back or a twist of his hips. Every shift of his body brought a burst of white light to explode behind his eyes, pleasure rippling along his nerve endings.

He fumbled for Rowland's hands, needing more of a physical connection between them, pulling them up to his chest, sighing in relief when the hands began to roam over his sensitive skin. The constant string of bright lights behind his eyelids shattered into major fireworks as his orgasm suddenly ripped through him.

Colin collapsed, wrapping himself tightly around his lover, who returned a welcome, equally fierce embrace. Taking advantage of the moment, Colin rolled to one side, urging Rowland to shift with him until he was pinned to the bed by his lover. He locked his ankles around Rowland's hips, letting his lips brush against his lover's surprised mouth. "Make love to me. Show me I belong to you. Make every pore in my body reek with your scent."

Purposely flexing his hips the tiniest bit, he watched the calm, gentle look disappear off Rowland's face. He deliberately clenched his ass, his channel still clinging to Rowland's buried cocked.

A growl of animal lust vibrated down through Rowland's chest to his ass as the vampire let his hunger loose. Every inch of Colin's skin was licked and tasted, and then tasted again. Nipples, throat, chin and jawline were sucked and marked. Lips and tongues clashed and dueled, palates and teeth were scoured, breath stolen, and rational thoughts erased.

Through it all, Rowland maintained a slow, steady rhythm of deep, powerful thrusts, every torturous, loving stroke aimed to rub over his lover's prostate. Colin was reduced to babbling incoherent half sentences and grunts. "I'm going to come, shit, shit! Rowland!"

Rowland intensified his thrusts, burying his cock deep, stroking slow, pulling out to the ring of muscle at Colin's opening, then easing back in to the base of his long, wide shaft. Colin thought wildly for a moment that he could feel Rowland reach his ribs. He'd never felt so deliciously full, and happy. It was like his lover had become a part of him, a necessary organ for life.

His orgasm began to build behind his tightening sac, and the rhythm of his bucking hips took on an urgent, primal beat. His release ripped through him just as he felt a burst of burning coolness drench his insides.

He turned his head, steeling himself for a flash of pain/ pleasure. Rowland bit down hard on his arched throat, breaking the skin. A cry of pleasure was pulled from Colin, the stinging pain quickly mutating into a flush of arousal that put his best orgasm to shame.

He moaned in contentment as the rush peaked and faded while Rowland finished suckling and bathed the slowly healing wound with his tongue to soothe the flesh closed. This was the part Colin liked best after sex, the time when Rowland nuzzled and kissed, lapping at the torn edges of his flesh for long minutes, making completely sure his blood clotted and the skin was healthy and seamless.

Reaching down, Rowland pulled up the covers. Rubbing a thumb over the area where he had bitten Colin, Rowland looked down, that faintly confused expression clouding his face. "There is an old expression that says 'Life is not measured by the breaths you take but by the moments that take your breath away'."

Colin stayed very still and silent, afraid of losing the extreme intimacy of the moment.

The vampire studied Colin's face, searching it intensely before speaking again. His voice turned husky and rough, his piercing stare suddenly warm and gentle. His fingertips caressed the line of Colin's jaw. "In over two thousand years, you have been the only one to make me wish that I could breathe again."

He slowly lowered his mouth to Colin's, so close their lips brushed each other's as Rowland whispered, "And you alone would be able to take it away again. You are my only 'moment'."

WALK

THROUGH FIRE

The night air was crisp, filled with the scent of pumpkin and chimney smoke. Hundreds of old trees dotted the cemetery grounds, their gnarled branches clinging to the last of the crinkled orange and red leaves that gave them voice when the wind swirled through their rustling tips. Dim and forlorn, a quarter moon hung low in the treetops, looking as if a single tear had been sliced in the black starless sky surrounding it. Off in the distance, a dog howled and two more answered it, a melancholy sound.

Caleb Archer slowly walked down the long, cobblestone path that led from the main cemetery lane to the area housing the oldest and largest crypts in this very large, old graveyard. He knew every stone and crack in the path. His footsteps carried him on his familiar, dark journey without hesitation. For the last one hundred and fifty-seven years, every All Hallows Eve, he traveled this path.

He didn't think about the chill in the night air, the heavy foreboding shadows hanging in the sky, or the dozens of masked and costumed children running past him. They were on their way to frighten each other and terrorize the town on this one night of legal mischief and mayhem, better known as trick or treat night, Halloween night, in these modern times.

Caleb was from a time before trick or treating. From a time when a man's profession became his name. Before a time of childish games and sugary gifts. Even before the time when this night was recognized as the eve to honor the dead that had departed from this world. He supposed if he thought about it, it was actually a night to honor him. He was dead, after all. All vampires were dead, soul-less. Just not their bodies, minds or, in his case, their hearts.

The groups of children tapered off and the last of the brazen huddles of white-sheeted ghosts and black-hatted witches raced away into the night, soaring past Caleb with a round of adolescent giggles and one high-pitched shriek of delighted terror.

A few feet away, a small girl, maybe six years old, dressed in a simple long smock with a ring of dried spring flowers in her pale brown hair lingered on the path, alone but unafraid. She seemed to shimmer in the moonlight, her pale skin nearly translucent. Her soft, doe-eyed gaze seemed to call to Caleb's long lost soul.

"Hello, Sarah Beth."

She smiled and Caleb smiled back, then nodded, prompting the child to come near and take his hand. She gazed up into his face, a sad expression on her unformed, sweet, childish face and they shared a moment of silent understanding before Caleb sighed, squared his broad shoulders and looked away.

And just like that, tall, towering, dark vampire and tiny wisp of a ghostly girl walked on, as they did every year, hand in hand, up the crumbling pathway.

Her slippered feet made no sound on the stone walkway. She was nothing more than a puff of fog to the humans that had raced by earlier, but the dead can see the dead and she was Caleb's yearly companion on this night.

Caleb's boots slipped stealthily through the leaf-strewn path without disturbing a single one. As they walked, more swirls of mist surrounded them on their journey, all eventually solidifying to pale, translucent forms of the human beings they had been once, long ago. Caleb ignored them all, save the girl, her chubby fingers grasped loosely in his own.

Looking up as they silently climbed, Caleb's gaze latched onto a massive marble crypt sitting on the crest of a hill. It was in the darkest section of the cemetery, surrounded by ancient trees and old-fashioned, spiked iron fencing. The tomb itself was a pale smear against the night, its once white marble structure, aged and cracked, marked by time, elements, and human hands. The pillars were towering posts carved with ancient symbols Caleb knew the meaning of and wished he didn't, along with the painted markings from more recent, less skilled hands. The paint looked like graffiti at first, but Caleb recognized the unholy crest and the smell of the human blood it had been written in.

He pushed through the heavy, iron gate and entered the crypt, lighting ancient but still usable torches that hung on the walls. He moved deeper into the silent crypt, suddenly assaulted with the decaying odors of mildew, feces, burnt flesh, and sulfur. The faint scent of a familiar rich, distinctive blood still hung on the stagnant air.

Caleb released the girl's hand and she reluctantly drifted away to stand in one corner beside a broken statue of a gargoyle, one who had failed in his job of keeping away the evil spirits from this once sacred place.

Five stone coffins were laid out in the center of the massive chamber. Three were broken and their seals removed, the bodies vandalized, their spirits part of the mists that had joined Caleb on his walk and that now hovered around the edges of the cold, dank room.

Placing the black duffel bag he had been carrying on a raised section of the floor, Caleb pushed it carefully out of the way, close to a still sealed coffin directly in front of an altar carved into the wall of the tomb.

Caleb rose and faced the altar. Where once had been the figure of an angel that now lay shattered on the floor, there sat the cracked, skinless skull of a woman, its jaw broken and the eye sockets still bearing the scorch marks where the eyes had been burned out decades ago.

Caleb knew her.

He knew her briefly in life and he knew her now in death. All dead things knew each other. Her spirit haunted this place along with the others, bound to her place of destruction until her debt in life was paid.

She had been Shaddal, beautiful seductress, spinner of lies, destroyer of love, and servant to Astaroth, Duke of Hell. She had been Astaroth's consort as well, indebted to the demon for six thousand years of tribute and service in exchange for power over men, and eternal youth and beauty.

But she had not been granted immortality.

When Caleb killed her, drained her of all of her blood, energy, youth and power, she became nothing but a hollow shell that ignited in his outraged hands. In the end, her firm, ripe, young body became nothing more than a pile of ash and the broken, scorched skull now on display in the shallow altar.

That had been one hundred and fifty-seven years ago, but Caleb still heard her screams echo off the walls in this place, remembered the sight of her eyes burning, and her flesh melting away to dust.

Astaroth appeared just as Shaddal had died, summoned by her earlier chants. He was too late to change her fate, accepting her death by one of his own creations, a vampire, to be binding.

He was accepting, but was also a vengeful demon. Shaddal had been his favorite.

So tonight, like every other Halloween night since her demise, Caleb came to make payment on the price of Shaddal's death.

His gaze flickered briefly to the little girl, still uncomfortable with her witnessing his payment, even after all these years. She gave him a solemn nod and he returned it. Then, for the first time in one hundred and fifty-seven years, a feeling of calm and strength he knew didn't belong to him filled his mind and body. He stared at her, marveling at the offered gift of comfort. His soul was long gone, but her tiny presence warmed him all the same.

Broad shouldered and muscular, with a vampire's speed and strength, Caleb still paused before accepting his fate once again. His own actions had brought him to this place and he had a debt to pay. Standing in front of the altar, Caleb pulled a knife from his jacket pocket. It was small and old, the blade honed down to a tiny sliver of metal by centuries of being sharpened and used, a small piece left over from a life Caleb had almost forgotten. He hefted it thoughtfully in his hand for a moment, and then swiftly slit his right wrist with it.

As the blood flowed off the end of his fingers, he drew a V over a blackened circle on the floor before him, then drew another one, this time inverted over the first. In the center of the enclosed shape, he drew the mark of the eye of the devil, then let the wound seal. It disappeared in seconds, leaving his skin unmarked. He knew there would soon be plenty of unhealed marks upon his flesh and none of them would heal this quickly.

Digging a handful of ashes out of his other jacket pocket, Caleb sprinkled them over the still-wet blood and began a harsh, guttural chant he memorized the first night he heard Shaddal say it in this very tomb. The night she had summoned her master with a stolen gift in hand. The night she had died by Caleb's hand.

She should never have tried to gift her master with what belonged to Caleb.

As he finished the chant for the third time, the ash ignited in a flash of blinding light and acrid smoke. A clap of thunder shook the stone foundation and a broken pillar split and fell behind him. Caleb didn't bother to run and look because before him stood the hulking form of Astaroth, Duke of Hell, treasurer of the underworld, keeper of check and balances. The demon Caleb owed the debt to.

Astaroth stood eight feet tall. His massive body was covered in plates of molten stone. The edges of his rock-like muscles glowed a fiery orange and wisps of smoke curled from between his joints. His face resembled a disfigured bull and his red eyes wept streams of blood to mark trails down the uneven planes of his massive snout. Fangs protruded from between his lips and razor like claws replaced his fingers. He smelled of death and fire, brimstone and ash. His voice rolled through the room like thunder, scattering the more timid of the ghostly specters to the rafters of the tomb.

A mournful wail filled the air. Though he knew it was meant as support for him, it nevertheless raised the hair on Caleb's arms.

Without looking, Caleb knew the little girl was still there. Unnatural warmth flushed his cold, vampire limbs and Caleb smiled. He could do this again. And again and again, for as long as he needed. The dead know the dead. She reminded him that love was the only thing left once your own mortality was gone.

And Caleb did this for love.

"You have come again, Vampire." Astaroth's voice mocked him, pity and contempt dripping like sap from an axed tree trunk. "I'm surprised you have not wearied of this yet."

"Not likely to."

Unperturbed, Caleb stood his ground, unflinching as Astaroth came forth and slowly strolled around him as he talked. The heat from the demon's body was intense and the air around him shimmered from it. "Your devotion is admirable. Valuable even, if one valued those kind of traits in a demon."

"You're the demon. I'm just a vampire."

"A vampire in love so it seems."

"You finally figured that out. Only took you one hundred and fifty-seven years, to do it in." Caleb gave the demon a tight, mirthless smile. "And they say demons are dumb."

"Insolent parasite!" Astaroth's voice trembled with rage and fire billowed from his mouth and licked at his blackened lips. He leaned in close to Caleb's face, forcing the vampire to turn his head in order to avoid being seared by the heat of Astaroth's vile breath.

"You have returned here for almost two centuries in the hopes of vanquishing my champions and winning the release of your lover." He snorted and sulfur-laden fumes choked the air.

Astaroth brushed Caleb's arm as he continued to walk around the vampire. Caleb casually patted out the flames the light touch left behind on the soft leather jacket.

Stopping behind Caleb, Astaroth breathed down the vampire's neck, singeing the fine hairs that grew there as he gleefully growled in Caleb's ear. "And each year you crawl away, beaten, broken, bloody and empty-handed. Who would you say is the unintelligent one, Caleb?"

Acting bored and disinterested, Caleb sighed and pointedly glanced over his shoulder at Astaroth. He stared the demon in the eye and quietly challenged him. "Bring on this year's devil spawn and we'll find out."

Holding Caleb's gaze, Astaroth narrowed his eyes then glanced critically over Caleb. The demon turned away from Caleb's unwavering stare, giving a dismissing snort. "I sealed the other vampire away in retribution for your pointlessly killing Shaddal and taking away her life debt of six thousand years of service to me."

"It wasn't pointless." Caleb found he could snarl as well as the demon could. "She died because she took something that didn't belong to her. She shouldn't have tried to give you Drew as a sacrificial offering. He wasn't hers to take or to give away. To anyone."

Caleb swallowed hard at the memory of Drew's face. The last time Caleb saw him, his body was contorted in pain, and his handsome face twisted in disbelief, as he was sucked out of this very crypt and into the black void of Hell Astaroth had just stepped out of. Drew had been a beautiful young man. Caleb wondered what he looked like now after nearly two centuries of Astaroth's company. But it didn't matter; it wasn't Drew's face that Caleb loved. "He belonged to me."

Smirking, Astaroth laughed, a harsh, bitter sound full of revulsion and mocking disgust. "And apparently, your heart and common sense belonged to him."

He was seething inside, but Caleb just slowly rolled his eyes at the demon's wide grin and sighed. "I'm tired of all this chit chat, Astaroth. You're beginning to bore me."

He felt a small stab of triumph in his gut when Astaroth's malicious grin twisted into a snarl. "Bring on your newest champion. The sooner we get this over with, the sooner I get Drew back."

"But will you want him? You already talk of him in the past tense. He's been sealed away all of this time, locked in a world of total silence, no one to feed from, no blood at all. No air, no sound, not the slightest touch from another being. For one hundred and fifty-seven years. How sane do you think he is by now? Are you sure he's worth fighting for anymore, Caleb?"

"I'll always want him back, Astaroth. He gave me something you never got from Shaddal. In all the six thousand years she was indebted to you as your consort she still never loved you. Worshiped you, pandered to you, obeyed you, yes, but love you? Neither of you even knew the meaning of the word let alone how it felt. You couldn't. Because love is pure joy and beauty and you'd destroy it the moment you touched it. You're not worthy of it."

"Insolent jackal!" Astaroth waved his hand and the floor turned to a carpet of glowing embers. Smoke and steam billowed up from the thousands of hot, amber coals and the air shimmered with the intense heat.

"You're just cranky because you know I'm right." Caleb jumped to stand on a step just out of the sizzling embers, then shrugged out of his long leather jacket, tossing it to land on the overturned gargoyle Sara Beth still stood serenely in front of. He flexed his broad shoulders and rolled his head on his neck, sparing a reassuring wink for the child.

Sara Beth nodded, but remained unmoving, a silent, grim witness to the coming devastating test of Caleb's endurance.

Dressed in loose fitting jeans, a plain black T-shirt and sturdy, steel-toed boots, he prepared for battle. He had yet to defeat one of Astaroth's demon champions, no matter how hard he fought. They were more powerful and stronger. But each year he returned and faced them again and again. The desperate need to rescue Drew from his prison in Hell grew.

Astaroth leapt upon the top of the lone, sealed, stone coffin in the center of room and stood atop it. It was where he always watched the coming battle from, center stage, smack in the middle of the action from which he could taunt and mock both Caleb and his own champion as they battled to the death.

So far, it had always been to Caleb's death.

No matter that Caleb was already dead. As long as he wasn't beheaded or staked through the heart with wood, he could be made to go through the agony of fatal injuries time and again, without actually ending his existence. One of the many 'benefits' of being a vampire, one of the undead.

Comfortably ensconced on his usual perch, Astaroth braced his molten body in a wide stance and clapped his smoldering palms together three times.

"We shall see just how bored you are with this demon, vampire."

"Bring it on, Duke. I have some trick or treating to do tonight." Caleb pulled the T-shirt from his torso and flung it off to one side, uncaring if the embers claimed it or not. He slipped off his boots and socks knowing from experience they provided no protection from the coals. They would just melt to his flesh and hinder him during the battle. He couldn't afford anything that slowed his movements if he was to eventually defeat one of Astaroth's champions and win Drew's freedom from Hell.

It had taken almost two centuries of trying, but he was discovering how to get and keep the upper hand in these battles. Through trial and error, Caleb had found that all of Astaroth's mighty demons had one common flaw. While they possessed great strength, they were short on quick thinking and slow on their feet. If he could stay moving, he lasted a lot longer, slowly wearing them down.

Heavy boots melted to his feet didn't help. He preferred the pain. Besides, it was only right he suffered some of what Drew suffered.

There came a clap of thunder and out of the embers on the floor rose a demon unlike any Caleb had faced before. It had eyes of glowing green attached to ends of six inch long, snake-like tentacles, all seven of them. Caleb could tell by the way it swiveled each eye that the creature could adjust his vision to encompass the whole room at once. It crouched low to the ground; its thick, hulking body bent and twisted, its back, head, and upper arms covered in sharp, crusted spines.

Between the spiny crusts, green slime oozed from open

sores over its entire body. Caleb could see tiny, pin-sized worms crawling in the pus as it dripped from its flesh and splattered onto the embers. The foul wetness hissed as it struck the glowing coals, releasing a stench into the stagnant air of the crypt that made even Caleb blink back the tears that stung his eyes from it.

Repulsed, Caleb muttered, "Well, aren't you just a blind date's dream?"

The beast hissed and advanced, arms reaching for Caleb before he was even in grabbing distance.

Barefoot, clad only in his jeans, Caleb stepped down into the area of battle, the soles of his feet blistering on the hot embers littering the tomb floor. The smell of burning flesh battled with the creature's stench and Caleb blocked them both from his mind.

There was only one thought, one focus, one desire for Caleb. This was his once-a-year chance to free Drew from the hell he had thrust his lover into. And if Drew had gone crazy from isolation and starvation, then Caleb would free him from that Hell, as well. He had to win this time; Drew didn't have much time left.

Caleb wasn't sure how much longer he could live with the fact that he continually failed to rescue his once playful, loving mate. Even after one hundred and fifty-seven years, Caleb still failed to win this yearly battle for Drew. First it had been about Drew's freedom, now it was about Drew's very existence and sanity. Caleb had to win this fight, this night, this time.

Both of their lives depended on it. His own faith in himself was faltering and without it, he knew this would be his last night on Earth if he should fail again.

Drawing on all his ancient powers, Caleb called forth the change and by the time the creature was upon him, he was vampyre. Suddenly transformed and formidable, he was full of ancient strength, channeling power from a thousand victims' life forces he had consumed, summoning all the magic and mystic spells he had taken the pains to learn over these last hundred years when he realized his own strength would not be enough to defeat a hell-spawned demon.

Eyes glowing a fierce yellow, fangs extended and eager, Caleb jumped into the fray, meeting his opponent head on.

The battle waged around the tomb, on every surface, whether it be broken coffins, upturned urns, shattered statues, or beds of sizzling, hot coals. Both Caleb and the demon suffered burnt flesh, bruised bodies and near-fatal injuries. The battle raged for hours, with Caleb taking the brunt of the blows. Each time he felt his strength waning, deserting him, he thought of Drew's horrified, beautiful face and he called on one of his new skills, fortifying his already awesome muscle and speed with mystical chants or spells of magic. But after a time, it became obvious even these powers would not be enough to defeat the demon creature.

Caleb was doomed to fail one more time.

He faulted and the creature took him down. He used his massive weight to pin a bleeding, broken Caleb to the floor, landing at the unmoving feet of Sara Beth. Inside, he was shattered and bleeding, his need to feed and repair paramount. He glanced up at her, a weak smile on his face for her unflinching, silent support, given freely one more year despite his defeat.

Sara Beth stood very still, gaze never leaving Caleb's face, her small, pale hand still resting lightly on the head of the fallen guardian gargoyle. Her presence touched Caleb even now, comforting and calming him.

Even the gargoyle seemed to take on her pale ghostly glow, the curve of his cracked ears and the length of his long tail, all faintly luminescent blue in the flickering light from the torches.

Unlike the other tortured spirits that roamed the room moaning and screeching their displeasure during the entire battle, Sara Beth hadn't moved since entering the tomb. Caleb regretted knowing such an innocent had been witness to the evil Astaroth and his minions embodied. One more debt owed to the dead.

His skin blistered and blackened, Caleb had no more energy left to resist. The last of his strength bubbled up and he used it to twist the panting creature's head sideways away from his own face. The foul odor from its breath was worse than from his body.

Laughing, Astaroth leaned down to stare into Caleb's eyes, a smirk on his snout and a mocking tone to his triumphant words. "You have failed once again, vampire. What good has 'love' done you? Only darkness holds the power of life and death. You'd do well to remember that for next year."

Astaroth glanced down between his feet at the sealed coffin he stood on. "But by then your lover might be completely insane and I'll have another unbeatable champion to add to my collection. Imagine how much devastation an insane vampire could bring upon the human race before they found a way to stop him."

Shaking his head solemnly, Caleb vowed, "I won't let you do that to him." Caleb grimaced in pain, and shifted beneath the crushing weight of the monster on his chest. The smell of his blood and flesh was becoming overpowering, blotting out the scent of everything else. "I'll kill Drew myself before I'll let you have him."

Jumping to the ground, Astaroth casually leaned against the stone coffin he had been standing on. "You may get the chance to do just that, if you ever manage to beat one of my demons, that is. I'd say better luck next time, but I don't think your little lover has a next time coming to him."

The Duke of Hell's hooded gaze slid sideways and Astaroth patted the coffin's stone lid. "Can't you hear him? He's growing more and more restless with each passing month." He rubbed a fiery palm over the stone slab until a section of its surface bubbled and pitted. "I doubt he has any fingertips left after trying to pry off this seal over the last a century and a half, don't you agree?"

Caleb's gaze darted to the coffin and his heart plunged to his charred toes. Had Drew really been inside that stone prison all this time? Alone and deserted, day after lonely day, laying only a few feet from Caleb each Halloween night? The unwitting centerpiece in each gruesome battle to win his freedom back?

Did Drew know Caleb had failed each year? Did he even know Caleb was trying to free him?

Their bond had been strong, but Caleb hadn't felt Drew near in all that time. Not even once. It stood to reason Drew hadn't been able to feel Caleb either. He'd been denied even that piece of cold comfort, left to think he had been abandoned, left to rot in a stone prison for all of eternity.

The soft scratching noise of mice in the debris around them reached his vampire ears and he imagined it was Drew digging his raw fingers into the stone lid. He fought against the demon's hold, but he didn't have the strength to throw him off.

"Finish him, for now. I grow weary of his pathetic struggles." Astaroth spit at Caleb, the wetness like acid, leaving a deep burn on Caleb's shoulder. "They are both mine for another year."

A massive fist punched his lower abdomen and Caleb heard and felt his pelvis crack and hip shatter. The agony the attack produced was nothing compared to the pain in his chest.

Shame rose up like bile and Caleb teetered on the edge of self-destruction. Defeated, he glanced up in apology to Sara Beth, once again disturbed by her innocent gaze. But this time, as their eyes met, Sara Beth's gaze held something more. There was a small, knowing smile on her tiny pale lips.

A slight movement of her fingers drew Caleb's gaze to her hand on the gargoyle, then inspiration filled his mind and his gaze traveled to the guardian's long, tipped, stone tail. The tail glowed, a bluish white, a weapon powered by an incorruptible source, the innocence and goodness of a child's love and devotion.

With all the speed and strength he could muster, Caleb snapped off the gargoyle's tail and shoved the short stone spear through the chest of the champion demon pinning him bodily to the smoking ember floor. The crunch of bone and cartilage was masked by the scream of agony. The creature roared in shock and instantly crumbled to ash before his cry had finished echoing off the crypt walls. The wails of the trapped spirits nearly deafened Caleb, as they sang his triumph to the night.

Stunned, Astaroth bellowed out his outrage and shock, but he called forth no new demons to take over where his last creature had failed.

Unable to move, needing blood and rest, Caleb lay crumpled at Sara Beth's ghostly feet, exhausted and spent, but not so weakened he didn't demand his reward. Panting between gasps of immense pain, Caleb clutched at his too-slow healing wounds. "Release Drew, Astaroth. Your champion is vanquished and your hold on both of us is absolved. The debt is paid."

Snorting his contempt, Astaroth stomped around the room to glower menacingly over Caleb's prostrate body. "Bold talk for a broken vampire that can't even stand up to accept his prize."

Caleb turned the full effect of his yellow-eyes on his tormentor and hissed from between grinding teeth and extended fangs, "Release him. Or does the Duke of Hell have no honor?"

Astaroth snorted again, pounding his massive fist on Drew's prison's lid. The room shook with the sound of his roar of displeasure. The ghosts huddled closer together and increased their wails. He let loose a deep breath on the coffin lid, belching white-hot flames. The stone melted away in a stream of molten lava, trails of liquid white marble splashing down into the fading embers.

The coals under Caleb's body died out and the floor returned to cold marble. The chill against his burnt flesh almost make Caleb sigh out loud, but a scrambling sound from within the open coffin grabbed his full attention.

The demon growled and then spit his words at Caleb, mocking ridicule in every syllable. "He will devour you, drain you of what little blood your broken body has left, and then the morning sun will claim him. I'll be rid of you both despite your victory." He spit at Caleb again and Caleb ducked to avoid losing an eye this time. "He's all yours, vampire. Enjoy having him back for the few minutes he lets you live."

Lightning crackled through the room, blinding Caleb, the thunderous clap of its energy deafening him for a moment.

When he opened his eyes, Astaroth was gone and a specter more horrible than Astaroth could ever be stood before him.

Naked, emaciated, withered, and nearly unrecognizable, the creature that crawled out of the stone coffin bore little resemblance to the beautiful lover Caleb had lost. Starved to the point of madness, isolated and confined for over fifteen decades, Andrew Wright had been reduced to a mindless animal, a vampire gone mad, a beautiful mind and body wasted away to skin and bones.

Any hope Caleb had that Drew retained some spark of his original personality died the second Drew sniffed the air, focusing on Caleb's bleeding wounds.

Drew's wildly flashing yellow eyes registered excitement and he growled, bared his fangs, and jumped on top of the only thing in the room he could feed from, burying his fangs to the roots in Caleb's exposed chest.

Snarling and hissing, Drew worked his way up Caleb's chest by pulling himself up with his fangs, hands, twisted into useless claws, leaving a trail of gaping, bloody wounds up the archer's naked torso. When he reached Caleb's neck, he knocked Caleb's head to one side with his own and tore into Caleb's willingly offered neck. Drew latched on tight and began feeding, wild and sloppy with need, draining his depleted lover's remaining blood from his beaten body.

And Caleb let him.

He wrapped his arms around Drew and held on tighter than he knew was good for either of them. The feel of holding Drew in his arms again was undiminished by the contorted, tortured shell of the being Drew had been turned into. Caleb pressed his lover's mouth harder against his neck and sobbed, tormented by the tremors that shook Drew's slender body. He ran his hands over Drew's back and arms, the feel of the once satin skin now like dry parchment paper under Caleb's palms.

Agony at the true loss of his lover overwhelmed him and Caleb's cries welled up and out of his chest, his agony and the pain of one hundred fifty-seven years finally given a voice. He clutched the wild feral thing Drew had become to him, tears streaming down his own contorted face, and he began rocking them back and forth, searching desperately for some shred of comfort for both of them.

Drew made a few muffled animal sounds and tore deeper into Caleb's flesh. Caleb tenderly kissed the wild strands of pale blond hair matted to Drew's cheek and neck, petting them down into place. He savored the feel of his lover in his arms for a moment longer, then his tears dried.

Realization that he had finally freed Drew from his prison and released him into a new hell of insanity, spurred Caleb to summon his waning strength and accept one final challenge to their centuries-long love. One arm still clinging tightly to Drew as he fed, Caleb used his free arm to drag both of them to the base of the coffin and his duffel bag.

Hoping for the best, Caleb had filled the bag with modern clothes for Drew, as well as blood bags to replenish himself after battle. Expecting the worse, he had packed two wooden stakes. Dragging the bag near, he fumbled through the pockets one-handed, then withdrew both long, slender stakes. They were made from smooth white ash, sharp and rubbed to a satiny finish to minimize the pain on insertion.

Biting back the tears once more, Caleb pulled one stake close and placed it between their bodies, pausing only long enough to lay his head on Drew's and place a tender, chaste kiss in his pale, brittle hair. He nuzzled Drew's ear and hoarsely whispered into it, knowing his lover wouldn't understand, but needing to say the words one last time himself. "I love you, Drew. Always love you, with my last breath."

Caleb summoned his ebbing strength and plunged the stake upward toward Drew's heart.

At least he had intended to.

Before the tip pierced Drew's flesh, Caleb's arm froze in place. He tried again, but again the stake would not penetrate Drew's chest. Confused and uncertain of what was happening, Caleb looked up to find Sara Beth staring back at him.

Freed from Astaroth's curse on their resting-place, the other ghosts had disappeared to find peace after the battle's end, but sweet Sara Beth had remained behind.

She smiled at Caleb and shook her head. Unsure what she meant, Caleb withdrew the stake and she nodded. Confused but listening, Caleb lowered it to the crypt floor and hugged Drew with both arms, gaze still locked on Sara Beth's, seeking direction.

The girl gently waved her chubby hand through the air and the duffel bag opened, spilling out bags of blood on the floor within Caleb's reach.

Uncomprehending, Caleb looked from Sara Beth to the bags and back again. "It won't help."

Tears broke through his tightly held control, making tiny rivers down his dirty, blood-smeared face. "He...he's gone."

He held on with both hands to the feeding, wild animal in his arms. "He's not Drew anymore. I can't leave him like this and I don't have much time left before he drains me."

She moved several bags of blood closer to them.

Shaking his head, Caleb picked up one and hefted it. "He's an animal now. He'll want warm blood, my blood, not bagged. And it won't change anything, he's gone mad. I took too long to win the battle. Blood won't bring him back." Caleb wiped his tears in Drew's hair. His voice hardened. "Not the part of him that counts."

Moving closer to them on soundless feet, Sara Beth bent down and touched Drew's head with both of her stubby hands.

Caleb felt Drew shudder and gasp, then the ravenous, mindless feeding gentled and slowed. The soft, pale blue/white light that always surrounded the little girl traveled out her fingertips and encircled Drew until his entire body glowed. Caleb felt the other vampire's skin tingle in his grasp.

Sara Beth released them. Giving Caleb a small serene smile,

she pointed to the blood and nodded again. This time Caleb understood her message. Already he could feel the difference in Drew, feel his body filling out, his skin becoming soft and supple again, his hair turning silky under his chin.

More importantly, Caleb could tell Drew's feeding had changed, becoming more of a lover's embrace than a death grip from a crazed animal. Sara Beth had restored Drew to him.

Caleb suddenly knew she was one of the failed gargoyles that had been charged with guarding this tomb. She was rewarding him for freeing its spirits, for doing the job the gargoyles had failed.

Tears in his eyes and his lover tight in his grasp, Caleb looked at her, an expression of near worship in his eyes. "Thank you."

Anything more would have been just useless words. Sara Beth knew his heart for the last century and a half. He didn't need to explain it. He buried his face in Drew's neck again and inhaled the scent of his lover, unchanged after all this time. When he looked back up, they were alone.

Cradling a more restful Drew to his chest, Caleb began to feed, allowing his lover to drain his fill from Caleb's body while Caleb replaced it with the tasteless, but nourishing blood from the duffel. Already he felt his body healing. By morning, Caleb's near-fatal wounds would be healed completely and his shattered bones perfectly mended.

Drew was sated, sleeping in his arms, face beautiful again, if still somewhat drawn. This last century had taken its toll on both of them.

Sleep would not come to Caleb, his heart too full and his mind too anxious, fearful that if he closed his eyes, he would awaken and find it had all been a dream. The weight of Drew's body, now lean and supple as it was supposed to be, anchored Caleb to the reality that their nightmare was over. It had been a harsh debt to pay for Shaddal's attempt at kidnapping and treachery.

The centuries to come would find them even more reclusive than they had been. Distance from both humans and demons would suit them both. Caleb planned on spending at least the next century and a half making love to Drew and showing him just how much he was missed.

Drew stirred and raised a drowsy head up off Caleb's chest and stared at him. His gaze darted over every line and feature of Caleb's face. He licked his lips twice to moisten them enough to talk without them cracking and then no sound came out of his open mouth. Disbelief and hope flashed in his sable eyes as fear made his limbs tremble in Caleb's tight embrace.

Caleb rubbed a hand over Drew's bare back and smiled, fighting back his own tears when twin rivers spilled from Drew's eyes as sudden comprehension dawned.

"Hey. Wondered when you were going to wake up." If Caleb had had a heartbeat, he knew it would be pounding in his chest waiting for Drew's reply. "I've been waiting for what seemed like forever."

Drew suddenly grabbed Caleb's hand and bit into his wrist, tasting the rich blood that flowed from the vicious tear. He licked at the flow, eyes locked on Caleb's the entire time. His body twisted around Caleb's half-nude form plastering his skin to Caleb's flesh. Lips still attached to Caleb's wrist, Drew leaned forward and buried his nose in Caleb's neck, inhaling his scent.

Abruptly, Drew let go of the wrist and licked the dry sweat and blood off Caleb's skin. It wasn't until then that he sighed and threw him arms around Caleb's neck, crushing the vampire to him. Drew crawled more completely into Caleb's lap, tucking his legs around Caleb's hips and tried to press himself under his skin. He stayed that way so long, Caleb feared for Drew's sanity again.

"It's you. It's really you. Not just some phantom dream come to torment me. I can taste you and smell you and feel you this time. You're really here." Caleb could barely hear Drew mumbling into his chest, but he understood as the other vampire's fingers dug into his shoulders taking a tighter hold on him.

"And you're free, peach. No more hell, no more prison." The sound of the pet name Caleb had christened Drew with their first night together brought a fresh round of tears to both of them. The sound of roughly gasped sobs echoed off the barren walls of the tomb.

Brushing his hands over the long, smooth curve of Drew's back and buttocks, Caleb soothed and calmed his lover. For long minutes, Caleb kneaded Drew's flesh, rubbing his sides and squeezing the firm curve of his spread ass. He loved the feel of Drew's backside, the firm globes reminding him of a freshly picked peach, and hence, the centuries-old term of endearment he had used earlier that had undone them both.

Drew's sobs soon faded away and his distress was replaced with growing arousal. The need to reaffirm their bond rose up in each of them, a ritual of vampire lust that couldn't be denied any longer. Arousal shoved aside all other emotions.

Caleb pulled Drew off from around his neck, breaking the strangling embrace. They exchanged a brief, lustful stare, and then Caleb yanked Drew into a scorching kiss filled with all the desperate need and aching desire he'd held inside since Drew had been taken from him. Caleb was trembling by the time he released Drew's lips.

He allowed Drew to draw back only a scant inch before he grabbed Drew's face and pulled him back for several short, intense, ravishing kisses that flamed both of their desires to a ravenous level.

Drew whimpered and whispered against Caleb's lips, "Still love me?"

Panting, chests heaving, Caleb twisted free once again and held Drew's head far enough away that he could look into his lover's eyes, a sight he thought he might never see again only a short time ago. Words seemed useless efforts for what he wanted to say, but he summed it up in one phrase he knew Drew would understand the import of for a vampire.

Voice halting, filled with love and a tenderness that went beyond words, Caleb stared into Drew's eyes. "I walked through fire to get you back."

All the doubt and uncertainty seemed to vanish from Drew's face and his body. He dove back in and kissed Caleb like he was never going to get the opportunity again, devouring him. He licked, bit and sucked at Caleb, drinking the trickles of blood his fangs drew, an urgent unstoppable need.

Words were suddenly too cumbersome to use, too inadequate to express their emotions. They fell into old mating habits and went at each other. Wild, passionate lovers with the strength and endurance of their vampire beasts let lose.

Caleb managed to release his swollen erection with one hand while holding Drew to him with the other. He could feel Drew's full cock nudging his abdomen, the beads of cum streaking over the ripple of muscles as he twisted and heaved to open his jeans without throwing Drew off his lap.

Slicing open the palm of his hand with his fang, Caleb stroked his cock with the resulting blood, lubricating himself with several swift passes. He grabbed Drew's hips and helped the other vampire raise up on his knees, then slammed Drew down onto his shaft, penetrating his lover's ass in one deep thrust.

Drew groaned and fell forward over Caleb's chest, his hips grinding down harder onto the shaft. He latched onto one swollen nub on Caleb's chest and suckled and bit, lapping the blood from the sweaty chest, moaning as he did so. His hands explored every inch of Caleb's skin he could reach, teasing and rubbing, reacquainting himself with his lover.

Stroking into his lover with every snap and thrust of his hips, Caleb wrapped his still moist hand around Drew's cock and stroked him in time to the manic rhythm of their frenzied coupling. It was hard, and dirty, and fierce, full of decades of unfulfilled want, desire, and love. It was short and sweaty and sweet beyond description.

With the final act of sharing their blood during an explosive mutual climax, they reaffirmed their life bond together. Exhausted, they lay in each others' arms, fangs slowly, reluctantly withdrawn, hearts finally on the mend together with their bodies.

Caleb had almost forgotten how sweet Drew's blood tasted, how rich and sinfully sensual it felt rolling over his tongue and sliding down his throat. It healed him in ways nothing else could. Holding his lover close to him, he tucked Drew's head under his chin and spoke to the room so he could maintain his control this time.

"I've missed you so much."

Drew paused before answering, pressing himself deeper into Caleb's embrace. His voice sounded frail and unsure to Caleb, like he was making a confession he didn't want to give voice to. "I thought you'd come for me so many times. I thought about it, dreamt about it, then hallucinated about it. I thought I'd go mad with wanting you and not having you beside me. I couldn't sleep, not without you."

One hand petted the soft blond hair on Drew's head, savoring the feeling of the silky, familiar strands of gold. Drew was Caleb's sunshine in a world of constant darkness. "I'm so sorry Drew. I wanted to be with you. I tried to be with you, year after year. I fought Astaroth's champions, but I couldn't defeat them until now." He took a deep breath and confessed, "And even then I needed help."

"Help?" Drew stirred restlessly on Caleb's chest, but didn't raise his head.

"A ghost of a little girl showed me the way." Caleb searched the room, but found no sign of Sara Beth. "I think her spirit used to guard this place. Once Shaddal desecrated it, her spirit watched over its souls until I freed you and them from Astaroth's hold."

He glanced at the shattered, carved altar in the wall, seeing the dirt outline of where a cross had once stood against the battered marble back. "I think she was an angel."

Drew sat up and looked off into the distance. Caleb's hands followed Drew's arms and held on to them. Eyes troubled, Drew frowned at Caleb. "I dreamed about a little girl while I was in that box. She would come to me when I would get wild. Trying to claw my way out through stone and such. She glowed, so I could kind of see her. She'd lie beside me and touch my cheek or rub my forehead and eventually, it would pass. She kept me sane, gave me someone to talk to. I thought she was just a dream."

"She was our guardian angel."

"Can't, Caleb." Even though his words dismissed the idea, his voice held a note of hope. "Angels don't help vampires."

"Maybe they do if the vampires lift a curse off a sacred place like consecrated ground. This used to be a chapel. That's why Shaddal picked this crypt, to defile it in Astaroth's name."

Drew seemed to think about it, then asked, "Think she'll come back? The little girl, I mean? I'd like to thank her."

Caleb glanced at the gargoyle that Sara Beth always stood by. It still sat in the corner of the room near the coffin where it always had been, but now Caleb noticed that it no longer tilted to one side and the debris and cobwebs had been brushed away. If he looked hard enough, he was sure there was a pale blue light glowing on its rough stone surface that hadn't been there before.

Brushing his jeans off, Caleb stood up and smiled at the silent, stone guardian before pulling Drew to his feet. "I think she knows we how we feel."

"But, an angel helped us, Caleb? Why?"

"Maybe she knew how much we loved each other." Caleb pulled Drew into an embrace and kissed the tip of his nose. "Maybe love really does conquer all."

Unsatisfied with just a chaste kiss, Drew captured Caleb's mouth and kissed him deeply, using tongue, lips, and fangs to make his point. Passions rose again. "Let's leave. We've got a bit of time to make up for, lover. Do we have a home to go back to?"

Caleb pulled out of Drew's arms and bent to pull clothing out of the duffel bag. He tossed jeans and a shirt at Drew, then zippered his jeans and pulled on his own discarded shirt, jacket, socks and shoes while Drew dressed in the strange new clothes.

"We do have a home." Caleb kicked the empty bag aside, covering the two discarded stakes with its canvas corpse. "But first we have something else to do."

"What's more important than going home?"

"There's still a little bit of Halloween night left, Drew." Caleb grabbed Drew's hand and pulled him to his side, heading for the gate out of the crypt. As they passed the gargoyle, Caleb tenderly patted its head. Odd warmth filled his hand at the touch.

Caleb smiled at his lover and tugged Drew closer. "Let's go and celebrate the dead."

Winner
Takes All

"All you have to do is nod and I'll end this quickly."

William Pray stared back into Malcolm Crane's harsh blue eyes and made very sure he didn't move a single muscle that could be taken as a sign of agreement. He wasn't going down that easily, no matter how much agony he was in. He couldn't afford to.

Malcolm huffed cold air into William's face, making his eyes water. "You never did know when to cut your losses and surrender graciously, did you, William?"

"Just a part of my charm."

Malcolm grinned and then buried his fangs deep into William's exposed shoulder, sucking blood and life from his opponent, just a little, just enough to weaken him further. As he pulled back, he tore viciously at William's skin, leaving a gaping wound that trickled precious blood onto the tarpaper roof of the abandoned apartment building. The wound showed no signs of healing anytime soon.

He ran a fingertip through the puddle of blood created beside William's battered face, drawing crude symbols on the roof's surface just far enough away that William could see them if he strained his neck and rolled his eyes. Malcolm knew William wouldn't be able to resist looking, and he couldn't. All vampires knew the ancient language. It was part of the conversion, a genetic imprint passed on to the newly converted, innate knowledge all vampires possessed after their awakening.

The symbols leapt from the gritty surface, their meaning searing into William's brain, unlocking his final waning reserves of vampiric strength. He surged up, his one still-functioning hand around Malcolm's thick throat. It was a pathetic attempt, but one William had to make. He managed to catch Malcolm by surprise, enabling him to throw the vampire off enough to roll on top of him, pinning Malcolm to the rooftop.

He tightened his fingers around Malcolm's windpipe before he remembered vampires as old as Malcolm didn't need to breathe. A malicious smile on Malcolm's face chilled William to the bone.

"Poor choice of defense, but I applaud your efforts to fight back." Pale gray-blue eyes studied him thoughtfully, a sudden intimate interest beyond the approaching victory lighting them. It would have made William blush if he'd had the blood to spare.

"You always could surprise me...in so many ways." Malcolm's stare turned colder still, and his lips twisted into a biting smirk. "I hope it's a trait you've passed on to your offspring."

William tried to pull back, but Malcolm held him in place and rolled them over together. A sharp metal roof vent impaled William through the back, and he screamed into the humid, still dawn-tinged air, the sound more an animal than human. With a powerful thrust, Malcolm used his considerable weight to crush William all the way down to the to the tarpaper surface.

Malcolm Crane had been taken in his thirty-second year of life during a bloody, vicious Celtic war. A celebrated, successful leader and brutal warrior, his body had been preserved for all time in its hard, thick-muscled perfection, honed by a human life of battle and grueling physical labor of the ancient times. Malcolm was broad, hard, and chiseled like a statue that paid homage to the perfect male form.

William's body reflected his prior life as a photojournalist. He was medium height, slender of build, with a keen mind and zero fighting skills. The most exercise he had ever done as human was jogging. He was no fighting match for Malcolm and he knew it, but there was more at stake than his undead existence. The blood markings Malcolm scrolled into the rooftop told him as much. But the pain, the pain was unbearable, agonizing, consuming.

Through the haze, William sensed Malcolm staring at him. He blinked to clear the tears of agony away and face his executioner with as much courage as he could gather.

He'd gambled everything he had in this long-awaited battle with Malcolm — his fortune, his power, his property and his very existence. He hadn't lost easily. Partly because that wasn't what Malcolm would want and partly because William had hoped if he gave the ruthless ancient a glorious win, the old warrior would be merciful and not take everything William's losing would entitle him. He had only been a vampire a few short years, but he had planned wisely, accrued power and wealth trying to make up financially for his sudden absence from his mortal life. He had been a creature of the night covertly arranging to pay college tuition.

William didn't care about his power or even the properties and money that he had hoped would go to his mortal heir, but there was one thing William didn't want Malcolm to claim. One very important thing he had to protect even if it was with his last breath. But he knew now that was lost as well. Knew it as clearly as he knew he was moments away from slipping out of existence.

He shuddered with the effort to pull in a breath deep enough to make his words heard, not caring if they sounded like a plea. "Don't make it hurt. Don't make him suffer, please."

Malcolm ran two fingertips down William's less damaged cheek, the touch sensuous and possessive, but with an element of hesitation.

"Why should I do that, William? What has earned him that privilege?"

Lying inches from Malcolm's handsome, angular face, with Malcolm's weight crushing down on him, William accepted the intimate touch in death that he had refused to accept in life.

He had always been attracted to the man physically, but Malcolm's sometimes brutally cruel warrior nature had been too great a barrier for William to ignore. It had even brought them to this closing chapter in their relationship. In the long run, Malcolm did not take rejection well.

"My dying request." William shivered and gasped, life draining away alarmingly fast, but he found enough will to lock stares with Malcolm hovering over him. He watched as Malcolm's cold glare churned to something dark, heated, and unspoken. "If you ever loved me at all, show him mercy."

The dark look froze, quickly replaced with a bitter stare. "Mercy?" Malcolm chuckled and traced the outline of William's swollen lips. "What is that?"

"Yes, mercy." Malcolm's fingers moved with William's mouth as he talked, and William didn't bother to shake them off, even going so far as to let his tongue flick against them as he moistened his lips between words, using all the weapons at his disposal to sway the vampire. "Have you lost touch so completely with humanity that you forget the meaning of the word? Isn't that one of the coveted traits of the finest of warriors? Mercy with victory?"

Malcolm's response was low, guttural, and cruel. "You know nothing of being a warrior nor of me!"

Now, even with nothing left to lose, the older vampire's ability to thrust paralyzing menace into mere words still made William cringe, but it didn't stop him from fighting back with more words of his own.

"I know you've won. I'm not sorry to leave this life. You've won this battle and, with it, everything I possess. If you're still are a true warrior, show him mercy. Don't lose touch with the human you once were, Malcolm. Don't lose *yourself* completely to this unholy existence. Please, don't make him suffer because of me."

"Always the altruist, even now when brute strength would have served you better." Malcolm's sneer had lost some of its sharpness, the bitterness replaced by a glimmer of something William read as grudging respect or maybe veiled affection.

He used it to push home his point as his last breath escaped his crumbling body. "You are the most powerful, Malcolm, the winner. But what will show the better man? The brutal winner or the merciful one?"

Malcolm's nostrils flared, his cold eyes narrowed, and William's heart sank. "Brutal or merciful, the *winner still takes all.*"

With a last defeated sigh, William's spark of unearthly life faded and his body turned to ash, dissolving under the weight of Malcolm's body, leaving the ancient vampire lying in the dust of the man who had once been his most steadfast detractor and his unachieved fondest desire.

His own hand was full of the ash that had once been William's left hand. Malcolm rolled the gold wedding band left behind in his palm. He read the inscription, then slipped it into his pocket as he rose to his feet. He didn't even try to brush the ash from his clothes.

§ § §

Malcolm couldn't believe the young man's name was actually Hunter. Hunter Pray. It was absurd and yet fitting at the same time. Since Hunter's father's demise five months ago by Malcolm's hand, the young freelance photographer had become the ancient vampire's *hunted prey*. Hunter was the last chip to be cashed in from the deadly high-stakes game that Malcolm and William had played and that William had lost. The twenty-four-year-old was the final acquisition for Malcolm. The one he had saved for last. The only remaining piece of his rival's most treasured possessions to claim. And the sweetest.

He had even begun entering Hunter's apartment while he slept, just to unnerve the human, play with him. He would enter by the perpetually open window and stand in the shadows until, even in sleep; the young man would sense a presence. Then he would vanish faster than Hunter's reactions could track him, always moving slow enough that the human's disoriented senses registered the flash of movement, the rustle of cloth, the swoosh of air as he departed out the sixth-floor window in the twenty-story apartment building. He knew from experience how unnerved it would leave his victims.

That was just the first three nights.

Now he came to marvel at how like the father the son was. William had had a small dimple in the corner of his mouth that never relaxed, not even in slumber. Hunter possessed the same dimple and the same full, deeply pink lips. So, entranced, Malcolm started watching Hunter from a distance during his waking hours as well.

When awake, the human's eyes shone with the familiar, intense, consuming interest in life that William's had held, and Hunter's physical mannerisms mimicked his father's -- rapid, impatient, energetic, and impulsive. Malcolm almost regretted his decision to end the existence of a human so enamored with living. But then, that would make the prize all the more sweet, wouldn't it?

Hunter was a beautiful young man with an underlying thread of confidence Malcolm could actually feel in the air when he got physically close to Hunter. The one time he allowed Hunter to see him face to face, he had been intrigued by the way the young man's gold-flecked hazel eyes met and held his. Intrigued and aroused.

The brief glance had been startlingly warm and open. It darted over his own sharp-boned features, wandered up to his closely cropped hair, and then dropped to his pale lips, moving on up to linger on his gray eyes with a stare that could have been interpreted as attraction if Malcolm had been prone to romantic notions. He wasn't. He couldn't even remember what romance and love felt like anymore, but he suspected it was right about then his interest in Hunter began to shift from quick-meal-and-prize-won to something more...intimate.

He had planned very carefully so that he could savor every moment of this victory kill. Malcolm imagined the young man's blood would be sweet, full of youth and strength, with a fervor for justice just like his father's — only better, innocent and untainted by even a short time as a vampire like William's blood had been.

Malcolm stalked him nightly. He followed Hunter home from his evenings out with friends. He sat in a darkened corner of the large, solemn reading room at the local library where Hunter spent most evenings reading, apparently researching some isolated, war-torn North African region. It was all unimportant, but Malcolm knew the value of learning about a victim. Plus he enjoyed watching Hunter in everyday moments, unguarded and relaxed, like now.

Face down, Hunter shifted and stirred under the thin covers, distress on his slumbering face, his senses already picking up on the intruder at his side. His nude body twisted in the sheets so that his lithe frame was outlined by the shroud of blue linen. A frown marred his forehead, and his lips parted to allow a soft gasp to escape.

Malcolm could smell the apprehension on Hunter's breath and in his sweat. It brought a slight twist of pleasure to one corner of his mouth. He picked up a pair of discarded jeans from the foot of the bed and brought them to his face. Pressing the button-fly crotch to his cheek, Malcolm inhaled the rich, musky smell lingering in the soft, well-washed fabric, delighting in the scent that was primitive and base, a dried, faint mix of Hunter's sweat and hormones.

It was pure and earthy, untainted by the tobacco, drugs, or alcohol that seemed to plague most of the humans Hunter's age. It was a natural aphrodisiac — ambrosia promising that his blood would be as sweet. Knowing he would have to leave soon when Hunter awoke, Malcolm couldn't resist moving closer. He tossed the jeans to a nearby chair and silently stepped to the head of the bed.

Hunter was short, like his father, not more than five feet eight, but the one hundred and forty-five pounds on his frame were lightly muscled and well-defined. One hand curled loosely under his chin, his faintly shadowed jaw framed by tousled fawn-brown hair that curled at his neck and fringed the wrinkled pillowcase.

A faded old scar under Hunter's right eyebrow glistened with a bead of sweat. Malcolm wondered what injury had had the pleasure of drawing this man's blood for the first time. He had a sudden urge to lick the tiny crevice of raggedly healed flesh.

First he imagined the taste of Hunter's terror-fueled sweat. Then his imagination questioned what the sweat would taste like pooling in the scar when created by wild passion and lust instead. Malcolm felt his passion rise, and the long-forgotten stirring in his blood almost made him recoil.

His prey stirred again. Hunter rolled onto his back, signaling the man's sleep-laden mind had finally registered his presence and was about to awaken. Dressed in black, a mere layer of darkness in the gray and black shadows of the room, he watched and waited until Hunter had actually started up in bed, disoriented and panting, to stare into the corners of the bedroom. Only then did Malcolm swoosh out the open window.

He heard the tap-tap of the window blinds swaying in the draft of displaced air along with a tense, "Who's there? Damn it, answer me!"

§ § §

"Who's there?" Hunter sat up in bed, staring into the deepest shadows in his room, searching for the source of growing disquiet that had invaded his life lately. "Damn it, answer me!"

But the bedroom was dark and empty. He knew it would be — it always was — but he couldn't shake the feeling that there had been someone, *something,* watching him. If not watching, than waiting for him. The last ten days of this feeling were beginning to play hell with his sleep.

"Freaking nightmare!"

Ten days had passed since he began to feel eyes on him, sense a presence with him in empty rooms. Sometimes it was beside him when he awakened at night, hair and sheets plastered to his skin with a sheen of sweat, even though the bedroom's air was cool and pleasant, a gentle breeze from his habitually open window. He'd close the window, but there was no reason to. There was no balcony, no fire escape, no trellis or drain pipe for an intruder to use, and he was too high for easy access. An intruder who got into his bedroom through the window would have to be able to fly.

Throwing back the damp sheets, Hunter swung both feet over the edge of the mattress and sat naked, hunched over his knees. He rolled his shoulders to shake off the tension and ran his fingers through his hair, grimacing when they came away clammy with sweat. Sighing, he turned on the bedside table lamp and made another quick visual scan around the dimly lit room before standing up.

Empty. The room was empty. Just him, the bedroom furniture, and a pair of jeans slung across the bedroom chair in a corner of the room. He was totally alone. He stopped and stared at the rumpled heap of worn denim, unable to force himself to walk toward it. Where before the night breeze had felt refreshing on his damp skin, he shivered now in the sudden chill, a flicker of fear skittering down his back. He stood naked, covered in gooseflesh, unable to grab his usual covering. After all, they were pants, just a pair of old jeans.

"Fuck."

Jeans that should have been on the end of the bed where he *always* put them so they would be handy if he needed them in the middle of the night. Because he always slept nude. With jeans at the end of the bed. Always.

"Well, just...fuck."

Suddenly, it wasn't the least bit reassuring that he was totally, completely alone. No roommate, no friend staying the night, no lover in his bed. Of course, he'd never had a roommate, didn't collect close friends, and there hadn't been a serious lover since college. He didn't have time for them. They could never adjust to his whirlwind travel schedule or his erratic hours.

The impact of his isolated life was never clearer than it was at this single moment in time. He'd been in war zones that hadn't made him this apprehensive. Something akin to menace seemed to linger on the air, dangerous, primal. Threatening.

Finding the willpower to move again, Hunter strode to the bedroom door. He found it still securely locked. Unhappy, he jerked the jeans off the chair and slid into them.

He tugged the jeans into place over his ass and moved to the open window, his cool, sweaty hands arranging his half-hard cock more comfortably to one side as he buttoned the fly. It was a tight fit. He usually liked the way the thrill of danger always made him hard, but tonight it was just inconvenient and slightly disturbing. This wasn't some foreign battle or prowling lion that he could run from by hopping a plane or boarding a safari Jeep.

He wasn't intruding on someone else's territory. This was something stalking him. Just him. Someone *had* been in the room.

It was about more than just a pair of misplaced jeans. He

didn't know how he knew it, but he did. He'd felt a similar but more fleeting sensation now and then over the years since his parents had died, like a lingering presence or an unexplainable force nearby. He had always consoled himself with the fairy tale that it was one or both of his sorely missed parents watching over him from beyond. The presence always had left him with a feeling of safety and comfort. This time it was the same — but different.

The tingle between his shoulder blades made him tense, restless, and sweaty with apprehension.

The breeze gusted up, and the blinds clattered softly against the window frame. Hunter raised the slats higher and leaned out the opening. The rush of air carried the smells of the city with it, but it still felt good on his skin, in his face, lifting the damp strands of hair and drying his scalp.

From his parents and their experiences, Hunter learned to love wide-open spaces and physical freedom. He'd spent most of his childhood and youth traveling with his parents from untamed country to the next primitive territory. They'd made him a partner in the family business as they photographed and chronicled natural disasters, military uprisings, and amazing events around the world. Hunter loved nature, craved the rush of energy the wind carried on it.

Except this wind carried something dangerous with it. Something or someone. He pulled back into the room.

"Burglar?" he asked the silent walls, but glanced out the window. "Nah. Nothing here to risk the climb for." *Six floors up in a twenty-story building? Not a real person.*

"Ghosts, then?" The thought of a ghostly apparition tweaked his memory. Something. *Someone* ghostly. "Crap. Maybe I got his picture this time!"

Tearing out of the room, Hunter headed across the hall and entered his spare-bedroom-turned-dark-room. Reflexively, he reached for and found comfort in the old, heavy, pebbled metal of the paper vault, part of his father's legacy to him. He used digital SRL camera for his assignments. But nothing satisfied his creativity in the same way as it did to take his personal photographs on film, to develop them on the enlarger and in chemical baths the way his father had taught him to do.

Soft, dim amber safelights glowed at the touch of a switch. He used the guest bathroom for the actual developing, but the final product of his recent photo shoot hung clipped to wires that crisscrossed a corner of spare bedroom.

"No, no, not that one. Where are you?" Hunter sorted his way through the drying prints, looking for the ones that had sparked his memory.

"Yes! Here you are." He tugged three pictures off the line and studied each one carefully, moving closer to the light to be sure he wasn't missing anything.

"What the hell?" He sorted through them three times and went back to the line to see if he had grabbed the wrong ones.

When a thorough search revealed he had the pictures he wanted, he scanned them again and still, again, found nothing in the frames but an empty chair and a glass of red wine. The very pale, intense, platinum-blond man that had been sitting in the chair across from him in the outdoor café yesterday evening wasn't visible in the photograph. But Hunter couldn't remember a time when the man had left the table when he had taken the shots.

Hunter had covertly snapped his picture from under a rumpled cloth dinner napkin. The man had been staring at Hunter, and Hunter couldn't resist capturing the man's animal magnetism on film, even without permission. Hunter found the man's intensity and boldness attractive. His flawless skin looked like fine marble, and his eyes were the same gray of an approaching thunderstorm. He was built large and muscular, with chiseled, high-boned cheeks and a thin streak of the palest of pinks for lips. The way the man held his mouth in a firm line made Hunter imagine a kiss from those powerful lips would be demanding and just as bold as the man's unwavering stare. Hunter had felt slightly undressed by the look. And aroused.

He examined the pictures more closely. Breath caught in his lungs and his throat tightened as he noticed the level of wine in the glass changed in each shot, decreasing slightly. But no one was there to drink it. Where was the man?

The photographs had been meant to fuel a few harmless wet dreams, but now Hunter had the unsettling impression this man could be the source of his disturbing nights. But that was ridiculous. He was just a man. Attractive and sexy, but a man.

"Must have been a bad roll of film. That's it. Bad film. That's gotta be it." But instead of tossing them into the wastebasket, he carefully took them out into the living room and laid them on a nearby table.

§ § §

Two nights had passed since Malcolm last visited his prey, nights spent thinking, examining, and planning. Two nights of questioning himself, searching his feelings and thoughts, reliving his past lives and lovers. They had been long, cold nights filled with few revelations. Malcolm had never been a man who deluded himself. He was harsh, unforgiving, the ultimate survivor over the long centuries. But he did so alone, unhindered by any of the human qualities William had prized. He considered mercy, charity, love human weaknesses. But it had been those very qualities in William that Malcolm had secretly admired, desired to embrace, if only vicariously through the other vampire. Maybe William wasn't the only one who could provide those connections for him. Maybe it was time for a change.

The sidewalk bench was made of concrete and wooden slats, both materials still warm to the touch in the last feeble rays of sunlight. The park behind him was still populated with restless children and chattering adults, all winding down from a Sunday spent together. It was a small park, mostly grass and swing sets, with no shadowed alcoves for unsavory types to lurk.

Malcolm settled onto the bench and waited, long black cashmere coat casually draping his strong, hard-muscled frame, forever preserved as it was on the final night of bloody battle when he had the misfortune to stumble across a creature feeding on the dying warriors on the battlefield. In a flash of teeth and pain, his human existence had ended.

He had been disoriented and outraged at first, but as he learned his new abilities, he reveled in his unimaginable power and strength. Regret over his lost human existence had never entered his warrior's mind or his warrior's heart. He had no close ties, his tribesmen all dead at his feet, and had found no need for any companions since. He preferred to face millennia alone, the way vampires were meant to live.

The chatter of tired children faded away on a sharp gust of autumn wind that brought a fresh scent to Malcolm. His nostrils flared, eager for more, and his lips twitched as he realized his mouth was watering, anticipating the first sweet taste of his prey's ruby-red blood. His teeth ached and his cock stirred, an obvious bulge in his finely tailored suit pants. He did so love the thrill of the hunt and the anticipation of the coming kill. He wondered how much terror he had managed to instill in Hunter these last few nights. Fear always gave the blood a sharp tang he had grown to appreciate and savor over time. Like fine wine and the most fragrant single malt scotch.

Shadows grew longer, darker, seemingly muffling the street noises like an old familiar cloak, wrapping the sky and surrounding trees in a blackened huddle. Only the sound of the rustling trees penetrated the cloak, the sky empty of moonlight and stars. Streetlights popped on one by one, but their yellow glare did nothing more than cast an eerie shimmer on the scene.

A foul stench struck Malcolm as a pair of twenty-something young men in too-large jeans that hung off their hips and bagged at their kneecaps strolled into sight, their sneering faces and curled lips so typical of the generation. Malcolm held their hostile stares until they could no longer face his steely glare, disappearing around a corner and out of sight. Their rough, uneducated voices carried easily to Malcolm's sensitive hearing.

"Let's go back an' roll that guy, Rock. Dude, he gots money. You see he got it. Let's go back."

"No way, man. You look at his eyes? Them dead eyes, Jam. I ain't messin' with a guy with no dead eyes."

"You a pussy, Rock."

"Fuck you. You do him yourself, you such a man."

"Fuck that. Let's jack a ride instead. Gotta be a BMW in this neighborhood."

The voices faded and so did their owners' foul scent. Any other night, Malcolm would have gladly relieved them of the burden of their directionless lives without a care, but tonight he had a sweeter toy to play with.

A battered Buick with a hole in its muffler rumbled past, nearly deafening with its choked wheezes, but the tapping of light footsteps under the noise made Malcolm cock his head to gather the sound more fully to him.

The soft tap of leather soles to concrete was distinctive now, a slight skipping gait that included frequent half turns and rapid shuffles to regain momentum. Hunter Pray walked like he needed to take in everything in his surrounds, constantly looking around him in a dizzying three-sixty spin as he journeyed through life. There was something about that restless, eager quality that caused Malcolm's chest to ache ever so slightly.

Casual and relaxed, the vampire settled back on the sidewalk bench, his gaze brazenly tracking the smaller man striding toward him, a light bouncing pace making Hunter's longish fawn bangs flop into his hazel eyes. One hand clutched a worn leather strap attached to a professional quality camera that was slung over his neck and one shoulder to keep it from swaying with each enthusiastic step. The other hand pushed the tousled hair out of the way every few seconds so he could see where he was going.

He passed under a streetlamp and paused, his gaze targeting the waiting figure on the bench. Malcolm's breath caught in his lungs as he inhaled deeply to capture Hunter's scent, the rich aroma of male hormones and worn denim.

The artificial light played over Hunter's face, highlighting his brow, his full lips, and emphasizing his straight, clean-shaven jaw, making the tantalizing scar under his eye appear luminous.

Like a siren's call, the tiny scar's glistening, ragged line begged Malcolm to touch it, to taste it, to feel the slickness of its shiny surface. His cock soared to full erection. Anger rose along with it as Malcolm was forced to draw his coat over his lap to prevent Hunter from bolting at the sight.

Hunter didn't pause under the light for long, but his carefree expression mutated to cautious interest. His eyes narrowed, but the slight smile didn't leave his face. Hunter's pace slowed, his steps no longer as jaunty as they had been, but he kept his questioning gaze focused on Malcolm's cool stare. He walked toward the bench, hands nervously fingering the camera. He began to hum a tune, his voice low and light, pleasantly on key.

It was a clever ruse, but Malcolm heard the click of the camera shutter all the same. It didn't matter. He could take all he liked. The pictures would never be developed, and if they were, they wouldn't show anything anyway.

Thirty feet away, the sidewalk and park now deserted, Hunter stopped humming. He pulled his dark brown corduroy field coat more tightly around him and the camera housing, leaving the uncapped lens casually exposed.

"This is, like, the third time our paths have crossed in the last few days." Hunter cocked his head to one side and brushed his hair out of his eyes, keen gaze studying Malcolm. "Should I know you?"

The scar grabbed the light again, and Malcolm's gaze was draw to it, his mouth watering at the prospect of tasting the shining crease of ravaged flesh.

"You should." He gave Hunter a glance with just enough lustful interest to be intriguing, but not enough to make the young man run for the hills. Malcolm wasn't in the mood to chase down his prey tonight. A few more soft, coat-muffled clicks of the camera touched his hearing. A flash of amusement softened his bold smile. "Get to know me, I mean." His stare moved down the length of Hunter's body, his intent and interest unmistakable.

"We seem destined to meet."

"Does kind of *seem* that way, doesn't it?" Now twenty feet away, Hunter kept right on walking, slower, more cautiously, but drawn.

Gazes still locked together, Malcolm eased off the bench, letting the full impact of his height and broad frame dwarf his surroundings, the nearby bushes, and Hunter. His level of interest and wonder rose when Hunter didn't blink or slow down. Even the moderate degree of fear Malcolm could smell in the air around the man didn't increase. He was surprised to discover that he was grudgingly impressed. He'd had the pleasure of watching seasoned, monstrous warriors tremble at the full sight of him, yet this small slip of a shutterbug did not. Malcolm found himself vexed, yet undeniably pleased.

From behind him came a screech of tires. Looking over his shoulder, Malcolm watched as the car's headlights suddenly veered and the car shot directly at him. The faces of the two street thugs that had passed earlier registered on him just before a solid mass struck him squarely in the chest.

With a muffled grunt, Malcolm flew off his feet and over the bench and landed hard on the ground. Instinct took over, his arms locking around his attacker, and both bodies rolled down the small sloping lawn to land at the base of a sturdy tree. Malcolm made sure he was the victor on top. Bits and pieces of the shattered bench flew through the air, then rained down and lay scattered in the grass around them.

The car tires screeched again, roaring off into the night, a litany of foul curses and shouted threats in its wake.

Underneath his two hundred and fifty pounds of solid weight, a pair of wide hazel eyes stared up at him, panic evident in them. It took a second before he realized the air had been knocked out of the man under him, his weight preventing Hunter from taking in a much needed breath.

He toyed with the idea of letting the man struggle, but Hunter's distinctive, alluring scent, now laced with relief as well as a larger fear, overwhelmed him. It made Malcolm weak in the knees, slightly disoriented, and hard as steel. Even now he could felt his swollen erection digging into Hunter's thigh, hot, hard, and eager. He knew Hunter could feel it, too.

Instead of rolling off and standing up, Malcolm tumbled onto his back, dragging Hunter along with him, until the human was lying stretched out over his chest, the man's legs splayed on either side of Malcolm's hips. Hunter's startled face hovered inches above his own. For an instant, he almost gave in to the compulsion to flick out his tongue and lick the silvery thread of scar tissue so close to his lips. One hand grasped the swell of Hunter's ass cheek and the other pressed between Hunter's shoulder blades, pinning the man to him.

Several rapid, startled breaths jiggled Hunter up and down, increasing the friction between their two bodies. Malcolm was inordinately pleased to detect a bulge of heat pressed into his lower abdomen as Hunter's erection grew to a mild firmness with each deep, anxious breath and resulting body rub. Then the gasps eased and Hunter tried to slide off Malcolm, but the vampire wordlessly tightened his restraining hold. Hunter got the hint and ceased to resist.

"You okay?" He cautiously eyed Malcolm, then hesitantly added, "Is this where we finally introduce ourselves?"

Warm, minty breath laced with the smell of adrenaline and worry wafted off the human in layers that teased Malcolm's senses and tantalized his already straining arousal.

The fear and worry weren't direct *at* him — instead they were apparently *for* him. His eyes narrowed. He increased his grip to the point that Hunter grimaced, creating tiny lines of pain at the corners of his eyes that Malcolm ignored, inexplicably angered by the man's concern.

Voice harsh and low, he still couldn't keep a current of disbelief out of it. "You attempted to protect me."

Blinking hard over a wide-eyed stare, Hunter adopted a Valley Girl *duh!* tone and answered, "Ah, yea-*ah*. Impending vehicular homicide makes me do silly things."

Malcolm stared back in a neutral, cold gaze for several long, tense seconds. He could smell the fear in Hunter shift to be more personal now, but the man's concerned gaze, fixed so very close to his own, didn't show it. It remained steady and open despite Hunter's instinctive awareness of the danger he was in.

He was so much like his father. Trusting past the point of good sense.

"It may not have been in your best interests to do so." His deep voice was deceptively soft but unerringly cold. When Hunter didn't flinch, Malcolm pulled him up his chest another inch and whispered against Hunter's parted mouth, "I am a danger to you." He felt the heat pressed into his abdomen jerk and grow, a swelling cock lengthening against him.

"Ah...well." A flash of pink tongue touched the parted lips hovering above his, and the urge to wet them down with his own tongue was too much to resist. Malcolm entangled his hand in the man's hair and held him in place as Hunter instinctively strained back.

His gaze fell to Hunter's mouth as he slowly ran his own tongue delicately over the trembling, silky strips of soft, full flesh. When he was done, he pulled back and eased his hold on Hunter's head. He found it intoxicating that Hunter didn't draw away once he had his freedom to do so. Intoxicating, highly arousing, and responsive.

Maybe the son wasn't so much like the father after all.

"I kind of figured that might be a possibility." This time it was murmured, a stuttered grunt heavy with lust and excitement. The man's heartbeat thundered in his chest, pounded against Malcolm's still breast in a rhythm that matched the pulse hammering through the shaft buried against Malcolm's abdomen.

"Yet knowing this —" Malcolm touched his tongue to his teeth, soothing the ache growing in them as the barely detectable scent of fresh blood suddenly reached him "—you risked yourself for me."

The scent of blood grew stronger. Hunter must have suffered an injury in the fall that was just now trickling to the surface from under his clothing. His blood scent was musky, like a spring rainstorm on rich black soil — clean and earthy, bold. Nothing like Malcolm had imagined. Yet another surprise from this human.

The night breeze rose higher, stirring the fallen leaves near them and carrying muted, distant voices.

"I find danger can be exciting." Shifting his hips, Hunter tried to ease his erection off Malcolm's stomach to one side.

Malcolm didn't stop him, surprised when he was relieved the sexual tension had lessened for the moment. This was too good to be over so fast.

The restraining hold gone, Hunter used one arm to prop his upper body off Malcolm's, but he didn't make a move to stand up. His tone was firm, but still laced with an undeniable apprehension.

"And…" He stared down into Malcolm's face, gaze searching the vampire's features as if he'd find there a reason for his own actions. "I'm not a person who watches while others get hurt without trying to do something to prevent it."

He started to lick his lips again, then paused, glanced at Malcolm's mouth, and swallowed nervously, a self-conscious, strained look on his face. Malcolm could see the man battle to force his thoughts back to the topic at hand. "It's kind of what I do."

Malcolm managed to deadpan, "Really? So you're a superhero?"

Hunter was silent for a full three seconds before he burst out laughing. He rolled off Malcolm and came to his feet, dusting dirt and dry leaves off his jacket and jeans. Hunter's laughter was genuine, musical and hearty, delight audible in it and in the startled grin on his young, smooth face. He looked more beautiful than his father had ever been.

Malcolm rose up smoothly with grace that belied his large stature.

"Not exactly. I'm a photojournalist. Freelance. I document the world's woes and the unfortunate people caught up in them. I try to bring media and world attention to people that need help."

"Ah. Even worse — a self-appointed savior." Malcolm mocked the righteous tone in Hunter's voice and watched with satisfaction as the man's eyes narrowed. He took advantage of his towering height and loomed menacingly over Hunter. His actions caused a spike in the scent of lustful hormones from the smaller man. He dropped his voice to a husky, growling whisper, more threatening than any shout. "Who comes to your rescue when *you* are in danger?"

"No one so far." Boldly leaning toward Malcolm's hulking presence, Hunter stared at the vampire's mouth, nervously letting his tongue trace back and forth across his own quavering lower lip twice. He then locked gazes with Malcolm and quietly said, "But I've always had this dream that some freaking tall, broad-shouldered, steely-eyed warrior would materialize out of the dark and save my ass when I needed it most." He blinked hard several times, but kept his gaze on Malcolm. "Know anyone like that?"

Malcolm felt a twinge of something sharp and hot twist in his chest. This sensual human was beautiful, confusing, impulsive, and unpredictable. Malcolm wanted to taste his blood and drink from him, here and now, but the faraway voices from before were drawing closer, and Malcolm had the sudden need to prolong this game, extend the claiming of his prize just a bit more.

"I might know someone." Malcolm reached out and ran his thumb over the eyebrow scar in what could only be described as a caress. Lust and the faint scents of precum mixed with blood filled his nostrils and invaded his mind, shaking his iron control. Taking this prize would be better than he had imagined. It was almost worth killing William to be able to claim it. "Why don't we go someplace private and discuss it?"

Hunter drew back. He cast a glance at a trio of people approaching from the end of the block, taking in the destroyed bench and the deep tire marks in the dirt and grass. "I don't feel like taking the time explaining this to the police right now."

He backed away from Malcolm and hurried down the sidewalk, away from the new arrivals. "I was thinking someplace more public." Walking backward, the usual bouncing step in his restless stride and a flirtatious, sultry look in his eyes, he smiled at Malcolm. "For now. Coffee?"

§ § §

The little diner was clean, cheery, and the food homemade. It was three blocks from his apartment, and Hunter was a regular there when he wasn't out of town on an assignment. The staff was mostly older women, social and good-natured. He was well known and liked there. People would remember seeing him and whom he was with if anything bad happened to him later.

The short walk from the park was a quiet one. He tried to walk beside the stranger, but the taller man's stride was difficult for him to match. He ended up doing his usual skip-and-bounce step. It kept him swaying back and forth on the sidewalk and made conversation difficult. His companion didn't seem to expect a lot of talk anyway, so Hunter just led the way.

He spent most of the time fighting off two urges. One to run far away, to get lost in a crowd somewhere — and the other, stronger urge to pull the seductive, mysterious, and admittedly dangerous man into the bushes and explore the firm body attached to the slick, sensual tongue that had lavished his lips earlier. The man's taste was like his scent, masculine and indefinable.

The front of the shop was partially plate glass windows. As they approached the diner, Hunter couldn't completely suppress a gasp when just his image was reflected in the sparkling clear surface. Behind him was only a wall of unbroken darkness dotted with starbursts from streetlamps. He walked more slowly, letting the man's physical presence register at his back, large and now more menacing than sexy. The plate glass still showed only one pale, dark-haired, startled face in the distorted reflection. He glanced over his shoulder to make sure the presence he felt was really there despite what the window was telling him. One look in the amused, steely gray eyes told him the man was aware Hunter had noted the missing reflection and he was patiently waiting for a reaction.

Shaken, Hunter pulled open the door, walked briskly to a table away from the windowed section, and sat down in a booth. "Want coffee? I come here for the coffee. Well, for the meatloaf really, but the coffee is great."

Hunter expected the man to sit opposite him, but he automatically slide further into the booth as the large man shoved the table forward with a nudge of his black designer boot and sat down beside him. Nervous, but turned on by the man's boldness and close proximity, he waved at a waitress, coaxing her closer to the table.

"I like it here. The waitresses are mostly older ladies, and they like to play mother hen to all the single guys that come in." He smiled and mumbled, "Kind of let's me pretend I still have a mom now and then." That was a piece of personal information he hadn't meant to reveal, but he couldn't take it back. "If that makes me sound weak, I don't care. I miss my mom. She died unexpectedly." All the same, he was relieved when the man only gave a single nod by way of acknowledgment.

He held the man's neutral gaze for a moment, then studied the design on the laminated tabletop. "I miss my dad, too. They were great people. They taught me to be who I am."

"Photojournalists, too, I gather?"

"Yeah. But they taught me more than how to take a good picture." He unwrapped his own prized camera from under his layers of outer clothing and placed it on the table between them, checking it for signs of damage from his recent activity in the park. He couldn't resist turning the lens toward the man and letting his fingers play over the shutter button. They itched to press it, but this close, the man was sure to hear it.

"I grew up traveling the world with them while they worked, seeing sights and living places other kids my age would have nightmares about. But not me. I loved the excitement near the war zones, on the fringe of riots, in a dark seedy alley in some poverty-stricken village. I dreamed about spending my life traveling, taking photographs, exploring the world few others see."

"Embracing the dark side?"

The man captured Hunter's gaze and held it trapped in his chilling, steel gray stare. It seemed to Hunter that the doors to hell could lie beyond those fathomless eyes.

Hell or maybe a dark version of heaven? He heard an invitation into that darker embrace in those low tones, smooth as fine brandy. Lust flared in the pit of his abdomen, and he became acutely aware of the wet patch on his boxers clinging coldly to his skin where his cock had wept during the car attack. He imagined he could smell his own scent. He gave the man a bold, honest look. "Flirting with it, maybe."

"That can have consequences of its own."

The man's intense stare seemed to transmit a new message, one that sent a thrill of excitement straight to Hunter's groin. Hunter impulsively let lust take control of the moment. "Yeah, I was, *maybe*, hoping it would."

The man's eyelids suddenly dropped to a sultry half-mast, and his nostrils flared, making Hunter wonder if he could smell his arousal, too. The whole imagined fantasy was enough to make his cock unfurl from the partially hard state it had retreated to during the walk to the diner. It forced him to shift in his seat to make more room in his jeans for it. Warmth rushed through his veins, heating his skin. He shed his jacket and scarf, letting them fall around his shoulders and down into the booth seat, fingers returning to the camera to toy with its levers and buttons.

"Do I get to know your name?" He looked up from the camera to capture the man's unwavering gaze.

The man's expression of firm reserve never altered, but his voice had just the slightest touch of surrender in it, as if he didn't give out the information entirely willingly. "Malcolm Crane."

Hunter wasn't surprised. It was strong and bold, just like the man. "Nice. It fits you."

"And you prefer to be called...?"

"Hunter. Hunter Pray." He held Malcolm's stare for a moment, then added, "But I think you know that already, Mr. Crane."

"One's name and what one wants to be called can be two different things. For example, you may call me Malcolm."

"Okay. Malcolm."

"Your name fits you as well -- a challenge, a worthy opponent to be stalked and, eventually, claimed." Something dark and unnamed flashed in Malcolm's eyes. Hunter's cock jumped, and his heartbeat pounded in his ears as Malcolm added, "Pray for the prey?"

"I don't pray anymore. Not since my parents died."

The dark look didn't fade from his stormy gray eyes. "Death is a natural part of living."

"True, but theirs came before their time."

"How so?"

"They were killed in a riot in a small, backward Romanian village where they were documenting atrocities in a local power struggle." Hunter took a deep breath, his fingers traveling over the camera, adjusting the lens and hitting the shutter lever as he turned the camera every angle he could while snapping pictures. He realized what he was doing only when a large, cool hand closed over his where it held the camera and stopped him from spinning the device. Staring into the man's unflinching, uncaring eyes, he let the shutter close three more time, aimed directly at Malcolm, before he stilled. "Nervous habit. Sorry."

"It is of no consequence." It was a short sentence, but it had an ominous ring to it. The grip on his hand was strong and commanding, and it didn't leave when Hunter stopped playing with the camera. The power in the mere touch was amazing. It sent a shiver down his spine he knew Malcolm could feel through their joined hands.

A waitress appeared, two empty mugs in one hand, a pot of steaming black brew in the other. At a nod of thanks from

Hunter, she set a mug in front of each man and filled them. Malcolm pinned her in place with a look, made an abbreviated, half-wave at her, and she turned hurriedly away without asking if they wanted anything more.

Hunter shot Malcolm a disappointed glare, but then decided the conversation was dampening his appetite. For food, anyway.

"You were left alone?" The hand finally slipped off of his. Hunter took a deep breath, relieved, even if a small part of him ached over the loss of contact.

"Yeah. The only child of two only children." Hunter took a sip of the steaming coffee, gaze dropping into the swirling dark brown depths, memories rushing in and making his eyes brim. It had been ages since he'd felt the urge to cry over his parents' deaths, but something about this man made the hurt of their loss feel fresh again. "It was an ugly death. They were attacked with axes and shovels. I only saw the pictures, but it wasn't pretty. Their bodies were shipped home, but only my mother's arrived. Backward province. Poor records. They said they lost my father's body before it was shipped It's never been recovered." He took another quick sip of the hot liquid to refocus his thoughts and drive back the ache of loss. "That was a few years ago, my freshman year in college. It was the first time I wasn't on assignment with them since I was eight." Regret crept into his voice. "If I'd been there, I might have been able to help."

"Or maybe you'd be dead as well." There it was again. That disturbing way Malcolm had of bringing danger and death aimed at Hunter back into the conversation.

"Maybe." He shook off the uncharacteristic melancholy and found the courage to look directly at Malcolm again. "My dad's motto was *flee and stay free*. I'm more of the *confront and confirm* type. Meet danger head on. Roll the dice and take my chances. Winner takes all."

Feeling bolder, he stared at Malcolm, but something cold and frightening turned the man's eyes a darker shade of gray, and Hunter swore a ring of blood red now encircled the gray irises.

A shiver that had nothing to do with sexual interest slithered down his spine, and the urge to continue flirting with the man faded away, held in check by a sudden sense of self-preservation.

"I probably taunt danger more often than I should." Cradling his camera, Hunter made a move to slide out of the booth, but Malcolm didn't budge. They shared a long, silent stare until Hunter realized his jaw was trembling.

Fear and attraction had always made for an intriguingly powerful sexual response for him, but the fear and attraction had never been in the same object of his sexual interest. Usually it was a setting of unrest or turmoil that created the fear, and Hunter would find a compatible soul in the chaos with whom to share the release of his sexual tension. Combining the two was proving to be a powerful aphrodisiac, but in this case real, honest-to-God, bone-chilling fear was overwhelming the intense attraction he had for the towering, pale stranger.

"Thanks for the coffee, but I think it's best if I go now. I…I guess I'm freaked out by the car crash thing. I'm not going to be good company tonight." Without another word, he pulled himself to a standing position on the booth seat and hopped over its high back into the next unoccupied booth.

Camera clutched to his chest with one hand and his coat in the other, he headed for the door without looking back. He didn't even stop when his scarf slipped from his grip, snagged on an empty chair as he barreled out of the diner onto the sidewalk. He was almost a block away when he realized he was still holding his breath. The last war zone he'd visited hadn't felt this dangerous.

§ § §

There was no sign Malcolm had followed him, but Hunter put the chain on the apartment door and slid the deadbolt into place as soon as the steel door closed behind him. He leaned against the cool, solid surface, the palms of both hands flat on the smooth metal. He found himself comparing the chill of the hard steel with touch of Malcolm's hand. The flesh had the same sense of solid strength as well as the smooth coolness. A flash of desire bolted through him, but he used the accompanying burst of fight-or-flight, fear-fueled adrenaline to push it away. This time his fear and desire were too entwined for him. A dangerous setting wasn't the same as a dangerous suitor.

Logically, there was no reason why a man like Malcolm Crane would be stalking him. By the cut and quality of Malcolm's clothing and his rock-solid self-confidence, the man was very successful at whatever it was he did and was used to having the finest things life had to offer. Why he was interested in Hunter remained known only to Malcolm. But Hunter felt sure Malcolm wanted him and especially him.

With a deep sigh of regret drawn through dry, pursed lips, Hunter backed away from the door, carefully setting his camera on the small desk by the entryway. He tossed his coat over one end of the sofa, losing a moment to a fruitless search for his scarf before he remembered leaving it dangling off a diner chair in his haste to put space between his impulsive libido and Malcolm.

It had been his father's scarf, one of the few treasures he'd kept and continued to use over the years. His mother had knit it using varied shades of blue and green to remind them of a particularly pleasant assignment in Northern Ireland. The blue of ocean and green of the traditional shamrocks highlighted his father's eyes and fawn-colored hair, just as they did Hunter's. Cursing himself for leaving it behind, he made a mental note to go back to the diner in the morning to try to reclaim it.

The adrenaline rush that had fueled his exit from the diner and his rapid trip home began to ebb. Lethargy crept into his muscles, and the crisp sheets and cool night breeze of his bedroom called to him, his fears fading in the familiar security of home.

He stripped as he walked, gathering the discarded items over one shoulder until he was completely naked by the time he entered the bath off his bedroom. A breeze gently blew in from the open window. Hunter inhaled the fresh night air, letting the familiar scents ease his rattled nerves.

Dropping everything but his jeans into an open hamper inside the door, he then moved to the curtained shower and adjusted the water temperature. Billowing waves of white steam filled the room, chasing away some of his lingering chill from earlier.

He stepped under the stream of water, relaxing into its soothing heat, letting the streams pulse hard against his flesh. The sound of the water filled his ears. He let the splashing beat invade his mind, blocking out everything else, including thought. Bowing his head, Hunter let the spray pound across his neck and between his shoulders, acutely aware of the rivers of cooling water that ran along his spine into the crease between his asscheeks and trickled around his ribs to the vee of his groin. Eyes closed and mind lost in the fog of steamy relaxation, he imagined the trail of running water to be a lover's touch, wet fingertips or, better yet, a moist tongue exploring his body.

Frustrated with the earlier rampant, yet ultimately unfulfilled sexual tensions, his cock jumped to full attention at the first slippery touch of his soap-lathered hand. Swollen and heavy, the circumcised shaft jutted up and away from his abdomen, a respectable seven inches, slender, but firm like the rest of his body. It was a shade darker than his abdomen, the head dusky pink. Its length was ribbed with veins that stood out close to the surface, like supporting steel cables pulled taunt along the structure.

His balls hung close to the base of his shaft, compact and unevenly suspended in their lightly furred sac of wrinkled flesh. They were very sensitive to touch, even more so than any of his lovers' sacs had seemed to be, especially the thin strip of flesh directly behind them. A slippery touch, a wet kiss, or just a bit of the right kind of pressure, and sufficiently aroused, he had more than once reached orgasm from that alone.

He fingered the sac, bringing it forward, feeling it tighten as the pulling caused a delicious pressure to tug at the sensitive skin behind it. He clenched his ass to still the immediate fluttering at his opening, his body begging for attention.

Rubbing two soaped fingers over the delicate strip, he fisted his cock with his other hand, sighing at the satiny smoothness of lather and hard flesh. Warm, moist air filled his nostrils and bathed his lungs. His skin flushed, his face aflame with surface heat and a growing internal glow of desire and need.

The last thing he wanted to think about right now was a menacing man who seemed to be stalking him and who made gooseflesh break out on his skin.

Yet Malcolm Crane, malevolent, ghostly pale, and intensely unnerving, was the only thing he could visualize, no matter how hard he fought it. As scary as Malcolm was, his pale, alabaster skin gave him a classic physical attractiveness. He radiated a raw sensuality and possessed an intriguingly dangerous quality Hunter had always found exceedingly appealing. Add the unexpected mystery of Malcolm's failure to appear in the first set of photos or in the diner window reflection, and Hunter was hopelessly entranced with the man, stalker attitude be damned. So, gooseflesh or not, head bent under the pulsing spray and body supported by one hand on the wall in front of him, Malcolm Crane was the face Hunter saw behind his closed eyes. His hand stroked and tugged, but Malcolm's large, cool hands were the hands he imagined. He gripped his cock firmly, almost roughly, the way he imagined the imposing man would do, occasionally rubbing a slippery palm over the swollen head, mixing pearls of creamy white pre-cum with larger dollops of bright white soap.

He formed a ring of index finger and thumb around the shaft and moved it slowly up and down in the slick coating of soap gel, letting his mind envision Malcolm's face at his groin and his pale, thin lips sliding up and down his cock. He increased the pressure so that the corona of the tip had to be dragged through the tight ring of his hand. Each upward pass made the supersensitive skin under the bulbous edge tingle and burn.

His asshole winked, his cheeks clenched hard, both searching for the long, thick monster of a cock Hunter imagined Malcolm possessed under those immaculately tailored trousers. Having experienced Malcolm's erection pressing against his body in the park, he tried to replay the incident in his head, savoring the feeling of the hard shaft. His leg tingled at the memory. His cock jumped, and flashes of heat infused his abdomen and limbs, fueled by the subconscious memory of at least nine heavy inches of thick fullness jabbing into his body as he lay under the fallen Malcolm.

Hunter groaned out loud, his own panting breath rasping in his ears over the pulsing water. He felt his knee weaken, the visual so real he had to stop himself from reaching down to tangle his hand in the short brush of hair on Malcolm's head.

Leaning his head against the wall to free his other hand, Hunter rested his weight on his forehead, shivering as the pulsing spray moved to stream harder into the small of his back and channel a river between his cheeks. He used one hand to part the globes of his ass, letting the trickle tease his opening before he reached under and between his spread legs to plunge two suds-covered fingers into his body. Placing his thumb behind his sac, he stroked over the sensitive spot, pressing just hard enough to make his eyes water. His balls jerked up the last centimeter as he twisted the two fingers jabbing deep into his ass. The memory of Malcolm's piercing gaze rippled through him, as did the memory of the other's tongue running over his lips. He sucked on his lower lip, hoping to reclaim the taste.

Electric bolts of pleasure shot out from the pit of his abdomen and groin, setting fire to his entire body. Gooseflesh prickled his skin. His knees locked, his asshole spasmed in a burning grip, and his eyes clenched tight while a strained litany of *"Fuck, fuck, fuck, Jesus, Malcolm, ffffffffffuck!"* poured from his panting lips. Opal threads of cum spurted from his cock and were instantly washed away.

Hunter slumped against the shower wall, tired fingers hurriedly finding new purchase on the tile surface to keep him upright. He felt drained and shaky, the orgasm one of the fastest and most powerful he'd experienced in ages. It left him weak-kneed and gasping. He was astonished by strange flashes of Malcolm's intense, victorious stare and wickedly satisfied smile, flashes so vivid that they seemed real.

His abandoned opening fluttered and burned, unsatisfied and still eager for more, fuller attention. Even his cock had only marginally softened. A knotted blaze of unleashed desire glowed and flared in the pit of his abdomen, making him squirm and gasp. His skin was hypersensitive to every touch as he rinsed the remaining soap away and stepped out of the shower.

Waves of gooseflesh broke out again. Hunter cursed under his breath and dried off, hurriedly toweling his hair into a tousled, but no longer dripping, mess. He tumbled into just his worn jeans, leaving them partially unbuttoned in his haste to leave the haunting visions behind, hoping they would disappear along with the fading mist of the shower.

He strode out into the hallway and sped through to the living room to retrieve his camera. It sat waiting for him on the stand, its single, all-seeing eye staring at him as he paced barefoot and flushed across the room. Despite the cool air from the bedroom, Hunter found the air thick and unusually still, like his hearing had become suddenly muffled.

A quick scan of the room revealed nothing unusual. His coat lay on the end of the couch, the same mail lay on the table by the camera where he had dropped it earlier, and the chain and deadbolt were still securely latched. Even so, he had a nagging sense of something being out of place. He turned the knob on the twin lamp sitting on the side table, snapping its second bulb on. The whole area brightened.

He searched the room a second time, but the lure of the new photographs he had snapped of Malcolm at the park and diner were too great to be ignored or delayed by a childish insecurity. The door was still locked. There was no one here. Hunter shook off the unsettling aura, hefted the camera, and padded off to his makeshift darkroom, shaking tufts of drying hair out of his eyes.

Dim amber safelights gave the darkroom a surreal, B-movie quality once he was sequestered behind the closed door to begin the labor-intensive job of developing the roll of film. Hunter worked through each painstaking step with an automatic sureness of hand that spoke of years of practice. So much of it was done without conscious thought, Hunter was mildly surprised when the film negative began to reveal its hidden secrets so quickly.

He stared it, examining each frame, eyes squinting to catch every detail and shadow on the ghostly cells.

He tried to tell himself that the shivers that ran down his spine and made him glance over his shoulder every few seconds were caused by lack of sleep and a lingering adrenaline rush from the hasty, dark walk home. But, Hunter couldn't rid his mind of the unsettling, passionate images of Malcolm in the shower. It seemed those would be his only images because Malcolm didn't appear to be on this new roll of film either.

With several of the newly developed photos held fanlike in one hand, eyes riveted to the pictures, Hunter moved out of the surreal dim of the darkroom into the light of the living area. He was still only dressed in his unbuttoned jeans, the flesh of his bare chest and bare feet bracketing the worn, button-fly denims.

Head down studying the pictures, Hunter came to a stop a few feet into the room. The same heavy, vaguely off feeling touched him again. The shadows in the room looked darker, thicker. Looking around the room, he scrutinized every gray-shrouded corner.

It took a moment for him to realize one of the bulbs in the lamp was out. Burned out, probably, but he couldn't keep his gaze from darting to the front door to check that the locks were still in place.

Not as reassured as he would have liked to see the chain still draped securely in the place, Hunter slowly began to walk toward the lamp to check the bulb. As he walked past the couch, he suddenly realized what had struck him as odd earlier, what he hadn't noticed, but what now he was sure had been there.

Haltingly, one hand still holding the pictures, he reached down to touch his scarf where it lay casually tossed on top of his coat. The scarf that belonged to his father, the one he had left behind at the diner during his hasty retreat a few hours ago. The scarf that couldn't possibly be here, behind his solid, locked door.

Mouth so dry his throat seemed to shrink closed, Hunter took a halting step toward the front door, wishing it were unlocked and standing open now instead of tightly sealed.

But after the first step, the need to know, the need to understand, the same need that made him such a good photojournalist, made him seek a sensible answer to an impossible puzzle. He turned toward his bedroom.

One of the darker shadows disengaged from the living room wall and shifted fluidly toward him. The eyes seemed to materialize first — cold, gray with a touch of red to them like in a photo taken with a cheap camera.

Hunter immediately stopped short, his heart choking him, pounding in his constricted throat. As the dim lamplight pushed the black shadows away from the shape, the towering, reserved figure of Malcolm Crane emerged.

Malcolm was still immaculately dressed in the same black overcoat, business suit, and black collarless dress shirt he'd worn earlier, his polished boots unscuffed and his trousers unwrinkled. If he had climbed the apartment building wall — the only way into Hunter's locked apartment — he was not only an amazing man, but astonishingly tidy as well.

Even though he wasn't truly surprised to see Malcolm, a bolt of fear shot through Hunter. His breathing turned to shallow panting that forced his heart rate to rocket until he could hear it pounding in his ears. Despite it all, or because of it, he was uncomfortably aware his cock was fully hard, pressing against the seam of his jeans, trying to jut out of the partially unbuttoned confines of denim. He stood still, ten feet away from the man, studying Malcolm's calm, almost expressionless, bold features.

Malcolm returned his silent stare and after a few seconds, maybe because Hunter hadn't run or screamed, the man's eyes seemed to warm with a hint of respect and a renewed light of interest. His pale lips twitched with the grudging beginnings of a pleased smirk.

Hoping to hang on to some tiny strand of control in the situation, Hunter glanced past Malcolm toward his bedroom. "How?"

"That's an old wives' tale." The smirk tugged harder at Malcolm's mouth. He didn't move, but his presence was filling the room, making it difficult for Hunter to breathe.

Thrown off base, Hunter blinked and stammered, "What is?"

"Needing an invitation to enter a dwelling for the first time." Malcolm slipped off his long coat and draped it over the back of a chair. He looked larger without it. His suit jacket followed. He slowly unbuttoned the neck of his shirt, eyes never leaving Hunter's confused stare while he talked.

"I meant, how did you get up to a sixth-story window?"

"It's not hard." Malcolm smiled, his clothes immaculate, no visible evidence of having climbed a sheer wall. "For me. With or without the invitation."

Malcolm hadn't made a move closer, but Hunter felt as if the man was invading his personal space, engulfing him in some kind of powerful aura. He took a small step to one side to escape it, instinctively gravitating in the direction of the front door. He stopped when he heard what sounded like a low hiss. The door was only a few feet away, but he knew he'd never make it.

Frozen in place with panic, Hunter tried to laugh. It sounded husky and raw, nothing like his laugh. His gaze dropped to the photos in his hand. His eyes were telling him the truth about his visitor, but his mind wasn't accepting it.

"I thought that invitation stuff was for vampires."

When Malcolm answered him with nothing more than an intense, knowing look, a shiver ran down his spine, so strong his shoulders shook. Hunter impulsively thrust the pictures at his uninvited visitor.

"You aren't in any of them." He paused to take a deep breath, then plunged ahead. "You should be in them. I know you *were* in them when I took them, but...you're not there." His voice rose by the last sentence. He had to clear his throat and swallow to bring the tone down. It came out a husky rasp instead.

He took a step closer to Malcolm, pictures held out accusingly.

"It's not the film. I thought it was, the first time it happened, but the film is good. Everything else is in the shot." He swallowed hard again, terrified and turned on by it, by the man in front of him. "Everything but you."

Malcolm made no move to take the photos from Hunter's hand. His gaze had become lazy, sultry, that light of renewed interest taking on a lustful, predatory quality. His long, thick fingers began to work off the links at his shirt cuffs. Once free, he dropped the glinting metal into his pants pocket.

Hunter's gaze followed every move. He had to wet his lips to keep them from cracking. The air in the room seemed to grow thin as he imagined all the reasons this man might need to remove his shirt. Keeping it clean of bloodstains took first place.

Since it had started to shake, Hunter dropped his hand. He tossed the photos onto the couch, where they scattered over his coat and scarf. The sight of the scarf made his stomach clench, and he looked up at Malcolm to find the man standing a mere foot away from him, bare-chested, sculptured, alabaster body boasting a hardened physique as perfect as any of Michelangelo's statues — and just about the same color.

Taken by surprise, Hunter started, gooseflesh covering his body, his pulse hammering through his veins, his hearing suddenly acute to the point that his breathing rasped in his ears. The scent of his own body and its primal, sexual reaction to this dangerous, alluring, predatory man filled the air between them. It was embarrassing to be so obviously turned on, but Hunter couldn't control it. He was attracted to danger, always had been, and this man — or whatever he was — was danger personified, all wrapped up in alluring muscle and mystery.

The room grew warm, the air heavy, sensual against Hunter's chilled flesh. The sensation increased the closer Malcolm moved to him. It was intoxicating, suffocating, delicious, and exciting.

Hunter stumbled back, colliding with the end of the sofa. Malcolm merely watched him grope for a hold on the couch arm in order to stay upright, no offer of help, no rush to rescue him. Hunter liked that. Too many of the larger men he was attracted to tried to treat him like a frail flower just because he was smaller. It was ironic that this man would treat him as an equal. But once again, the minute he regained his footing, Malcolm was standing a breath away. Hunter never saw him move.

"Who are you?" He barely stopped himself from adding *what are you?* "Why are you here?" A clean, slightly tangy scent surrounded Malcolm, one Hunter couldn't place but found mildly exciting.

Malcolm's eyelids drooped, and his gaze shifted to look at the scarf on the couch, then slid a heated stare back up to meet Hunter's. "Just before he died, I promised your father I would visit his son." The words were cold, factual, but something hot and needy lit up Malcolm's eyes.

Hunter leaned back to give himself breathing space, attraction and lust battling fear and, now, confusion. This wasn't a direction Hunter expected the conversation to take.

"You took your time." Despite a lingering sense of survivor guilt, Hunter had accepted his parents' deaths long ago. It was an effort to hear even his own voice over the steady pulse echoing in his head. Somewhere in the back of his mind he wondered if the pulse was his own. "My father's been dead for years."

"From his mortal existence, yes." Malcolm extended one sinewy, powerful hand and ran a single fingertip up Hunter's bare arm, over his shoulder, and down the shallow valley that defined his chest, dropping away just as it reached his belly button. "But his immortal life ended just a few months ago."

"What are you talking about? Immoral life?" Even as he said it, Hunter knew what Malcolm meant. Knew it, but didn't want to believe it. Couldn't believe it.

"He was vampire."

It was short, simple, and carried a weight so heavy Hunter stumbled back. This time Malcolm did reach out, but it was to pull him brutally forward, both upper arms held immobile in a pair of cool, callused hands.

Their bare chests and stomachs rubbed skin against skin.

The silky sensation was full of waves of excitement like static electricity that rippled across Hunter's flesh and seeped into his muscle and bone. It was hard to catch his breath. He couldn't look away from Malcolm despite the fear that knotted in his belly. Close-up, Hunter could see the blood-red ring that flared around the man's irises.

"I don't believe you." It was indistinct, nothing more than a whisper of near soundless air, but Malcolm smiled, and his eyes told Hunter he had heard him. Then the smile grew, and the sharp, pointed tips of Malcolm's pearly white canines were visible. Light danced off them as they grew longer, and the reality of who — *what* — had him in its embrace struck Hunter squarely in the gut.

Vampire. Mythical creature, folklore demon, living dead, nightmare fodder, unreal.

Someplace deep inside, someplace locked far away, primal and old, told him it was true. He knew it was true. Just as he had known for some time that this man in front of him wasn't a man. Not any longer. It terrified him, and yet, goddamn him, it excited him more than anything else or anyone else ever had.

Malcolm's stare was mesmerizing. Hunter shivered, unsure whether it was from the possessive gaze or the seductive caress. Both made him weak in the knees, a fine sheen of sweat popping out on his skin as he struggled with the concept of the deadly creature before him and his own ingrained, if foolhardy, desire to court danger in all its forms.

The tangy scent radiated off Malcolm, sharp and faintly metallic. He stood so close, a powerful tower of sculptured white stone, suffused with sensual force and a dominating presence that captured Hunter's most base desires.

He released one of Hunter's arms to reach into his pants pocket. Alarmingly, Hunter found himself wishing for the cool grip back, distressed by the loss of even a little physical contact with this...*this what? Vampire?* He could barely make himself think it, let alone say it.

A gold band appeared in Malcolm's hand, the vampire holding it so Hunter could see the inscription on the inside. It read, *forever, my true desire*, with a date. Today's date but a year from the past. His parents' wedding date of twenty-six years ago. Malcolm had known his father.

"He was like you? A vampire? That's why his body was never returned?" Hunter's personal history suddenly fell apart, unraveling to re-forming in a different pattern. "My parents weren't killed in a riot?"

"Yes, they were initially. By villagers who had discovered William and his wife had been attacked and bitten by a local vampire that preyed on visiting foreigners. They knew if your parents weren't destroyed properly, they would rise as vampires. Your father awakened early and escaped, only wounded. Your mother was spared the awakening altogether."

"Awakening?" Slowly, his parents' deaths were making sense, more sense than they had years ago.

"The conversion from human to vampire. It is somewhat... unpleasant." Malcolm extended the gold band.

A peace offering or a gift, Hunter took the proffered ring in his free hand, clenching it in his fist, eyes closed and heart aching anew. A dull throb that ebbed to a pinpoint of pain. "It's weird, but I always felt like my father was still near until lately."

He felt the burn of tears but blinked them back, suddenly seeing a different side to this whole surreal situation.

"Did he like being a...vampire?" There, he'd said it out loud, and no one had laughed.

Malcolm stroked his thumb over Hunter's cheek, again and again tracing the line of his jaw up under his ear and then down his neck, mapping the artery that ended under Hunter's breastbone.

There was a deafening pause while Malcolm stared into Hunter's face, scrutinizing every detail. Hunter knew how much he looked like his father. He knew Malcolm was comparing them at this moment. He could see the recognition in the vampire's expression. Finally, something clicked in Malcolm's eyes. His ramrod-straight shoulders relaxed, and his harsh façade slipped just a bit.

"No. He didn't. He hated every moment of it." Malcolm sighed and dropped his hand away from Hunter's cheek. Something exasperated, even affectionate, entered his voice, something he couldn't hide with harsh words and a piercing stare. "As ridiculous as it was, William regarded suicide, even as an unholy creature, as out of the question." He glanced at Hunter's fist, where the wedding ring was still tightly clasped. "He felt it would lessen whatever chance he still had of seeing your mother in the afterlife." A fire blazed to life in the vampire's eyes, anger and pain obvious. His words were sharp and clipped, resentful, spat out between gritted teeth. "He was full of idealistic theory and foolish sentiment."

"But you liked him." A flash of insight hit Hunter, leaving a jolt of excitement and, surprisingly, jealousy in his chest. "You had feelings for him, didn't you?" Malcolm sneered at him, but Hunter could see the pain and loss. Malcolm's feelings for William were transmitted in one flashing glare before they were smothered by a murderous scowl, but Hunter had seen and he knew. "You loved him."

It took several seconds for Malcolm to respond, the words resigned and slightly bitter when they did come. "William's heart belonged only to your mother. Forever, just like the ring's inscription says. He hated every single day they were apart." It wasn't an answer, but it told Hunter everything. Malcolm had loved his father. *An unrequited love.*

As shocking and unreal as all this was, standing in the harsh embrace of a flesh-and-blood vampire, touch as cool as the late autumn breeze and fangs glinting sharply in the lamplight, it made sense. The pain of Malcolm's fingers digging into his arm was real. The thrill of excitement in his stomach and the heat of desire at his groin were real. The revelation of his father being newly dead meant little. William had been long gone from Hunter's life, if not his memories, for many years. The renewed loss he had momentarily felt dimmed and slipped away.

"And now he's gone. Not so immortal after all. Another old wives' tale?" He didn't expect an answer, and he wasn't disappointed. He didn't think the vampire was going to offer up a list of viable ways to end a vampire's existence. Certainly not one Hunter might be tempted to use at some point. "How can you be sure he's gone?"

Malcolm pulled Hunter more tightly to his chest, his cock stiff and tall in his pants, pressing into Hunter's bare belly. Hunter's cock answered, full, eager to escape out the top of his partially unbuttoned jeans. Malcolm bared his fangs slightly, the effect at first chilling but ultimately fascinating to Hunter.

"I know because I killed him." It was a guttural growl, but something choked and painful entwined around the words like an unwelcome, clinging vine crumbling the mortar between once solid brickwork.

Hunter searched Malcolm's face, so close to his own, looking for some sign of weakness and finding none except a shimmering, elusive need for...what? Him? His father? Or maybe just a need to feel something again.

"Why?" He was surprised at how calm he sounded, how calm he was. There was no animosity toward Malcolm for his deed, just a growing sense of amazement.

"We had a bet." A hand grabbed his waist, slipping around it, traveling up his spine to grip the back of his neck, forcing him to arch back to keep a distance between his bare flesh and those glinting fangs. "He lost."

Hunter knew it was meant to sound cold and uncaring, but Malcolm's eyes betrayed him. Experience created by years of courting and then embracing or eluding danger gave him an instinctive ability to see more than one side of a situation. And there was definitely more here. "You know what, Malcolm? I think my father won."

The grip on his neck became bruising. Malcolm shot him a murderous glare but said nothing. The silence was as telling as the spoken truth would have been. "You freed him from an existence he hated, when he couldn't do it himself. You gave him his chance at being reunited with my mother."

Malcolm's nostrils flared, his mouth pinched until he ground out, "I cut out his heart and watched him crumble to ash underneath me." It was merciless.

Hunter stared, unfazed, into the unyielding gray eyes boring into his own. His answer was short and sincere. "Thank you."

And apparently unexpected.

Malcolm flinched, just a little, before he brought himself back under control. "An idealistic fool, just like your father."

Disdain. Harshness. Intolerance. They were all there, along with a twist of grudging wonder. Malcolm's gaze traveled searchingly over Hunter's face, and Hunter had the feeling the vampire was memorizing him, drinking in everything about him, looking for something. Hunter decided to throw the last thread of self-preservation to the wind and give Malcolm what he was looking for.

"Maybe. But there's one way we're very different." He relaxed the arch in his spine, feeling the grip on his neck lessening as his muscles shifted, bringing his face closer to Malcolm's mouth, his lips almost brushing the pale, thin ones as he talked.

"Do tell." Malcolm made no move to stop Hunter, his breath teasing Hunter's purposefully parted mouth.

"My heart doesn't belong to anybody yet, and... I'm not inclined to rebuff your advances. If that's why you came here."

Hunter stroked a thumb over Malcolm's lower lip. A light passing touch to one canine unexpectedly produced a small cut on the ball of the digit. He jumped but didn't pull away.

A stonelike tower of control, Malcolm waited, a faint narrowing of his now red-ringed eyes his only reaction.

Hunter took a ragged breath, watched the red eyes as they dilated. He rubbed his injured thumb over a pale lip, smearing it a ruby red, then slid his thumb into Malcolm's parted mouth.

Malcolm's tongue instantly laved it, blood wiped away, a groan vibrating in the back of the vampire's throat so husky and raw, a shiver of anticipation raced down Hunter's back and burst into a thousand little bolts of pleasure.

When the blood stopped flowing, Malcolm tilted his head up and carefully forced the thumb from his mouth. "I came to claim my winnings."

Hunter was left panting, hard and more aroused then he could ever remember being. He was still afraid, but it was nothing compared to the passion and need he was experiencing. The warm flush, the dizziness, the sheer craving to be touched and satisfied.

The smell of lust and sweat filled the air between them, musky, potent, intoxicating. Hunter was enveloped in the vampire's power and strength, captured, restrained, cradled. He felt unsteady just standing still. The air in the room grew thicker. His next breath was hard to drag into his protesting lungs and then suddenly the hard-won air was locked inside, his mouth sealed to Malcolm's cool lips.

It was a rough, raw, ravenous kiss. Hunter's lips parted for Malcolm's questing tongue, and his mouth surrendered without a fight, opening wide to the invasion, his hands clenched on Malcolm's smooth alabaster shoulders. He swallowed, and the taste of copper washed down his throat, spicy and sharp, a more exotic elixir than the blood he knew it was.

Blood. Malcolm's blood, vampire blood, thick liquid ambrosia that literally burned like whiskey and left him more intoxicated. It was like sucking the syrupy brown sauce off his favorite Chinese dish, full of bite, sharp and spicy, a little burn, a little sweet, all delicious, making him quest further down Malcolm's throat, yearning for more.

In his mind he could see the blood coating the roof of his mouth, trickling over the crevices in his tongue, creating tiny rivers of black-red to tantalize every taste bud it touched. He felt it slide down his throat and seep into his cells, staining everything in its path. It felt like it had a life of its own. He wanted more.

It was...addictive.

That he was going to have a lifetime of savoring this rolled though his mind, and he sobered slightly. He flinched. A frown knitted his brows together, his eyes narrowed, and his heart tripped into high gear, uncertainty pushing lustful needs aside. He never thought of the long term in anything. Why would he feel that way now? He lived every day for the moment, never planning ahead, and certainly not planning a future with a vampire as his lover.

He wanted to lose himself in the fierce embrace, but a nagging itch kept tickling his brain until he pulled back, panting, flushed, sweaty, and reeling. He didn't think he could take a steady diet of this without stroking out. His lips and arms wanted to dive right back into the kiss, but he needed to hear one more old wives' tale shattered before he could fully enjoy it.

Head tilted back by Malcolm's grip, Hunter let his lust-heavy eyelids flutter up to study Malcolm's chiseled, pale features, hoping to see the answer in the vampire's expression as well as hear it in his throaty voice. "If a vampire tastes a person's blood, can they really know his thoughts? Control him?"

"No." It was said in part smugness, part disdain. "A vampire is merely nourished by a human's blood."

"That's a relief." Hunter drew in a deep breath to sigh out his gratitude, but the air was pushed from his lungs with a grunt. His back slammed up against the wall by the bedroom door, his body pressed chest to chest to Malcolm's iron length.

The vampire's hand wove its way into his hair and tugged, bowing his back slightly and arching his groin out to grind on the thick thigh forced between his legs. It was delicious, if unexpected, demanding yet wholly seductive. As powerful, as swift, as the lift and slam had been, Hunter knew Malcolm was being restrained, and the thoughts of what more lay beneath that restraint thrilled him as much as it frightened him.

Harsh, raw, and unapologetic, Malcolm murmured, "It's after a human tastes a vampire's blood that the mental and physical binding occurs."

"Fuck."

The taste of spiced copper and vibrant, liquid lust lingered on his palate and burned the corners of his mouth. The tip of Hunter's tongue immediately darted to one corner to wipe it away, but captured it instead as though it was the finest ambrosia. His skin prickled at the thought of what he had just done, what Malcolm had just said. He believed the truth in the vampire's words, felt it coursing in his own veins, heard the whispers weaving ghostly tendrils of control through his mind.

"Well...just...fuck."

Hunter sucked in a deep breath to tell Malcolm to stop, to let him go, to move away so he could think, but his hands, one still tightly clenching his father's ring, moved to the vampire's neck instead. Once there, they hung on. He pulled the taller man closer and wrapped a leg around him, his hands now busy undoing both their flies, his fingers suddenly thick and uncoordinated, fumbling over the remaining buttons on his own jeans and battling with the zipper tab on Malcolm's dress pants.

Bracing them both, Malcolm let him work, merely transferring his own lips to rain attention on the line of Hunter's jaw and the curve of his sweat-slick neck.

It took too long, but finally both cocks sprang free. Then things moved too fast for Hunter to process. Air whipped around them, vibrating with electricity, leaving his flesh feeling slightly scorched. One minute he was pinned between his living room wall and Malcolm's body, and the next he was gasping for air, lying completely naked, pinned between his bed's mattress and the vampire's cool, hard weight.

His pulse pounded in his head, and his cock matched the hammering beat with its own throbbing rhythm. Hunter's nerves were so hypersensitive, every lick to his neck felt like a wet stroke that ended at his weeping cock. The scent of pre-cum filled the air, and the bump and grind of cock on cock turned slick as satin on steel.

He struggled to fill his lungs, the air heavy despite the light breeze from the open window. Lips moved from his neck to his mouth, devouring, dominating, and delicious. Malcolm's rough, wet tongue sucked on his lower lip, teasing its sensitive lining, urging his teeth to open. His mouth surrendered, and Malcolm invaded full force, crushing Hunter's mouth to his, arms wrapped tightly around him, hand holding his head in place by a powerful, possessive grip on his hair.

The kiss was deep, powerful, all encompassing. It made the room spin and the dim bedside lamplight glow like a supernova. It stole Hunter's breath, his rapidly diminishing resistance, and his last lingering doubt that this was real. He knew with certainty that it was not some bizarre erotic dream. Or nightmare. The creature who had him locked in his arms was a vampire after all. But any fear he had over what making love with a vampire might entail was overshadowed by the passion and desire consuming him.

A deep moan of pleasure escaped him, and there was an answering murmur that could have been admonishment or agreement. The murmur vibrated through his chest, sending shocks of need and want straight to his groin. His balls pulled up and his cock jerked, frantic for more than belly friction in its own wet droplets. Hunter craved the heat of a thick, hard shaft, slick and supple as satin-capped steel sliding into his body, piercing him to his heart, stoking the fires of passion until it burned him from the inside out.

Suddenly the spicy hot burn of slick copper washed over his taste buds. And this time Hunter gulped greedily at Malcolm's blood, hungry for the connection that intensified every nerve in his body, every touch and stroke, every response from his willing lips to his eager cock and spasming opening. He hungered for it all, his soul consumed by the need as much as his body was consumed by Malcolm's mouth and hands. The vampire's cool-as-ivory cock skated alongside his as the taller, larger man hunched over Hunter, curled around him from on top, lips to lips and cock to cock, weight and ravenous hunger enfolding him as completely as Malcolm's arms did.

Skin sweat-slick and fevered, Hunter clenched his ass and tried to buck his hips, desperate for more contact, more friction. He moaned and whimpered, the sounds muffled by tongue and lips, but the tone clear. The grip in his hair tightened, but Malcolm didn't relent in the kiss or his dominant, unyielding position. As frustrating as it was, Hunter felt a thrill wash through him as Malcolm pinned him more fully to the mattress and renewed his oral assault.

It was passionate and powerful. Hunter couldn't resist the lure of stroke and rub, his own tongue drawn into a dance of slide and savor with Malcolm's agile mouth. His ass fluttered and spasmed wide then clenched, his gut achingly empty, longing to be filled, ridden, stretched, and claimed. The cock sliding across his belly felt so long, so cool, so hard on his heated flesh. The mental image of a huge penis-shaped ice sculpture filling his ass flashed across his mind. His cock jerked, and he felt it spill a small pool of pre-cum, boiling hot to sticky cool in seconds as the chill night air stole its heat. He writhed and turned, his fists pounding on Malcolm's shoulder, first pushing the vampire away, then pulling him closer, fear and lust battling in every touch, grunt, and moaning whimper.

There was a light pinpoint prick to the side of his tongue that made Hunter start and pull his tongue back. One of Malcolm's thick, square hands grabbed his jaw, holding him in place and his mouth open as the vampire's tongue lapped at the lining of his mouth and suckled at the bleeding wound. The sting of the cut intensified, then spread, fanning out to run tiny rivers of fire down his skin. He felt like he'd been doused in gasoline, skin raw, burning, ready to ignite at the first hint of a spark. And then the whispers where back in his head, a mellow, rich baritone, smoothing away the burn and extinguishing the pain while they fed the passion and desire.

Hunter stopped pushing Malcolm away. He wrapped his arms around the vampire's neck and returned the fervor of the kiss in kind, giving Malcolm control but without giving up his own desires. He freed a leg and threw it over Malcolm's hip and ass, locking it around one of his heavily muscled thighs, heel digging in as hard as he could.

Malcolm wrenched Hunter's head away and stared down into his unrepentant eyes.

"I want more, Malcolm. I want you to fuck me. If you're going to own me, do it right. Claim every part of me."

A hard, penetrating glare sliced through Hunter. Malcolm had gone still, his grip on Hunter's jaw and in his hair like a vise, menacing, reminding Hunter who and what he was in bed with.

"I don't take orders." It was a silky whisper, more frightening than a bellowed roar. A single, chastising kiss ghosted over his lips. "From anyone."

Hunter had to work to keep from tearing up from the painful hold in his hair. "If you want, think of it as a last request." He felt his heart pulse in his neck, felt the skin tighten over it, heard the rapid thump-thump-thump in his ears. He knew Malcolm could see his pulse by the way the vampire's look flickered to his neck between narrow-eyed glares and sneering, lethally whispered words.

"If I want?" It was light, amused even, a sudden change in attitude. "Is that what you want as your last request? To be fucked?" Malcolm rolled his hips and tilted his groin, causing a grind and rub of cool cock against hot cock.

Hunter groaned, biting his lip to keep from crying out, frustrated need boiling in his gut, scalding through his veins and nerves. "Since I don't think I stand a chance in hell of surviving this?" The cold, predator's glint in the vampire's eyes caught his attention. He swallowed hard, fear gaining a new foothold. "Yes. I'd rather it was something more, but yes, I'll settle for fucking."

"Why something more?" Malcolm frowned. "The physical act is enjoyable without the emotional attachment." Hunter tried to arch and grind again, but Malcolm pressed him firmly onto the mattress, stilling his movements by sheer greater weight.

"Honestly?"

A slight narrowing of Malcolm's gaze gave Hunter permission to go on. He felt his face heat. His tongue darted out to moisten his lower lip, and Malcolm's gaze flickered down to watch. Hunter tasted spiced copper. The knowledge that it was left behind by Malcolm made his mouth water and his gut burn with need.

"I guess I've got nothing to lose by saying it out loud. It's not like there's going to be a morning after to get embarrassed over sappy cock talk, right?" Tears stung his eyes, and he gasped a little to bring them under control before they had the chance to humiliate him by falling.

The hold on his jaw lessened. Hunter worked his jaw to ease the stiffness in it, then sighed, eyes focusing on Malcolm's steady gaze. "It's just...you're everything I've ever fantasized about in a lover. You make me feel everything I've dreamed about. Passion, danger, power, need, animal attraction." His fists balled on the muscled ridge of Malcolm's broad shoulders, pressing hard on the alabaster surface. "If things had been different, maybe even... love."

He snorted a weak laugh, knowing he sounded like a schoolgirl. "I guess that's why you're not human." He snorted a short laugh again, and this time a single drop of moisture managed to trickle out the corner of one eye and into his hair. "To be my perfect fantasy lover, you'd have to be unreal, wouldn't you?"

Malcolm was still and silent for so long, cold gray eyes boring into his, Hunter began to think something was wrong with the vampire. Even the whisper in his head had gone silent, but he could still feel its power drifting in his mind, a constant presence, as if a cool mountain stream trickled through the nooks and crannies of his brain.

Something shifted in Malcolm's stare, the icy stare, one thumb moving to caress the line of Hunter's cheek. It was alarmingly affectionate, the deep, low voice now raw and oddly pitched. "Do you want to survive this, Hunter Pray?"

Red tendrils fanned out from the edges of icy-icy gray in Malcolm's irises, turning the whites of his eyes to pools of scarlet.

Hunter's breath froze in his lungs, and he had to gasp to keep the growing dizziness at bay.

"I don't know." In his head, the whisper crooned soft and low again, and a renewed rush of thrilled desire made his skin prickle. Passion and lust battled with a sudden panicked urge to flee. "Will I want to survive?"

"I don't know." A thin smile flickered across Malcolm pale lips, his gaze taking in every inch of Hunter's face, evaluating him. He worked the gold ring from Hunter's unresisting fist. Without looking away from Hunter's wide-eyed, lust-filled stare, he tossed it on the bedside table and then raked a heavy, manicured nail over Hunter's exposed jugular, a predator's gleam in his eyes. "No one ever has."

A shudder ran through Hunter, but he didn't honestly know if it was from fear or anticipation. Both sensations prompted him to suck his lower lip between his teeth and bite down. He flinched at the sharp sting, but the thick, slippery liquid that washed over his lip and bathed his tongue tasted rich and warm.

The grip on his hair became almost intolerable. He knew the vampire didn't breathe, but he was sure he heard a small gasp that wasn't his. Past the point of no return, Hunter touched the tip of his tongue to the blood, deliberately smearing it over his parted lips. "Let's find out, then."

Malcolm pounced before Hunter drew his next breath. Skilled hands and cool, firm lips were everywhere at once but never in one place long. His mouth was ravaged, his eyelids kissed, face caressed, and ribs traced with blunt, callused fingers. His hair was pulled to arch his neck, the faintly shadowed skin exposed, only to be licked and nuzzled, scraped with blunt teeth, and then ignored. His skin was lapped at, scoured, sucked, and nipped from his chin to his taut, burning nipples, then down across his quivering belly, the wet trail ending in the crease of his thigh where leg met trunk, and back again. All the while Malcolm's large hands gripped his wrists tightly. Hunter's frustration mounted, accompanied by an undeniable wanton desire to be claimed and marked in any manner the vampire wanted. Hunter felt almost suffocatingly full, a second presence in his thoughts, but his body was empty and yearned to be filled as well.

He screamed silently for relief. His fear swung from fear of being bitten to the fear of not. He wanted Malcolm more than he had ever wanted any other lover. He could blame the mental link the vampire declared was created when Hunter swallowed Malcolm's blood, but he was honest enough with himself to recognize that he had wanted this mysterious, menacing stranger long before that. His flesh burned for more, his cock so hard it pulsed with the rapid pounding flow of blood from his hammering heartbeat.

Every cell of his body tingled. Every touch of Malcolm's tongue was like a cool caress that chilled him and pumped the flames of desire higher. Hunter twisted and bucked, his hips and thighs pinned to the mattress by the weight of Malcolm's upper body nestled between his spread limbs.

He yanked on his wrists, desperate to free them from their immobilizing hold. He wanted to run his hands over the rippling muscles and chiseled perfection of broad shoulders, to see how crisp the short hair on Malcolm's head was, to pull his face toward him and kiss his pale, firm lips. Instead he was forced to endure a thousand sensations battering at his senses with no relief or respite. His groans and gaps filled the night air with the sounds of pained pleasure, broken occasionally by a rumbled grunt of appreciation as Malcolm's hands and mouth brought Hunter to the brink of climax and back down again. His cock was untouched as yet but for the irregular bump of cheek or chin as Malcolm explored the bony ridges of his groin or mouthed the nest of fawn-colored hair.

It came as an unexpected shock when Malcolm's mouth closed over his cock. Hunter jumped at the delicious slide of wet flesh sucked vigorously down over the spongy tip. Then he squirmed and bucked at the unanticipated sting and burn of razor-sharp teeth raking down the shaft as Malcolm swallowed his erection to the base. Now he knew why his hands had been confined. The pain flared, a bright flash so intense, sweat broke out and ran in rivulets to the sheets. Then as suddenly as it burst on him, the pain faded, replaced by a velvet vise filled with warm honey, gliding over his abused cock, soothing the wounds and making him harder than he had been. Hunter realized Malcolm used his lips to capture the blood as it flowed, holding, using it to wet his cock, bathing it in his own blood, lubricating and feasting on him at the same time.

Looking down, eyes forced open by desire to watch his ruddy pink cock disappearing between those blood-smeared lips, Hunter found his breath caught in his throat. The sight of Malcolm's mouth, pursed, wrapped around his shaft, pink cock and pale lips now the same shade of glistening black/red, the contrast shocking, exotic, revitalized the flash of pain he felt when the blood was drawn. It sent bolts of ecstasy sizzling through his body, muscles spasming, skin flushed anew and his asshole clenching, empty and wanting.

He turned his hands until his fingertips could grab hold of some of the flesh of Malcolm's hands, and he dug his nails in, refusing to be denied a human connection to his vampire lover. The excitement, this pain, this glory was meant to be shared. He felt a growled groan of heated lust vibrate through his cock and into the pit of his stomach. The sound shattered the last barrier to his climax. His hips reared up, cock planted deep in Malcolm's throat. His whole world exploded. Cum boiled up from deep inside. He could trace its path with his senses. It left his abdomen, ripped through his balls and up his cock like a tiny volcano erupting, scalding liquid cascading from his body in pulsed ribbons, all of it consumed by Malcolm's measures, sure swallows and sucking lips.

Hunter was flying. The force of his climax echoed in his chest, welled in every bead of sweat, jumped in his synapses, and left a buzzing in his ears. He hung in a euphoric cloud, bathed in the heat of intense pleasure, wrapped in a sheet of strength that was at once both comforting and restraining. His mind slowly drifted back to make contact with his body, a heavy, sated exhaustion blanketing him. That orgasm had come from the center of his being.

Languid as a drug addict floating on the effects of an unprecedented high, Hunter didn't resist being rolled onto his stomach. Malcolm stretched out full length along his back, the vampire's powerful thighs pushing Hunter's open and up to allow Malcolm's thick cock to nestle snugly between his cheeks.

A low murmur growled distinctly in his ear, and anticipation shot through every fiber in Hunter's hypersensitive body as the vampire announced, "Now that the edge is gone from your immediate need...we do this right."

"Edge?" His voice was breathless, his throat hoarse, dry, from panting. "That was a whole lot more than my edge, Malcolm."

"You just think it was." A hard nip of teeth pinched the flesh at the curve of his neck. Hunter shuddered, waiting for a solid bite. Nothing followed except Malcolm's whispered, "Trust me, pet, we've just begun."

Hunter tensed, expecting a sudden and harsh penetration. His skin tingled, gooseflesh erupting as tiny nibbles and wet, soothing licks bathed his shoulders and back. *Malcolm*. Malcolm lazily lapping the sweat off Hunter, tasting the flesh from his neck to the small of his back.

The shock wore off quickly, arousal returning, planting a twisted knot of anticipation in Hunter's belly and coaxing his limp cock, if not to fill, to at least take notice of the renewed attention. Malcolm inched down Hunter's back a lick and nibble at a time. He paused at the small scabbed cut on Hunter's back made by the flying bench pieces, sucking and worrying the raw flesh until Hunter squirmed and grunted his discomfort. Then he tore open the scratch with a razor-sharp slash of a tooth. It burned like being sliced with a honed paring knife.

Hunter could feel his blood well to the surface before Malcolm's greedy mouth sucked it away. The vampire's tongue pressed into the wound, spreading its edges so it bled more freely. It was painful in a small hurt sort of way, but Hunter's mind moved from the discomfort to realizing how erotic Malcolm's mouth felt pressed against his back, how sensually the vampire's lips massaged his flesh while they suckled, how stiff and blunt the tongue probing into his body felt, these same mouth, lips, and tongue that had just given him a blowjob like never before. It all became seductive and exotic, the pain now a tingling warmth that spread out and down to his groin.

His cock stirred and filled, rubbing over wrinkled sheets trapped under his hips. Before he could start thrusting against the linen for friction, Malcolm slid down between his legs, nudging his thighs open with his shoulders, giving silent commands to Hunter by a touch of his hand. A palm pressed lightly on the inner thigh told Hunter to raise his leg higher; a tap to his arm that was fumbling under him for a hold on his cock told him to remove his hand. He reluctantly obeyed without understanding how he knew what to do.

Hands massaged his ass cheeks in a slow, kneading rhythm that pushed them together tightly then moved them apart so the cool air struck the tight, hidden bud of his opening, making it ache with need. God, how he wanted to be filled, taken, claimed the way Malcolm had threatened to do. He wanted a long, thick cock inside of him, and more than that, he wanted it to be Malcolm's cock. He wanted Malcolm to take him, ravage him, make love to him. If he was going to die, this was the way to go.

A sudden stab of slick wetness mixed with the cool room air. Hunter grunted and jerked, his hands twisting the sheets in his fists to keep from rearing up out of bed. A firm bluntness probed at his eager hole, and Hunter groaned out his pleasure into the pillows. He couldn't stop himself from arching his back and raising his hips, pushing back onto the slick pleasure of Malcolm's jabbing, stroking, questing tongue. It was too much and not enough. Roughly thrilling against the sensitive nerve endings of the tight ring of guardian muscle, yet too little to dissolve the gaping, empty void of needing to be filled.

"I want more. I need more."

Gasping, Hunter tried to rise up on his knees, to press back and impale himself as deeply as possible on the tongue now bathing the rim of his opening. A hard, thundering slap to one cheek made him gasp and freeze, the firecracker of sudden pain unexpected. A large hand placed on the small of his back froze him in place on his knees, supported by his own hands and trembling thighs in an awkward half-crouch. He stayed that way, panting and trembling, silent, Malcolm's tongue still teasing the rim of his asshole. Finally, the hand moved from his back to one hip, steadying him, drawing Hunter into a more comfortable angle.

A fingertip played over the moist opening, rubbing light circles over the wrinkled, puckered edges, pushing into the yielding center just enough that Hunter could feel the stretch and anticipate the coming fullness. But the finger never ventured further, retreating again and again to rub big and small loops on his skin, its tantalizing trail occasionally made slicker by a darting jab of tongue.

Hunter could barely stay upright. His body trembled with need, and his skin prickled with sizzling bolts of growing desire. His cock hung free between his spread thighs, full and heavy. With his forehead pressed into the mattress he had a good view of his cock jutting out from his belly, its dusky rose length curved to his navel, clearing the bed by several inches in its erect state. Beyond his legs, between them, stood sculptured slabs of pale marble thighs and a pendulous sac surrounded by curls of coarse hair. He couldn't see Malcolm's cock, but he could feel it bump against the curve of his ass now and then, and he could see it in his mind's eye, knew it was inches away from his open and ready ass, glistening, thick, and heavy.

He tried to lower his groin enough to touch the bed, to gain friction on his cock's head, but another hard, stinging slap to his already sensitive butt cheek stopped him. He couldn't stop the choked groan that escaped. Flushed and fevered, every nerve singing for relief, his mind felt as if it was stuffed with cotton, disoriented and slow. Only his cock and ass seemed to have a clear connection with his brain, both parts overwhelmed by sensation and need. But every time Hunter's passion began to arch toward climax, Malcolm changed his tactics and the glow faded, then built again under a new rhythm of stroking caresses.

Finally, the touch stayed long enough that Hunter felt the stirring of an orgasm coiling deep in his abdomen. It gathered energy, his entire focus narrowed to the pattern of licks and jabs on his opening and ass, building higher and higher toward the point of no return. He sensed more than heard the low, deep murmur in his head say something he couldn't comprehend at that moment, and then, like a light bulb gone bad, all stimulation was instantly gone, taking with it the building buzz and pressure of climax.

He pounded a fist on the bed sheets, uncaring if it earned him punishment. But nothing happened, absolutely nothing. Malcolm's solid presence remained behind him, but the vampire had apparently moved back enough that no part of him touched Hunter.

Hunter's first urge was to roll off the bed, away from this maddening creature, but that little murmur in his head told him that would be the short and sure path to non-survival. Besides, he didn't want this to end. He never wanted it to end.

"Bastard, you really are a monster! You're killing me here. Do something. Please." Ass in the air, thighs spread, face pressed into the bed, Hunter knew he must look like an eager rentboy, a slut, a whore begging for a hard fuck.

"I will decide when and how I kill you, pet. And when I do, rest assured, I will not start at your delightfully red, handprint-marked ass."

A flush of embarrassment heated Hunter's face. Then inspiration hit him. His heart hammered in his chest, and his breath came in shallow pants triggered by excitement and fear.

Forehead taking the strain off his upper body, Hunter spread his knees as far as they would go, squatting low to the mattress, balancing his weight so he could reach around behind and grab his ass with both hands. He parted his cheeks, exposing his opening, then tightened the ring of muscle and relaxed it, a wordless beckoning to Malcolm's cock.

A sudden sharp intake of breath let him know he had the vampire's attention, and that awareness sent a thrill through his body, making his ass wave slightly. A hand fell on his hip and stayed there, long fingers digging into his flesh hard enough to leave bruises. Hunter imagined the blue-black fingerprints on his hip, the red, glowing handprints on both sides of his ass, the healed but still tender bites on his back and cock. His balls pulled up and his dick tapped his belly, pulsing to the beat of his racing heart.

But still nothing happened. No spank, no bite, not even a ghostly hint of a breath on his skin.

He presented himself more fully, but when he remained untouched, Hunter moved one hand to his cock and pushed it back between his splayed legs, pointing the dusky shaft, its tip glistening with dabs of creamy white pre-cum, directly at Malcolm. He swayed back and forth, rubbing the creamy liquid into the sheets, releasing the musky, pheromone-drenched scent into the air. The hand on his hip twitched. Hunter closed his eyes to clear his mind, knowing the whispering murmur was still there, quiet, and let his mind form the question he wanted to ask out loud but didn't dare to. *Bored with me already?*

The room stayed silent as a tomb for several agonizing seconds. Then Hunter felt himself lifted and flipped in the air. He landed on his back on the mattress, eyes wide open, legs folded back at the knees so his heels rested on the bed, his raised hips resting on Malcolm's muscular upper thighs, legs bracketing Malcolm's thick, firm waist. His wrists were captured in a loose grip at his sides. The air had been knocked out of him, and his head spun.

Malcolm leaned over him, eyes blood red, fangs extended, lips curled back in a hissed growl that vibrated through every fiber of Hunter's body. Malcolm was magnificent and deadly-looking — power, animal attraction, and control mixed with stamina and amazing strength. He was the predator at the top of the food chain.

The vampire slowly bent down until he could latch on to Hunter's lower lip with his teeth. Tugging on it, he let it slip out of his grip centimeter by centimeter. The tension split open the healing bite Hunter had given himself earlier so that a small bead of blood welled to the surface when Malcolm released it.

Hunter could feel the warmth of the blood on his lip. Eyes locked on the vampire's unearthly gaze, he deliberately pressed his lips together, smearing the droplet over both of them, then parted them slightly, the invitation clear.

"So vibrant, rich, so alive. No one has ever made me miss the warmth of being human, until now." Lips only inches away from Hunter's, Malcolm spoke into Hunter's parted mouth, deep voice husky and raw with want. "I have begun to fear, Hunter Pray, I will never be bored with you."

Touching his pale lips to Hunter's blood-smeared ones, Malcolm gave him the briefest, chaste kiss, barely making contact. He then nuzzled his cheek and jaw over the wet opening, streaking his pale skin with strokes of deep red, all the while sniffing and inhaling the scent of the rich, coppery blood.

It was erotic and primal, and it thrilled Hunter to see himself written across Malcolm's face. The marks only remained on his skin for moments before they faded, seemingly sucked into the vampire's very flesh. Hunter reached out and touched Malcolm's face, wishing his mark were still on the vampire.

Slowly drawing back, Malcolm slipped out of Hunter's touch. Once he was sitting back on his heels again, he pulled Hunter's hips toward him in a powerful yank that slapped cock to cock.

Hunter groaned as his erection curled forward, swollen and hot, but his gaze stayed glued to Malcolm, watching, breath held, as the vampire used his fangs to slice open the first two fingers of his own hand.

Blood, viscous and dark, flowed out of the wounds. It dripped like honey, full-bodied and glistening wet in the dim bedroom light. Malcolm let the blood pool in his palm, then used his hand to stroke his stiff, pale cock, anointing the shaft and head with a liberal coating until the wounds closed. He made to lick the remainder off his palm, but Hunter reached out a beckoning, open hand. Flirting with danger, always pushing the limits.

Wordlessly, Malcolm placed his bloodied hand in Hunter's, his eyes dilated, his lips parted in anticipation. Hunter strained up to lick the tips of Malcolm's fingers, then sucked each one into his mouth to scour it clean with his tongue, swallowing down the spicy tang of vampire blood, feeling the bond between them strengthen and grow. Once they were both clean, he licked the smears from Malcolm's palm, teasing the sensitive surface with light, lapping caresses until he felt more than saw Malcolm's hand twitch. Then he sucked both healed fingers between his lips down to their bases, only to slowly slide his pursed mouth off again. Malcolm's riveted gaze took in every swallow, every lick, every seductive gesture.

A faint sheen of sweat made the vampire's skin glow a golden ruby, the whites of his eyes red, his gray irises now flecked with threads of yellow gold. His large square hands clenched into fists but relaxed long enough to pull Hunter's hips up and push his legs back, one hand guiding his blood-slicked cock into Hunter's ass.

The burn was immediate, the pain a fleeting shock that instantly melted into waves of pleasure. Every measured thrust and withdrawal spread the fiery glow deeper into Hunter's abdomen. His asshole flared and clenched trying to pull Malcolm in, the slow, tempered thrusts maddening. Hunter moaned and bucked, feeling the tip of Malcolm's cock brush over the small nub of his prostate. Every rub and jab sent tendrils of electric excitement scurrying along his nerves. Pressure built at his opening as more of Malcolm's wide girth eased into his channel. A similar pressure began to uncoil in the pit of his abdomen. The pressure grew and grew until Hunter was squirming and writhing, only Malcolm's hands and iron grip keeping him firmly in place.

Whimpers and gasps joined groaned oaths and curses that intensified as Malcolm's strokes became more rapid and deeper.

Hunter reached for his own cock, but found his fingers trapped under Malcolm's hands, pinned to his own bucking hips, his erection taunt, bobbing with each new thrust, splatters of tiny white droplets spotting his chest. His opening was spread wide, the base of Malcolm cock slamming hard against the clenched ring, coarse hair tickling the tender flesh around his hole, adding a sensation he'd never been aware of with other lovers.

Everything about this coupling was new and different, like it was his first time. He felt more, sensed more, not just what he was feeling but what Malcolm was experiencing too. He felt the ridges and bulging veins on Malcolm thick cock and the deep rim of the head as it passed over his hidden gland and up his ass, but he also knew the satiny tightness of his hot, slick, wet flesh around that cock. It was dizzying trying to sort out which sensations belonged to whom. In the end, he gave up and immersed himself in all of them, encouraged by the indistinct hum of pure pleasure in his head.

Each thrust hammered deeper into him. So deep, the delicious fullness reached the uncoiling threads of ecstasy loosing in his gut, nudging them to unfurl faster. He wanted more, harder, to be taken like he'd never been before. Hunter was consumed by the need to have Malcolm fully inside of him, his body impaled on Malcolm's, Malcolm enfolded by his. This was ecstasy, bliss, the binding act that Hunter knew was needed to link them together forever.

Now all that was left was the claiming. The taking of his blood, the final joining, the completion, the ultimate bond that would either take Hunter's life or give him a new one.

Death or life as a thrall to a vampire master. His protector, his future, his lover. Which one Malcolm had in store for him, he couldn't tell, but he was beyond caring, at the point of no return. Malcolm had won the bet with Hunter's father, and he deserved his prize.

One of Malcolm's hands moved to pluck at his painfully stiff tits, but Hunter seized it and quickly pulled it to his lips. Not giving himself time to think about his actions and what the vampire would do if he were displeased, Hunter snagged a tiny bit of the thin skin over Malcolm's inner wrist and bit down hard. Blood welled out of the wound, coating Malcolm's wrist.

A sharp intake of air, more surprised than pained, rewarded his efforts. The grip on his hip became almost crushing for a moment. Malcolm plunged his cock deep into Hunter, then stayed there, grinding his hips, stretching Hunter's opening impossibly wide, forcing his full length into the core of Hunter's body. The pleasure was so great, Hunter almost blacked out. Wildfire blazed in his gut, pulled his balls up tight, and made his cock christen his chest with more droplets of liquid passion.

Teetering painfully on the brink of coming, Hunter sucked the trickle of blood out of the rapidly healing wound. When the flow stopped seconds later, he let the last beads of red elixir linger on his lips, painting them in the dark scarlet. He raised his gaze to meet the vampire's, deliberately licking the coating off with his tongue.

"You play with fire, pet." Malcolm's voice was raw, rough, barely audible, but Hunter heard the words in his head as well. "I have never experienced one such as you."

"So burn me. Leave your mark on me. Claim me."

Malcolm's eyes swirled with mists of red, and the yellow threads in his irises seemed to grow luminous as his fangs descended longer. Malcolm reared back slightly, and Hunter took that as a signal to turn his head to one side and arch his neck.

Bright pain tore through his shoulder and neck unlike anything he'd ever felt — vicious, searing, and pure agony. And then it was gone, replaced by a building sense of excitement. Bold threads of electricity pulsed along his skin, through the fibers of his muscles, and into the cells of every one of his organs. Even his bones throbbed with desire. His heart pounded against what now seemed like his fragile ribcage. His breath was held captive in his stunned lungs. His cock exploded, stinging strings of hot cum marking both their abdomens, adding the musky scent of sex and his own sweat to the heavy air.

Malcolm arched over him, long, sharp fangs embedded in his upper torso while his long, blunt cock was buried balls-deep in Hunter's lower torso. He could feel Malcolm erupting into his ass, pulsing shot after shot of cum into his body at the same time as Hunter pulsed mouthful after mouthful of blood into Malcolm's eager mouth. It was like an unbroken circle of desire and bliss beyond any Hunter had experienced or would again. He knew it was only possible like this, with Malcolm, with a vampire lover.

Lethargy from blood loss hit him, his breathing shallow and labored, his mind clouded with soothing words and the buzz of climax that refused to recede. Hunter decided it really wasn't such a bad way to end his search for the most exciting and dangerous lover. Or such a bad way to meet an end to his life, either, if it came to that.

His eyelids flickered closed, but not before he caught sight of the gold ring on the bedside table. Death by vampire. Maybe he was more like his father than he thought. He'd ask him if they met in the afterlife.

§ § §

Hunter shifted his head to look up into Malcolm's face. He had awakened what had turned out to be two days later, cradled naked in the vampire's arms in bed, his cheek pillowed on Malcolm's still, broad, hard chest, his arms curled around the creature's body like he was clinging to a life raft. Once fully awake, he hadn't seen the need to change his position, content to lie in his lover's powerful embrace, a faint, pleasant hum in his brain reassuring him all was right in the newly altered world into which he'd been drawn. The hum, the connection, gave him the courage to test his boundaries.

"Did you come here to kill me?"

The all-consuming red swirls were gone from Malcolm's eyes, but a flicker of yellow glinted in the bedroom light, hard-edged and cold. Hunter made sure he didn't drop his gaze, waiting and watching.

Malcolm twitched and blinked. His eyes turned back to a stormy gray-blue, and the odd expression of warmth, desire, and wonder transformed his stony features. Hunter liked this look.

Pursing his lips in what Hunter thought was an effort to hide a smile, Malcolm sniffed, then pulled Hunter further up onto his chest. He entwined their legs, Hunter's soft cock pressed into Malcolm's solid abs. Locking his arms around Hunter's waist as if he thought he might try to escape, Malcolm stared directly into Hunter's eyes. "Originally, yes."

"And now?" The whisper told him the answer, but he wanted to hear it out loud, from Malcolm.

The vampire paused a moment, the shadow of unexpected wonder in his face deepening along with his voice. "No." It was just one word, but it sounded harsh and hard won.

It scared Hunter just enough for him to make light of it. "Why?"

Malcolm's eyes narrowed for a heartbeat. Then a smile tugged at the corner of his mouth. He successfully fought it off. "Do I need to show you again?"

He pulled Hunter's head down and nuzzled his throat, nipping the thin skin at the crook of his neck, working his way up until he could suck on the tip of Hunter's chin. In between nips and licks, he asked, "Could it be you were not paying attention earlier?"

"Hardly." Hunter pulled back so he could look down at Malcolm. He searched the vampire's face, gauging Malcolm's expression with the hum in his head, trying to learn to read both of them accurately. "Are you going to convert me?"

"No."

There hadn't been a flicker of hesitation. Hunter wasn't sure if that was good or bad for him. Did Malcolm love him for who he was, as he was, or did he just not want Hunter around forever?

"Why?"

The sigh and scowl were closer to real this time. "That is becoming a very irritating word in your vocabulary."

There was that scary tone again. Hunter fought it off with more humor. "Why?" Irritation flashed across Malcolm's face. Hunter leaned down and kissed him, deep, hard, and slow. When he was sure the scowl was gone by the sudden arousal jabbing him under his own lengthening cock, he pulled back and smiled at his lover. "Give me more than one-syllable answers, and I won't have to keep asking why."

Hands gripping Hunter's face, Malcolm's gaze darted over every surface and plane, studying it, searching for something. Hunter wasn't sure what, but his survival instincts told him to relax into the vampire's hold and let his mind fall open. All resistance flowing out of him, all his walls and defenses dropped. He laid his emotions and thoughts bare to all scrutiny, his fate resting, just like his face, in this creature's powerful hands.

"Because I want you as you are." Malcolm's tone was deep, raw, and husky with desire and possessive hunger. It sent a thrill directly to Hunter's hardening cock. "Unchanged, unaffected by the awakening. I want your love of life and the feeling of your warmth next to me." Malcolm wrapped a leg around Hunter, embracing him with his entire body. "You are a connection to my past, a part of me I had discarded, but now find I want to reclaim. Since I can't, I shall claim you instead." A callused but tender thumb stroked Hunter's cheek, a lover's gentle caress. "I shall keep you as you are."

"I'll die eventually." Hunter nudged the palm holding his cheek, wanting more but settling for a touch.

"Thralls live much longer than mere humans. Partaking of my blood in small amounts will lengthen your life span considerably."

"I can live with that."

"Yes, you can and will. Live."

"Hey, I'm with you on this one."

Leaning across Malcolm's solid chest, Hunter grabbed his father's wedding ring from the nightstand and toyed with it, the inscription *forever my true desire* playing over and over in his head. He looked from the ring to Malcolm's face, still seeing the intense possessiveness and claiming lust for him in the vampire's heated stare. "When you won the bet, this ring became yours, right?"

Taking the ring from Hunter's hands, Malcolm studied it for a moment, flashing the dim bedroom lamplight on it, reading the inscription again as if Hunter didn't know the vampire had it memorized. Suddenly he handed it back, his manner curt and authoritative. "It's yours now. Put it on."

Unable to hide his pleasure, Hunter put on his most innocent expression. "You're giving it to me?"

Malcolm's eyes narrowed suspiciously, but he answered, "Yes."

A mischievous smile nudged the innocent look off Hunter's face. "It says, *forever my true desire.*"

"I am aware of that." There was a long-suffering impatience to his words, as if the vampire was well aware Hunter was baiting him.

"You want me to wear a wedding band? From you? One that proclaims me to be your true desire?" There was a teasing note in his tone, but Hunter really wanted to hear Malcolm said it out loud.

"Will you always need this much reassurance?" Malcolm grunted slightly as Hunter rolled and sat up, straddling the vampire's hips, his firm, bare ass sliding back to wedge Malcolm's growing shaft between its warm, smooth globes. "Because if you do, I'll be forced to drain you right now and save myself the frustrating burden of a high-maintenance lover."

"Do I frustrate you?" Hunter rubbed his ass against the hot cock that branded his flesh from asshole to low back. A sultry, seductive smile teased his lips.

The smile instantly vanished when Malcolm took his face between both his cupped hands and pulled Hunter to his chest, eyes filled with an intensity and heat unlike anything Hunter had ever seen.

Hunter's heart jumped into his throat at the low, raw sound

of Malcolm's rasping voice. The vampire whispered mere inches from his lips, eyes locked on Hunter's now serious expression.

"Like no one has frustrated me in all of recorded time."

Hunter was dragged down into a kiss that etched the word *forever* into his mind and his heart. It was rough and demanding, almost brutal in intensity. Hunter knew his lips would be bruised and swollen later. Without pause, the kiss suddenly gentled into a passionate embrace, full of desire and caring so tender, Hunter's eyes flashed open to make sure he was still kissing Malcolm.

When it was done, Hunter panted heavily, body flooded with warmth, both emotional and physical. He touched his tongue to the tender corner of his mouth, enjoying what the tiny ache told him about his lover's feelings that Malcolm couldn't say out loud.

Eyes ablaze with wonder and want, he ran a finger over Malcolm's parted mouth, pricking his fingertip on one barely extended fang. He slid the bleeding finger across Malcolm's lips, then into the vampire's mouth. He felt the groan from Malcolm's chest vibrate through his entire body. His cock jumped, and the heat at his ass grew thicker, the tip rubbing a sticky spot into his spine.

"What do you say we see if we can make up for some of that unsatisfying recorded time of yours? We've got forever, right?"

LAURA BAUMBACH is the award-winning author of numerous short stories, novellas, novels and screenplays. Her favorite genre to work in is manlove or m/m erotic romances. Manlove is not traditional gay fiction, but erotic romances written specifically for the romantic-minded reader, male or female. Married to the same man for almost 30 years, she currently lives with her husband and two sons in the blustery Northeast of the United States but is looking for a warmer location to spend the second half of her professional and family life.

Laura is the owner of ManLoveRomance Press, founded in January of 2007. You can find Laura on the internet at:

http://www.laurabaumbach.com/

http://groups.yahoo.com/group/laurabaumbachfiction

http://www.mlrpress.com/

http://groups.yahoo.com/group/mlrpress/